IT HAS FINALLY COME UPON THEM...

When his son died, the victim of a failed talisman of glass, Pelask the fisherman called upon the sea god Etma for revenge. He cursed the Vigen, Master of Glass, saying: "Let no man's son apprentice to the glassmaker, lest he become a sacrifice to Etma's wrath!"

Yet his curse had no power over a woman, and when the Vigen took his niece Kyala as apprentice, Pelask's curse was turned back on its creator, and Etma's sea demon wreaked deadly havoc on fisherfolk and landsmen alike.

Then the Vigen, too, died, and only Kyala, Mistress of Glass, remained. But with fisherfolk and landfolk turning against her, could Kyala and her loving friend Bremig the wood-carver summon the true Power of Glass and subdue the angry god's fury?

◆ ◆ ◆

ALSO BY M. COLEMAN EASTON

Masters of Glass
Iskiir

Published by
POPULAR LIBRARY

THE FISHERMAN'S CURSE

M. Coleman Easton

POPULAR LIBRARY

An Imprint of Warner Books, Inc

A Warner Communications Company

POPULAR LIBRARY EDITION

Cover art by Victoria Poyser

Popular Library books are published by
Warner Books, Inc.
666 Fifth Avenue
New York, N.Y. 10103

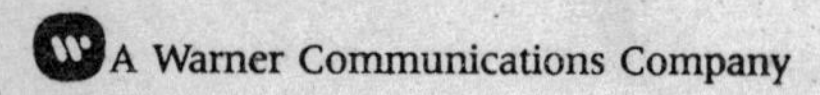

A Warner Communications Company

Printed in the United States of America

First Printing: February, 1987

10 9 8 7 6 5 4 3 2 1

The Laying of the Curse

*A**LONG* a northern coast, far from the busy settlements of more temperate climates, there stood a fishing port that served also as the center of commerce for the surrounding farms. And in this town of Darst the seamen and landsmen generally distrusted each other, each group following customs the other found repugnant. So the two factions kept apart, meeting only when there were fish to be traded or goods to be bought. Yet circumstances sometimes forced an alliance between a fisherman and an artisan of the town.

It happened that the fisherman Pelask shared a boat with his younger brother. Each brother took his eldest son to assist him, but there was no place in the small vessel for Pelask's second son. Nor could the family afford to build another boat at that time. Reluctant to send his younger boy to serve with strangers—always a chancy enterprise—Pelask decided to find him a landsman's trade.

Methodically, the fisherman canvassed the shops of Darst. He tried tinkers and weavers and cobblers, but was turned down wherever he inquired. One craftsman had no need for an apprentice; another found the boy unsuited to the skills he must master. And at last, when Pelask despaired of finding a calling for the lad, he happened by a glassmaker's shop.

The man inside, Pelask knew, was no ordinary artisan. He was a Vigen, a maker of glass talismans, whose arcane knowledge was both admired and feared by the townspeople. Despite the mystery of this craft, the fisherman entered the shop with his boy in tow.

Watnojat, as the glassmaker was called, turned from his workbench with interest and listened politely to Pelask's request. "I've sought an apprentice for some time," the Vigen confessed. "Let me have a look at your boy." The youngster, barely ten years old, pushed away the blond hairs that hung over his eyes and stepped forward nervously. "The lad's growing nicely," observed the glassmaker. "I need a strong boy in this line of work."

With that, the glassmaker began to describe the rudiments of his art. He pointed to shelves that held bottles filled with mineral powders. These scarce pigments, he explained, were essential to producing glass of various hues. "This is an iron earth," said Watnojat as he shook out a few grains of dark powder into his palm. "And this green is an ore of copper."

To control the colors of his glass, the Vigen hinted, was an art that took a lifetime to master. The minerals must be correctly chosen and the other ingredients properly mixed. The fuel for the kiln must be selected with care, and the heating and cooling precisely controlled. This first step—the casting of glass batches—was followed by other difficult procedures until finally a talisman was produced.

Such talismans had a long tradition, and Pelask was familiar with the reputation of the craft. A bead of the proper color, it was said, could halt charging beasts and even send them whimpering into the forest. Farmers protected their flocks with the Vigen's beads, and travelers depended on them for safety when crossing wild places.

Like other fishermen, however, Pelask had never used a Vigen's talisman. As a man of the sea, he felt safe so long as he placated the demon Etma. So he could not say from his own experience how effective were the glassmaker's charms. Yet, having found no encouragement elsewhere, he felt he must pursue this possible career for his son.

"Tell me, Tem Vigen," said the fisherman. "How can you know if my Torged has a bent for this work."

"I must test him," said Watnojat. "As I've tested dozens of others. The chance of success is small, but well worth trying."

Pelask saw his son staring up uneasily at the bearded Vigen. "Do what he tells you," the father said in an insistent voice, for the fisherman knew that glassmakers were well paid for their talismans. Though their art made use of mysterious powers, it was a calling that earned both respect and a good livelihood.

At once, Watnojat took glossy beads from a pouch and held them for Torged to inspect. A bar of daylight passing through one of the Vigen's windows ignited the brilliant orange hues of the talismans. "This will be a game," said the Vigen. "All you need do is look and touch. Can you see which bead is darker than the other?"

To Pelask's eyes, the colors did not much differ. But his son answered quickly, and the Vigen nodded. When the artisan brought out a third bead, the boy correctly told which of the first two most closely matched its color.

Then the Vigen displayed reddish-brown talismans, showing one pair after another to the boy. Pelask blinked, but could see no difference at all between two the glassmaker called siennas. Torged spent a good while before making his guess, but to his father's surprise he was correct.

The glassmaker, not yet finished, suggested a test that made Pelask shake his head in dismay. He wanted the boy to close his eyes and distinguish colors by the *feel* of the glass. Who had ever heard of such an ability? It was no wonder that the Vigen had rejected so many candidates.

Nonetheless, the boy was willing to try. "This one feels colder," he said, holding a dark mossy-green.

"Excellent," said the Vigen. He offered a golden pair that, to Pelask's eye, looked a near match. Yet again, Pelask's son sensed a difference in the warmth of the glass. The boy had skills in his fingers that no one had ever thought to try!

At last, when the testing was done, Watnojat smiled and clapped the fisherman on the shoulder; he offered at once to take on the boy. Pelask hesitated only briefly. The cryptic nature of the Vigen's craft troubled him, but no other artisan had shown interest in his son. And Pelask wished to spare the boy the cruel alternative—a seaman's apprenticeship with masters not his kin. After a short deliberation, he turned Torged over to the Vigen's training.

The fisherman and the glassmaker did not become friends, for they had nothing but Torged in common. During the brief summers, Pelask would not see his son at all; the glassmaker and his apprentice spent every warm month searching the mountains for rare mineral pigments. And during the long winters the two put in many hours at the kiln. When Pelask visited the shop, he often found his son too busy to talk with him.

From time to time, however, Pelask was apprised of the boy's progress. With a smile, Torged would lay glossy beads of his own making before the fisherman. "That one can halt a bear," he would say, pointing out the colorations that matched the talisman to the creature's eyes. Pelask understood that only with such a match was the glass thought to be effective. "That one can stop a wild dog." The father nodded, happy for his son's progress; but never once did he request a bead for his own protection. He trusted only weapons of iron when he entered the forests.

And so Torged grew to manhood while the Vigen's beard turned white and the hairs vanished from the old man's head.

Soon, the glassmaker promised, he would turn over his shop to his apprentice. Pelask awaited this moment eagerly, for he was proud that his son had succeeded in mastering such a difficult art.

But one day, late in winter, Torged could not be found either at home or in the glassmaker's shop. Sent in the morning to cut hardwood, the young man had not returned by dusk. And so, accompanied by the Vigen and by two younger sons, Pelask drove his sledge into the forest.

There had been talk of strange creatures in the woods, of the Lame Ones that once had been the scourge of the region. It was believed that they feared men now and, at worst, would only attack their ponies. Was it possible, Pelask wondered, that his son was even now making his way home by foot?

Night had fallen, and a fresh storm sent snow swirling against the fisherman's face. With Watnojat at his side, Pelask drove up mountain roads, following with a torch the fast-vanishing tracks of other travelers. His ponies shivered with fear, but the fisherman could sense no danger. All he could hear was the incessant whining of the wind.

Suddenly the baying of wild dogs rose above the storm. The fisherman fought the frightened ponies, then turned over the reins to one son while he reached for his bow. His other boy nocked an arrow as the baying grew louder. These packs, Pelask knew, might hold a dozen dogs or more.

A gleam of teeth emerged from the darkness. Arrows felled one dog, then another. Pelask dropped his bow and took up his spear as the remaining beasts prepared to charge. There were too many; they came at him from three directions.

Suddenly a voice shouted hoarsely above the commotion. "Scatter!" Watnojat called to the dogs. Pelask was only vaguely aware of the old man's words. "Run—or feel the beads' power!"

How was it possible? The fisherman watched in astonishment as the baying gave way to whimpers of pain. "Be gone!" shouted the Vigen. The lead animals crouched in submission, then turned away from the sledge. A few dogs lingered to snarl, but soon they too plunged into the forest. In moments, the pack was gone.

Pelask turned to see the glassmaker on his knees clutching a lantern in one hand and talismans in the other. "Vigen, those are powerful charms you hold," the fisherman said with measured awe. "I only hope that my son is as well protected."

"Torged carries such beads," Watnojat assured him. "Many of the townsfolk carry them."

"Forgive me, Vigen," said Pelask. "I'm a man of the sea, not the woods." He looked down at the weapon in his hand. "I feel safe only with an iron point in front of me. But tonight, I could not have saved myself."

Fearful of what other hazards the night held, the fisherman calmed his ponies and soon got them underway again. In this dense part of the forest, the falling snow did not penetrate easily. Instead of a steady fall of fine powder, occasional torrents spilled from high branches and tumbled to the ground. The lead ponies, still skittish from the dogs' attack, reared as a brief cascade crossed their backs. Then they began to race forward, and the other two were obliged to follow. Pelask stood up, shouting "Soso" and tugging at the reins. Suddenly the animals whinnied, twisted, and nearly toppled the sledge as they brought themselves up short.

The way was blocked by another sledge and by four lifeless grays sprawled in the snow.

With a cry, Pelask rushed closer, heading for the figure that had fallen across the driver's bench. Above the dead man his lantern still burned, illuminating his open mouth in his final expression of astonishment and of defiance. *Torged!* A spear lay beside him, its point blood-smeared and matted with coarse hair that could only have come from a Lame

One's coat. And as Pelask lifted the torch, his mourning wail already pouring from his throat, he saw the string of talismans—the Lame Ones' eyes—clenched tightly in Torged's fist.

What false hopes this Vigen had given! His charms worked against wild dogs; against Lame Ones they were clearly worthless. Pelask's first impulse was to skewer the old man on his spear and hang his body up for all to see. But no. He held back his anger as he dragged his sad burden back to his own sledge. He would have vengeance, but the Vigen's suffering must be prolonged. For now, he must let the old man live.

No words were spoken on the long journey home. The snow blew harder than before, but the fisherman barely felt the cold. The ride down the mountain seemed endless, yet when they reached the bottom at last, Pelask could not recall any of it. He left the glassmaker by his door, then went home to tell the grim news to his wife.

It was not until morning that the fisherman decided the manner of his revenge. Torged had been the Vigen's sole apprentice, and now Watnojat had no one to carry on his work. Pelask resolved that there would be no other. Let the aged craftsman die in his own time, the fisherman decided. Let him live months, even years, knowing that he would leave no successor.

To achieve his goal, the bereaved father knew he must call on the sea demon Etma. For the sea had lost a son and justice must be served.

Late the next day, as the time for Torged's burning neared, Pelask sought an offering to the demon. The previous night's storm had lifted. The tide was low as evening approached. Carrying a large sack of sailcloth, the fisherman walked through the snow that reached almost to the sea's edge. He followed the rocky shoreline, then climbed out onto the flats, where a thin crust of ice lay atop the sand and debris.

He stepped past slender ribbons of seavine and kicked aside mounds of bladderwrack. Farther out lay a bank of black rocks that was visible only at low tide. He bent over the craggy surface, peering into trapped pools of water. Here he hoped to find a morsel that would gain the demon's favor.

But what should he choose? A sea urchin? A starfish? Such were the gifts one made for good sailing on a cloudless day. A rarer present was needed for this occasion. Pelask bent closer to the pool, pulled off one sealskin glove, and dipped his hand into the chilly water. What was the shiny thing with claws? he wondered. The crab hid instantly, but the fisherman saw the gleam of its pincers below the jagged edge of the pool. He plucked the little creature out and dropped it onto the dry part of the rock before it could snap at his fingers. Then he smashed its shell with the side of his hand.

The crab was not quite dead. Pelask bent down to study the iridescence of its pearly covering. He could not remember seeing one of these before. Drying his hand on his sealskin coat, he waited for the thing to stop struggling. Then he dropped it into the sack that lay at his feet.

Straightening up, the fisherman turned to search the flats for another gift. He walked slowly, scanning the soft bottom for an item of rarity. Beyond the rocks he found a broad fluted leaf of sea lettuce with an unfamiliar texture. Perhaps, Pelask thought, it had been carried here from some far-off sea. And so he stuffed the leaf into his sack to serve as a wrapping for his gift. Now he needed one token more, preferably something long dead.

Darkness was coming fast, but he pulled his glove onto his near-frozen hand and trekked out toward the mouth of the harbor. Something suitable might have beached farther out, he hoped. All he saw were shells, dead herrings, and enormous strands of kelp. Ribs of a broken boat stood in his path. He sidestepped to avoid the wreck and suddenly cried out in delight. A dead sea turtle, belly-up, lay almost hidden beneath the smashed keel. Quickly he lifted the rank creature and added it to his sack of booty.

It was time to go home. Pelask turned and saw lights flickering in the town. By now his other sons had readied the funeral pyre. He must finish his task and meet them at the town square.

As he walked, however, a vague dissatisfaction grew. His gifts for the demon were good, but perhaps not good enough. To assure the Vigen's punishment, Pelask considered what else he might offer. At last, finding an answer, he pushed up his cap to expose his left ear to the biting wind. At home, he hurried to his unheated workshed behind the house, chopped open the belly of the turtle, and cut out the fetid liver. He warmed the sea lettuce, now stiff with cold, between his hands. Then he placed the broken pearly crab and the bloated piece of meat in its center. One more thing . . . He carried the offering into the house.

"Ola," he said to his red-eyed wife, who sat by the fireside waiting for him to escort her to the pyre. "Ola, you must do something for me. Ask no questions." He picked up her sharpest paring knife and passed it one time through the flame of the hearth. Then he bent down and showed her his earlobe, now numb from exposure.

At last, his package complete and his cap hiding his mutilated ear, he walked with Ola to the town square. The pyre was ready. In accordance with his instructions, Torged was garbed in a fisherman's sealskins so that all might forget he had followed a glassmaker's calling. The body lay atop a bier of pine boughs that rested on the pile of oak.

"The torch, father." His oldest son handed him the brand as he came to the base of the pyre. Then the other family members stood back while Pelask faced the onlookers. He lifted his offering to the demon, carried his torch high in the other hand as he paraded about the bier so all could see. Then he stopped, directly facing the Vigen, who had dared to stand at the front of the crowd.

"My son was a brave fisherman," Pelask shouted. "He was a man of the sea. That is what you should recall of him. And I burn this token to Etma so that all of you will be saved from my fate. Beware this Vigen . . . this false maker of glass. His work is a sham and his talismans are worthless. Stay clear of him, I say. And if any man sends him a son, let him suffer as I do; *let him lose that son.*"

Pelask placed on Torged's chest his packet of gifts—taken from the newly dead, the long dead, and the still living. Then he touched the fire to the pitch-soaked wood. The flames leapt up, the oak logs crackling as the heat spread. The fisherman stood back from the smoke, and the others edged away also. But Pelask saw that the Vigen remained in place, flames reddening his streaming cheeks. Torged burned, and his ashes flew out over the western sea. And the other offering burned too, its essence drifting toward the demon that Pelask hoped to please. Etma, rising at night to survey her domain, would breathe the scent and understand his desperation. The demon would bring him justice.

But the fisherman was impatient. That night he broke into the glassmaker's shop, tore the hide of the Vigen's huge bellows, knocked down his kiln, swept the jars from his shelves. There would be no more glass made in Darst, he exulted, not even while the old man lived.

In the following days, Pelask listened eagerly for talk of the Vigen's plans. He even affected landsmen's dress, slipping into the Oxtail Tavern and standing in shadows to overhear the talk of farmers and shopkeepers. At times he was forced to bite his tongue to keep from shouting his views. Many voices supported the Vigen, praising his work. The talismans, said one farmer, had protected him from foxes year after year. And another man, whose wife had almost died of a fever, attributed her cure to the glassmaker's intervention. Not one voice denied the value of the Vigen's works. Yet Pelask knew how they had failed his son.

Despite the sentiment in the old man's favor, the fisherman was gratified that no one offered a boy to take up the Vigen's trade. The landsmen did not live in daily fear of Etma's wrath, but they would not willingly cross the demon. Everyone had heard of great waves crashing over the shore, of waterspouts sucking up a coastal village, of sea creatures plaguing land as well as ocean.

And so, for several days, Pelask was content. The Vigen would find no new apprentice; soon his wheezing breaths would end forever. There would be no successor in Darst, and Pelask understood that few Vigens remained elsewhere. The rest of his kind would soon be gone. So much the better for everyone.

One day Pelask returned to the Oxtail, however, to hear startling news. The Vigen had taken an apprentice, after all —Balin's daughter. *Daughter!* How could that be? A woman Vigen was as unlikely as a woman fisherman. Never had anyone heard of either. Pelask pushed his way out of the tavern and vented his feelings in the solitude of the open air. At first he began to laugh. His curse had spoken of sons, so a daughter had been chosen instead! The wily old man had evaded the curse, only to make himself the laughingstock of the town. The girl could not become a Vigen. The glassmaker would leave nothing behind, and so the fisherman had won his victory after all.

Pelask had triumphed, had he not? Yet the matter of the curse troubled him. He had meant to deprive the Vigen of an apprentice, but his words had carelessly allowed one anyway. The demon could not rightly take action against Balin, for Balin had given no son. Etma was stirred up now. How would her ire be spent?

The fisherman brooded over this for days. The townspeople in the Oxtail also expressed their concerns. Evading a curse by trickery was no light matter. Who could guess Etma's reaction?

The grumblings continued, and the Vigen must have sensed the people turning against him. For to Pelask's relief, he packed his belongings and his new assistant onto a sledge and departed for a journey that few expected him to complete. And so Darst was rid of Vigens, at least for a time.

But Pelask drew little comfort from the old man's absence. Each time he departed for his boat, he took leave of his wife as if he would not be returning. Even when the sky was clear and the water perfectly calm, a dread came over him as he walked toward the sea. For he knew there was still a matter to be settled.

CHAPTER 1

SWEATING under the noon heat of summer, Bremig the wood-carver wiped his brow before reaching down to select a narrow-bladed chisel. Bare-chested except for a pocketed leather apron, he studied the half-finished piece that stood on a stump outside his workshop. He had promised that the figure would be ready for painting by tomorrow. But the uncommonly warm weather had hampered him, and he was not sure he could finish on time.

When completed, the carving would resemble the head of a three-eyed snarling ox, with great fangs and a scraggly beard of seaweed. This was, so Bremig had been told since childhood, the image that the sea demon found most pleasing. By hanging it from his prow, a fisherman believed he could placate fickle Etma. Since such carvings were a mainstay of his livelihood, Bremig had little reason to dispute the practice.

The carver, not yet thirty winters old, was lean of face and body. Most mornings he scraped the dark whiskers from his cheeks, and so spared his friends the uncommon sight of a black beard. From the time of his youth, he'd been judged too awkward and weak for a seaman's work. Fortunately he'd avoided the fate of his cousin Torged. Rather than learn a landsman's trade and work in a town shop, he had developed his early whittling skills into a trade of his own.

Still without a wife, Bremig often overheard his brothers laughing about his shyness. But the girls of Darst, with their flaxen hair and gleaming eyes, always scowled when the wood-carver passed them. Whether he was truly ugly he could not say. When he gazed at himself in a bucket he saw a flattened nose and a face that ended in a jutting chin. His black hair, roughly trimmed by his sister-in-law, was stiff and unruly. And his long neck showed a prominent apple. Surely, he admitted, these features could not be called handsome.

Bremig again wiped his brow with the grimy cloth that hung from his belt. No more time for wandering thoughts, he told himself as he lifted his mallet to the chisel; the piece was due tomorrow. Slivers of oak flew as he began to detail the texture of the figure's beard.

Suddenly his concentration was interrupted by footsteps and a high-pitched voice. "Bremig, Bremig," his young brother, Wek, shouted. "He's cold as a starfish."

The wood-carver looked up in annoyance to see the intent small face, the tawny hair blowing about his brother's ears. Wek was fond of riddles, and disliked saying anything straight out. "I'm busy," said Bremig, trying to conceal any hint of curiosity. Otherwise, the game could go on for the rest of the afternoon.

"But don't you want to know?" Wek's voice rose to a whine. His brother shrugged and lifted his mallet.

"It's the old Vigen. Finally got what he deserved."

"The glassmaker?" Bremig frowned. The incidents of last winter were still fresh in his mind. His cousin Torged had been killed in the hardwood forest despite the old man's beads. But after that, the Vigen and his new assistant had vanished; no one expected their return.

"*She* brought him back," the youngster continued.

"The apprentice? Balin's daughter? Then there will be plenty to talk about tonight," the carver replied irritably. "Now, I have work to finish."

"But don't you wanna see him burn?"

"Do they light pyres at noon? Go bring me something to eat if you want to be useful."

"But they're goin' to cut the biggest oak in the whole forest," Wek protested. "We could go watch, if you'd hitch up a cart."

Bremig took out his longest chisel and pointed the blade toward his red-haired brother. "Maybe I ought to shave a bit off your nose," he said. "That bump's always bothered me. Come closer."

Wek sucked in his cheeks to make a vulgar noise, then turned and ran for the house. "All you wanna do is work!" he shouted when he was well out of reach of Bremig's long arms.

The rangy man laughed, then picked up a thin blade again. The beard was the part of the figure that required his greatest skill. He shut out other thoughts while he carved, and was surprised when he looked up to find that someone had left him a pickled fish and a torn chunk of bread.

Wek made it clear at the evening meal that he was going to watch the burning even if he had to walk up to the town square alone.

"It won't be at the square," said Bremig's father, Lanorik. The head of the household stared moodily into his chowder. His face was pockmarked and creased; even in lamplight the roughness of his weathered skin was evident. "The burning's at Widow's Knoll," he explained after a pause.

"The Knoll?" said Wek in surprise. "Then I'd better start now."

Lanorik gestured with his wooden spoon. "Finish your meal first. You'll see the fire from here."

Bremig watched his brother suppress his reaction until their father was looking elsewhere. Then the boy screwed up his face, thrusting out his chin, pushing his lips into an ugly pout.

The grimace vanished, but Wek did not give up his plans. As soon as the meal ended, he begged Bremig to harness a pony. "You can't do nothin' in the dark," the lad insisted. "Not real work. Carvin' whistles don't count."

Bremig sighed. He had never felt comfortable with landsmen, and the matter of the Vigen and his apprentices had left him even more uneasy than before. What would it serve, he wondered, to hear eulogies for a man so despised by Darst's seamen? Yet Wek's pleadings at last evoked a sympathetic nod. The carver took a lantern and shuffled out into the cool evening air.

The stable stood adjacent to his shop, and he paused within to rub the neck of his mare, a bay roan with white patches about her muzzle. Aside from the tools of his craft, this horse was all he possessed. He knew of no other fisher family keeping an animal strictly for riding. That he was thought strange for this landsman's habit mattered little. He was viewed as a misfit in any case by nearly everyone he knew.

Bringing his father's pony to the traces, Bremig readied the cart. Wek hopped up to sit beside him and soon they were rolling through the streets of the town. As the two brothers neared the hill the traffic grew heavier, until Bremig decided they would leave the rig by the roadside and walk the rest of the way. Every farmer in the district, it seemed, had come for the glassmaker's burning. And as Bremig climbed the path, he noticed more than one fisherman at the edge of the crowd. Hecklers, he thought. That was why Wek had been eager to come.

At the top of the hill, a low rock outcropping made a natural seat. From that bench, it was said that anxious wives scanned the sea for their husbands' boats. But Bremig doubted that any wives had time to trek this far from the harbor. It was more likely a place where landsmen, joyful in their bones that they would never risk the sea's challenge, watched the sun drop below the waves.

On the flat hilltop behind the seat, the pyre soared. "You see!" Wek shouted. "They did cut the biggest oak. It had to be!"

The carver pulled his younger brother aside. "Let's stand over here," he said, heading toward a cluster of men in sealskin boots and loosely knit sweaters. A few fishermen nodded at Bremig's approach. One of Lanorik's friends traded banter with the boy. But, to his surprise, the carver did not see his uncle Pelask in the group. Where was Torged's father? Surely the bereaved fisherman should be present to witness his enemy's burning.

Then a murmur went through the crowd and all heads turned. The torch was on its way up the hill, but who was carrying it? Bremig watched a slim figure approaching. Clad in goatskin jacket and breeches, she climbed slowly, her face pinched with sorrow, her eyes on the crest of the hill. *This must be Balin's daughter*, he thought as his companions began to mutter. *The one who replaced Torged*. He found himself edging closer to have a better look at the subject of so much controversy. In the shadowy torchlight, her cheekbones showed prominently; above her narrow face, her short hair appeared uncommonly dark in shade.

"It's Kyala," someone hissed. "I hear she never was any good at . . . ooof." His vulgarity evidently was cut off by someone's playful blow. "Not good for anything else, either," the voice continued in a louder pitch. "So they tried to make her into a man."

"What do you know about it?" another fisherman taunted the first. "I hear they tried to make you into a g—" His voice trailed off, and Bremig heard sounds of scuffling and laughter. If Kyala heard any of this she did not show it. Walking stiffly, she reached the hilltop and clambered onto the stone bench.

Bremig looked up with curiosity. She was taller than he had expected. She was dressed in masculine garb; she did not even wear the neckband of an unmarried woman. Yet he found an appeal in her features that he could not explain.

"Some of you know," Balin's daughter began in a wavering voice, "that this seat I'm standing on was a favorite of the Vigen's. In his last years, he came here nearly every evening to watch the sun join the sea. And so I asked that we meet here and together send his smoke up to Ormek." She paused, and a few murmurs of approval rose from the onlookers.

"We've come to send off a man who has done much for us," she continued. But at these words, the fishermen began waving their caps and hooting. Bremig turned in annoyance, and then wondered why he was scowling at the hecklers. Undaunted by the jeers, Kyala raised her voice and continued. "I ask you to recall his years of service—how he gave his talents for the sake of us all. Many farmers can tell you of flocks protected by his talismans. Many travelers have Watnojat to thank for their safe passage through the forests."

The fishermen's objections rose feverishly, and Bremig felt himself jostled by churning fists and elbows. He shook his head in dismay, wondering how she expected these men to forget Torged. Yet others in the crowd shouted for quiet. "Hear what I have to say," she continued when the clamor died back. "Listen first, and then judge this man. You say his beads failed, and surely they did—*once*. In a long life, only one time did his talismans let us down. That was a great misfortune, but now it has been avenged."

Avenged? Bremig's eyebrows raised. Not everyone had heard this, and her last words were repeated from mouth to mouth. Kyala paused, allowing the muttering to continue awhile. Then she lifted the torch and shouted the rest of her news.

"Hear this, friends. The Lame Ones are finished! The beasts who killed Torged are dead! Look behind you and you'll see what the Vigen has done for us . . . with Ormek's help." At that, the onlookers stirred, turning and shouting with surprise. Coming up the hill were three more torches, each accompanied by a grisly trophy on a post.

At first, Bremig saw atop the closest pole only a shapeless dark mass. But as the first bearer approached, he discerned what was surely a beast's head, a mass of boils and protrusions covered by dark hairs. The jaw was propped open to show the great canines and the long, narrow tongue. The huge eyes, reflecting the torch's gleam, seemed still to have life.

Though Bremig had never seen such a creature alive or dead, he recalled descriptions from wayfarers' tales. Many stories had exaggerated the details, but he could not doubt that this had been the head of a Lame One.

At once the onlookers began to cheer. "The Vigen was a hero," declared the nearest pole-bearer. Bremig recognized the tones of Arod the ironsmith, the one Darst townsman he viewed as a friend. "Let's send his smoke to Ormek with this triumph on our lips." Arod was risking his good relations with fishermen by honoring the old glassmaker. Yet glimpsing this proof of the Vigen's victory, Bremig could find no fault with the smith. He watched with wonder as the heads were paraded up and down the hillside.

Soon the carver's attention returned to Kyala, who waited patiently until the noise settled a bit. "He was an old man," she continued, "and he carried a spear where young men wouldn't follow. The beasts knocked him to the ground, but he stood up and attacked them again. Even when he could barely hobble, he went after them, only to be battered once more. And now . . . now he has earned his reward. Ormek awaits him."

Some fishermen continued their hooting, but their voices were lost beneath the roars of approval. "He gives life and He welcomes it back again," shouted Kyala with a wave of her brand. Then she stepped down and bent to ignite the pitch-soaked kindling at the base of the pyre. The flames rose quickly through the pile of oak, and the onlookers' cries of encouragement grew louder. In disgust, the seamen turned and began to push toward the rear of the crowd.

"They're all goin'," said Wek with disappointment. "This is the best part." Bremig shrugged, and stayed with his brother until the pine boughs under the bier started to burn.

"Enough!" said the carver. He and his brother were now encircled by landsmen, and Bremig did not like their unfriendly glances. Despite Wek's pleas, he grabbed the youngster's arm, then turned to join the fishermen descending the hill. Though he tried to will it away, Kyala's face kept appearing before him as he made his way to the cart.

The next morning, the carver had difficulties finishing his prow-piece. He stalked about the yard, studying the figurehead from different angles. Now and again, he would make a small change, shaving a bit here and there, but he was not satisfied. The image should be frightening—fear was Etma's delight—but to Bremig, the features were laughably ugly and nothing more.

Concluding that he could only make matters worse, Bremig put his tool apron aside. Perhaps the customer would not notice the inferiority of this work. Possibly, it was no different from his other prow-pieces. Something in his attitude had changed, Bremig suspected; today he had no interest in staring at grotesqueries.

Did his mood, he wondered, reflect his concern over his uncle's whereabouts? Torged's father had been absent from the burning and had not returned to his home last night. Bremig could not say if his uneasiness this morning stemmed from Pelask's strange disappearance or from an entirely different cause.

The carver had other work waiting. There were weather rods, staffs bearing manlike faces with thick, downturned lips and toothy mouths, to be shaped. But he would let those orders wait. The pilings in the harbor already bore so many similar poles that he wondered how a few more could matter.

Bremig sprawled on a bench in the shady side of the yard. His customer would come soon, and then he would be free to go into town. He rubbed at his forehead. *Shops?* Why was he thinking of shops? He had no need to visit Arod the ironsmith, and what other business did he have?

The figurehead was soon collected by the satisfied boat owner, who took it in a cart to be painted. Bremig began to pace around the yard. Then he went into his shop and pulled away scrap wood and a hide that concealed some of his personal carvings.

Here were works that he kept to himself, works that no fisherman would encourage. Seamen had little interest in Ormek the Sun; they felt their fortunes to be governed solely by Etma. But Bremig sometimes secretly turned his hand to carving Sun disks of the kind that landsmen hung from eaves and rafters and harnesses. Now he picked out the one that pleased him most, admiring the decorative border that surrounded the sun's image. A circle half the size of a cart's wheel, this disk was larger and, he thought, more handsome than any he had seen in town.

Bremig understood that landsmen gave such images as tokens when a loved one was lost. Only half aware of his intentions, he wrapped his work in a piece of sacking, then covered up the other carvings. Hurriedly, before Wek could find him and follow with curious questions, Bremig headed toward the rutted path.

The streets were busy with pedestrians and carts. On this warm day, all the shop doors stood open, and the air carried odors of leather one moment, of wool another. Bremig made a point of avoiding the street where Arod's forge stood. He did not want the smith inquiring after his errand.

For a moment, the carver hesitated, trying to recall the route to his destination. He had visited Watnojat's shop now and then, occasionally looking in on his cousin's training.

Bremig wondered now whether it was true, as people said, that Kyala would carry on the old man's trade.

Even if people doubted the power of talismans, they still needed windowpanes and colorless glassware. A Vigen who was willing to produce such ordinary work would have a good business, he thought. Yet who had heard of a woman engaged in that craft?

And surely, even if she planned to carry on his work, she would wait for a few days after the Vigen's burning. Nonetheless, Bremig continued toward the glassmaker's shop.

At last he neared the stave structure that lay between a cobbler's workplace and a potter's shed. To his uneasy surprise, the shutters were open and the door stood slightly ajar. People brushed past him as he stared at the weathered planks. At last he rapped with his knuckles.

There was no answer, so he pushed the door open a crack more. The air inside was stale and musty, as one might expect of a room closed for so long. Within, a figure suddenly turned. Kyala? She seemed so young, barely a woman, but this was certainly Balin's daughter. A ribbon of daylight crossed her face, and he saw fresh grief. Her nose, reddened from crying, stood out above thin, pale lips. Unexpectedly, Bremig felt his pulse throbbing.

"I . . ." she said hoarsely as he continued to stare at her. "I'm not ready for business. Come back . . . in a few days."

The carver shook his head. "I need no glass today. I've . . . brought you a token. For your lost Vigen, though he was no friend to me." He summoned his courage, and pushed the door open wider. Before she could protest, he slipped inside, unwrapped the bundle, and presented his gift.

Drawing closer, he noticed the rich blue-green of her eyes. Her short chestnut hair was unkempt, yet when the light caught a few strands they gleamed. Tentatively she reached to take the disk, then turned it slowly from one side to the other. "I've . . . never seen one like this. Who could have made such a fine thing?"

Bremig felt his face flush and did not answer. He turned away, glancing at the shelves and bench where bottles made of bubbly glass stood in disarray. He could see hints of color within—the brown of dark ale in one, the gold of a buttercup in another.

"This is a wonder," she said, still staring at his carving. "But why would a stranger give me such a token?"

The carver could not explain himself. "Torged was my cousin," he managed. "But I don't blame old Watnojat for what happened to him. No charm can be perfect. Fishermen believe in their snarling figureheads, yet Etma swallows a few boats every year."

Kyala shook her head. "Etma is at the bottom of the sea where Ormek chained her. The storms tip the boats; no demon has a hand in that."

"You believe one thing, and we another," Bremig answered softly. "I would be happy to think that the demon lies anchored in the depths." He sighed, knowing he must now confess his trade. "As it happens, I do a brisk trade in carvings to please Etma. But now and again, I turn my thoughts to the Bright One."

"Then this is your work?" Kyala studied the disk again. "You shouldn't waste your talents on the other."

"Will you accept it? I know nothing of Vigens except for what Torged told me. And he said that Ormek's power was behind the talismans . . ."

"So it is," said Kyala with sudden enthusiasm. "And I'll be glad to hang your gift above the center of the shop. It's exactly what I need in this gloomy place."

Bremig nodded, pleased that now someone would benefit from his secret labors. "Then you'll continue the glassmaker's trade?"

"I'm trained for nothing else. My mother tried to teach me cooking, and I learned how to scald milk and how to turn a good fish into charcoal." For a moment her face brightened into an impish grin, and Bremig felt bathed in its warmth.

"Yet this art is said to be full of mysteries . . ."

"My studies were brief, but I know the Eighteen Fires and the proportions of all the mixtures. And, by Ormek's gift, I have a talent with colors. So in time, I may succeed."

"Then I wish you . . . Ormek's blessing," said the carver. The unfamiliar words came surprisingly smoothly. "But now I must leave you to your work."

"I still don't know why you came." She tilted her head and looked at him with a faint smile of curiosity.

Bremig began to laugh. "I've asked myself the same question, but I don't dare answer it."

"Then come back when the shop is ready, and I'll show you talismans. And tell you what each one is used for."

He wanted to promise he'd return, but he managed only to nod.

When Bremig reached his woodworking shop, he could not recall how he had gotten there. Though he'd walked through the streets of Darst, he retained no memories of the journey. All he could recollect of his visit to town were Kyala's face and voice and the musty smell of the shop.

He must take his mind off Balin's daughter, he told himself. Yet his thoughts kept returning to how different she was from the other young women of Darst. The fishermen said ugly things about her, but Bremig disbelieved their spiteful tales. Why, he wondered, could she not be a glassmaker and a woman as well?

To distract himself from such musings, the carver took a stout ash pole and carried it to the yard. He clamped it to a stump so that he could work comfortably while sitting on a stool. After donning his apron, he began to shape the topmost face of the weather rod.

"Bremig!" Wek's voice startled the carver. Bremig had already begun the fourth distorted countenance in the rod's progression, and his fingers were feeling cramped from holding the tools. He stood up and stretched while his brother raced across the yard.

"Uncle's still missing," shouted the youngster. "Can't find him anywhere."

"And what about the dory?"

"Still gone. Some boats out lookin' for it."

Bremig frowned while he fingered his chisel. Pelask's behavior had been strange in the months since his son's death. But to go off alone in a dory with no explanation . . . "Call me when the men come back," he said. He bent again to the pole.

Neither Pelask nor the boat had been found by evening. Lanorik was moodily silent, and a gloom settled on everyone in the household. After the meal, the carver slumped on a bench and put his head in his hands. By now he was willing to believe that his uncle might be dead. Bremig felt his grief rising as he wondered if the fisherman had met the fate he'd predicted for himself.

Again, the next morning, the carver was unable to concentrate. He finished the weather rod, surely one of his poorest efforts, and could not muster the energy to start another. For long stretches he did nothing but sit on his outdoor bench and stare at the shaving-littered ground.

It was not until afternoon that Wek came running with his unwelcome news. "They found Uncle Pelask's boat!" he shouted. "What's left of it. But no Uncle."

"What are you saying?"

"Beached and smashed . . . up the coast a ways. But Uncle's gone."

"These past days the weather's been calm," Bremig said angrily. "How does a dory break up on a quiet sea?"

"It's got to be the demon's revenge," the boy insisted. "For the curse . . . Etma *made* Uncle go out, and then she sent something after 'im."

"Something? And what might that be?" But Wek raced back to the house without giving an answer.

That night the mealtime talk was only of Etma. Lanorik, whose eyes appeared weary with sadness, muttered darkly about a gathering of his comrades. "We must warn the town," he said. "End this, before it ruins us all."

Bremig's older brother Juukal was grim as he waited for his food. Juukal's wife brought boiled cod to the table, while his mother Hekina sat apart, her eyes closed while she chanted softly to herself. Alternately crossing and straightening her fingers, Hekina seemed to pay no attention to the others.

"We don't know what happened to Pelask," the carver protested. "You said there wasn't even a scrap of his clothing. For all we can tell, he stepped ashore somewhere and then the dory got away from him."

"Got away from Pelask?" Lanorik retorted bitterly. "I've spent more time with my brother on the sea than I have with your mother in our bed. Pelask's bones lie with the demon. You can be sure of that. And if this isn't stopped, Etma will be looking for *me* soon. First me, and then my sons." He reached his huge, callused hand toward Bremig, then shook his shoulder roughly. "For you as well, my landbound man. Even if she has to come up here to take you."

Though Lanorik had said nothing directly to Wek, the youngster cried out and jumped away from the table. "I'll hide in the woods!" he said. "No demon's gonna get *me*."

His mother's chanting continued, and it was left to the boy's aunt to comfort him. But Lanorik refused to halt his ominous talk.

"What good does it do to frighten the boy?" asked Varva as she held quivering Wek's face to her apron.

Ignoring his daughter-in-law, Lanorik pounded the table with his fist, rattling the planks and the wooden platters. "All our woes come from the glassmaker and his vixen. *She* slipped under the curse. *She* came back to stir up the demon again. But we can save ourselves if we act. I say let's be rid of that—Kyala!"

This outburst made gooseflesh rise on Bremig's arms. If Pelask indeed was dead, then it was not because of demons or curses. But what if others took Lanorik's views?

Seeing the depths of his father's anger, the carver abandoned attempts to calm him. In a few days, when the first grief faded, the elder would probably become more reasonable. At any rate, without proof, Pelask's passing would not be proclaimed until a full month of his absence. Perhaps by then the coincidence of Kyala's arrival with the accident would be forgotten.

The carver continued to brood, however. After last night, he'd hoped that the ill feelings against Watnojat would gradually subside. He hadn't foreseen that the old hatred might now turn toward the Vigen's successor.

That night the problem of Pelask's disappearance was not allowed to rest. Shouts roused the household as all were preparing for sleep. The voices sounded all at once, and Bremig had to struggle to separate the words. "Come see Etma's message," he picked from the babble outside. "Written on the flats for all to read." Bremig, Juukal, and their father pulled on boots and sweaters and hurried to the door.

Wek ran in and out of the doorway crying, until his aunt caught him and dragged him aside. Bremig rubbed his eyes and stepped into the cool evening air. The moon was bright, revealing the milling shapes of a half-dozen men who waited. His tall cousin, Draalego, Pelask's oldest son, appeared to be the leader of the group; certainly he was the loudest in his exhortations.

Moments later they reached the harbor. The tide was low, the boats resting on the dark bottom at the foot of the quay. The breeze carried an odd odor, deeper and more rancid than the usual smell of the exposed seabed. And in the damp sand farther out, showing clearly in the moonlight, were markings that made Bremig's hackles rise. The harbor's floor had been gouged and scraped over a broad area; troughs ran all the way out to the water's edge. The usual debris—seavines and broken planks and old netting—lay piled as if a monstrous hand had pushed them aside.

"There's your proof!" shouted Lanorik. "First Pelask, now this. Etma has given us two warnings. We won't wait for a third."

"We know what we've got to do," said Pelask's eldest son. "Let's get all the others. And plenty of torches."

"Burn out the Vigen. Let's do it tonight."

"Hurry! Call the rest of 'em."

For a moment, Bremig was dizzy with confusion. His feet were leaden and his head would not turn. He saw Kyala's shop in flames and the young woman clutching her disk of Ormek while the fire took her as well. Then, suddenly, he understood what he must do. While the others made for the cottages, Bremig began to run toward his father's stable.

CHAPTER

2

THE streets and houses were lit only by moonlight as Bremig drove feverishly up into town. He had no time to think about his route, yet his hands worked the reins and somehow brought him to the glassmaker's shop. The pony whinnied in surprise as he jerked the animal back.

In an instant he was pounding on the locked door. When no answer came, he knocked his fist against his own forehead as punishment for his stupidity. Where would Kyala be at this hour except in her bed? And Bremig did not know where to find her.

There was but one townsman he could turn to—Arod the ironsmith. Mounting the cart in one bound, Bremig called an order to the pony. A hasty swing into a broad lane, and then the carver jumped down in front of another shop door.

Bremig beat on the planks and raised a shout that echoed from the lifeless buildings. Arod lived in a cottage behind his forge, and might not hear this commotion. Past a stave gate, the carver knew, a passage led directly to the house. He turned, found the gate locked, and stretched up to see if he could scale it. But his fingers would not quite reach the top. He kicked at the staves and shouted again for Arod.

"Stop that," cried a huffy voice from within. "Or I'll split your head for you and make your ears ring for a month."

"Balin's daughter . . ." The carver tried to keep his voice low, but his tongue had a volition of its own. Everyone on the street must be hearing this, he thought. "They're coming . . . to drive Kyala out."

"Who's coming?"

"Pelask's kin. Mine too." The last erupted in a tone of despair.

Bremig leaned against the rough partition and waited five heartbeats. Arod, he knew, had been the old Vigen's friend. Would he help Kyala now?

A sigh came, and Bremig felt the gate pulled away from him. The smith, his stocky figure in shadow, his pale beard disheveled, reached up to rub at his eyes. "I warned Balin there'd be trouble," he said sharply. "Didn't think it would come this soon."

"Just tell me where to find her. I'll do the rest."

The smith peered out at the modest cart. "You'll need more wagon than that. Wait for me by the wide alley around the side." He pointed, then turned and strode back toward the house. Bremig realized that the man had not yet even put on his boots.

But Arod was not gone long. He returned driving a two-pony wagon, and hurriedly led Bremig to Balin's nearby cottage.

A stranger to this household, the carver stood aside while the smith spoke to Kyala's yawning mother. Though Balin had wrapped her short, full figure in a quilt, Bremig saw how she shivered in the cool night air. Suddenly Kyala was at the door, her anguished face lit faintly by the lamp she carried. Fully dressed, wearing her now-familiar goatskins, she rushed into the street and stared at the cart and wagon. Openmouthed, she looked to Bremig for an explanation.

"Pelask's dead," said the carver hoarsely, taking a step closer. "At least his kin think so. And they're blaming you for it."

"Pelask!"

"Fishermen are coming with torches. We've got to get you away." He reached to pull her toward the cart, but she jumped back from him.

"*Away?* To where?"

"To your aunt's farm," said Balin suddenly. "That's far enough inland for safety. If they can't smell the sea, the fish-gutters get weak in their spines."

"And leave my shop?" Kyala looked defiantly at her mother. Bremig made another grab at the daughter's arm and caught her sleeve, but she broke free.

"And what of my pigments? The colorings took two life-times to gather."

"Are they worth losing yours for?" he asked. "I know those men . . ."

"The pigments can't be replaced." Kyala retreated toward the doorway of the cottage.

The carver closed his eyes and tried to guess how much time remained. He hoped the mob would seek courage in numbers, gathering everyone who subscribed to their foolish notions before setting forth. "Then let's take your storm-cursed colorings with us," he shouted. "But get up on this cart!"

"Go," said Arod to the young woman. "I'll take care of the rest of the family. Can you find your way to the farm?"

"I can find it."

"By moonlight?"

She nodded. "But I'll need this lamp for now." By then, her brother and her grandmother had joined Balin at the cot-tage door. Kyala glanced back at them.

"We'll be fine," said Balin bravely to her daughter. "No-body cares about us. It's only you they want."

Bremig could not stifle his impatience. He reached around Kyala's waist, but she slapped his arm and squirmed from his grip. To his relief, she then made for the cart, and mounted of her own volition. Bremig jumped up and took the reins, and before she could seat herself, they were moving.

Their first stop was the Vigen's shop, where, once inside, Kyala began frantically pulling down vials from the shelves. "Find something to pack these in," she shouted. The lamp sat on the bench, but the corners of the room were deep in shadow. Bremig stumbled against a barrel, lifted its lid, and reached inside.

"Sand?" he said with surprise as he felt the dry grit slide through his fingers.

"To make glass," she called back. "The purest white sand. But dump it out. All of it. I can get more."

The carver grunted at the weight as he tipped the barrel over and let the contents spill onto the floor.

"We need straw . . . for packing," she insisted, bottles clinking together in her hands. "Through the back door and behind the potter's shop."

Bremig struggled with the warped door, found his way out into the alley. He cocked an ear toward the harbor and thought he heard muffled voices. Quickly, he swept up an armload of bristles and rushed back inside. Kyala began to pack the barrel with bottles and wads of straw.

"You do this for me." She thrust a handful of vials at him, then fell to her knees and began to wrestle with a heavy crock. Some of her bottles were bulbous, as large as a fist, while others were the size of a thumb. Continuing to pack, Bremig noticed Kyala bring up a small box from its hiding place beneath the floor. "Now you know one of my secrets," she said as she placed the box carefully atop the contents of the barrel, then heaped more straw around it.

At last the shelves were bare. Kyala and Bremig rolled the keg to the door, then gave a great heave and lifted it onto the cart. She ran back into the shop and the carver called after her. "Take nothing else!" Now he was certain he heard the crowd, angry voices rising from the lower streets. He ran back to find her climbing onto a stool in the center of the room.

"Not even this?" She cut down the disk he had given her, glanced once more around the shop, and picked up a few small items. Her cheeks were wet, but she made no sound of grief. She led him back to the cart, leaving the door open and the lamp burning as if in welcome to those who would come.

Bremig knew nothing of the inland roads. He was content to take Kyala's orders, turning where she told him, only vaguely taking note of the route. "How far?" he asked her once, and that was all he said for half the journey. It was enough that she sat beside him, her shoulder or arm sometimes bouncing against his as the cart rattled over ruts. She turned often to look at her cargo, and Bremig feared that the ride might break a few vials.

"This trouble," he said at last. "This trouble with Pelask's kin must end. They can't blame you for every bit of ill luck on the sea."

"And how can it end? Do you think they'll forget?"

"In time. After all, Darst still needs a glassmaker."

Kyala shook her head. "The ones who know that won't dare speak. Poor Watnojat was driven out and nobody stood up for him."

"But I was at his burning. I heard cheers for your Vigen."

"Memories can be short. He was a hero until the curse was laid. On the next day, the townsfolk all hid their faces from him."

"I don't understand," the carver confessed.

"They were afraid—afraid he'd treat them like beasts and cast talismans to match their eyes. Then, if people turned against him, he could always force them to do his will."

Bremig shook his head. "Torged told me about his ability to control animals, and I believed him. But is such power over *men* possible? Even my Vigen-hating kin scoff at the idea."

He turned to witness a bitter smile on Kyala's face. "It has been done—and I have seen it. Better that your kin doubt—"

"Then you argue against yourself," Bremig interrupted. "By your own words, we should trust no Vigens."

Kyala did not answer at once. In the soft moonlight Bremig saw her fists tighten and her expression grow rigid. Finally, in a hoarse whisper, she said, "I don't know if I can trust myself."

Bremig could say nothing to that. Feeling a chill that did not come from the night air, he stared down the straight road. Her bleak mood, he told himself, would pass. For now, he must think only of delivering her to her destination.

The cart was descending a hill, and he thought he glimpsed a hint of movement far ahead. His pony increased its pace, and soon Bremig realized that he was gaining on a wagon. The bulky shape grew clearer. "It's Arod," he said when they were close enough to smell the dust raised by his wheels.

He spoke no more as he followed the smith through open country. They turned into a narrow track, passing outbuildings that crouched like rabbits against the bare ground. Bremig heard goats bleating, and a sharp barnyard scent reached his nostrils. They rolled up to a long stone farmhouse with a wide door set into the middle.

Balin stepped down from Arod's wagon and took upon herself the chore of waking the household. "Go back, before you're missed," said Kyala quietly to the carver. She climbed behind him and began to tug at the barrel.

"I don't know where to leave that," he replied, ignoring her suggestion.

"Put it on the ground. Anywhere. We'll take care of it later."

"But . . ."

"What will happen if your cousins figure out where you've been? They won't thank you for this night's work."

Bremig had not yet considered that problem. Suppose he simply returned the cart to his father's stable? In the evening's confusion, who would know he'd been gone? But he felt compelled to linger.

She was straining with the load. He turned to help, and they set the keg gently at the side of the track. "Go, now," she said. "You've done a great kindness. Don't waste any more thoughts on me."

"Waste?" He could not turn from her. Balin was off by the farmhouse door with the rest of her family in a cluster around her, but Bremig had no concern for the others. He grasped for words to express the vague hopes he had nurtured. If he was to leave Kyala now, then he must have the answer to at least one question. "Do you . . ." he stammered. "Do you think me foolish to care for you? Some say I'm ugly . . . or worse."

"Not ugly. And too good a man to risk what you have for me. All I can bring you is misery."

Bremig's mouth was dry, and the words he wanted did not come.

"You should talk to a farmer named Jelor," she said. "Then you'll listen to my advice."

Feeling his knees weaken, he steadied himself by leaning against the cart. "And what . . . what would I learn from this Jelor?"

"That I'll be no man's wife. He asked me three times, and I refused all his pleas—as I'd refuse yours." She took a quick stride toward the carver and reached up to cup his cheeks in her hands. Her palms burned against his skin. "I know your needs," she said in a shy voice. "But you must find someone else—a woman who can mend your breeches and won't let your soup boil over." She gave him a final glance, which he dared not interpret as one of affection, and then she was off, running to the open doorway of the house.

* * *

Kyala tried to put aside her last glimpse of the carver's anguished face. Her coldness had been unkind, perhaps even cruel, but her reasons were sound. She had sworn to her mentor that she would carry on his art, and a glassmaker's shop was no place for raising a family.

Perhaps she might have explained this, but too many other thoughts intruded. If only she could forget the events of this night. If only this could be a summer like so many before, with Balin's family arriving to help with the haymaking.

But this year they had come too early for the harvest. As Kyala neared the doorway, she saw Aunt Findren's arms about Balin; both were weeping. The daughter's steps slowed and she could not meet Uncle Ridrune's gaze. After all, it was she who was the cause of this suffering, she who had precipitated this disturbing visit.

"Come into the house. All of you," said Ridrune gruffly. He gestured with his broad hand, and Kyala followed the others inside. Only one lamp burned in the lengthy room, and the embers in the central firepit barely glowed. Pallets lay on raised floors that edged the two longest walls. Kyala saw small heads popping up as sleepy children peered after the source of the commotion.

From the far end of the house, girls came with bedding for the unexpected guests. Kyala enlisted the aid of two brawny cousins, who pulled on their boots and went out to retrieve her barrel. Then all settled down and tried to find some sleep before dawn.

It was not until she closed her eyes that she gave any further thought to Bremig. Her first impression had been his curious appearance, his long, delicate fingers contrasting with the rough features of his face. He had asked if she found him ugly, and the truth was just the reverse. But she would not tell him so. Not after Jelor.

She tried to force her mind to other matters, but could not

dispel Bremig's image. What if he were beside her now, touching her as Jelor had done, pressing himself against her? There was a woody scent about Bremig that one might expect from a carver. In the dark farmhouse, she thought she sensed that pleasant odor again.

A brief joy brushed her, until she recalled again Jelor's anger and confusion when she refused to wed him. As unfeeling as she now must seem to the carver, she had acted to prevent such deeper hurt later. For she would not abandon her promises, despite being driven from Darst. Surely there was a town somewhere that would accept a woman for their Vigen . . .

In the morning, Ridrune sent one of his sons to ride into Darst for news. Assigned chores, Kyala spent the morning in the main barn shoveling manure. She emerged tired and dusty at noon. Approaching the house for refreshment, she glanced longingly up at the lumpy turf roof where she had often climbed for sport. A goat was grazing there. Had it been any other summer, she would have clambered after it and chased it back to the meadow.

The air in the barn grew hot that afternoon, and the smells worsened with the heat. Kyala kept stopping to listen for her cousin's return, but heard only her labored breathing. He must come soon, she thought, though she dared not think what he might tell. Grabbing the wooden barrow by its rough handles, she trundled it to the next stall in the row. With a grunt she leaned into the shovel, but suddenly was distracted by shouts from the road.

Racing out of the barn, Kyala saw the rider on his sweating horse. She nearly stumbled as she hurried across the yard. "They burned the shop!" he shouted. "And a few more with it. Balin's house is safe."

She continued to run toward him, wanting more news than he might have. "What of the people who helped us?" she called, her heart hammering as she spoke. "Were they found out?" But the rider merely shrugged as he rode past her.

Not until evening, when the family had finished eating, did Ridrune's son tell more of his news. The front door stood open, letting in the cool night air. Children sat at the edge of the high floor, swinging their feet against the stone risers. The adults sat on benches, the men smoking tobacco in long-stem pipes.

"There's trouble on the coast," her cousin said, pushing back a lock of blond hair that kept falling onto his forehead. "That's the part I've been saving to tell you. It started with strange doings last night. Huge ruts and gouges on the tidal flats."

"Someone has a good imagination." Ridrune laughed.

Kyala's cousin scowled at the remark, and for a moment she feared he would not finish. "Later that night," he continued, "when the tide came in, two fisher cottages were smashed—broken to bits. And someone saw what did it." He wrinkled his brow. "Something from the sea bottom."

"And what could that be?" asked the father calmly, blowing a long plume of smoke. "Seaweed that walks? An army of marching mackerels?"

"The fisher folk say . . ." He hesitated, then finished in a whisper. "They say Etma sent something."

"Etma?" Ridrune scowled, his good humor instantly gone. "We don't speak of that one here." He made a sign of Ormek with thumb and forefinger.

"But I saw it, father," the youth protested.

"Saw a beast crawl up on land to attack the houses?"

"No . . . But I saw its tracks. Gullies in the shoreline that a man could lie down in."

"From stormwater runoff," Ridrune said sharply before taking another long draft on his pipe.

The youth seemed unwilling to continue in the face of his father's disapproval. He lowered his eyes and began to speak instead of the goods he saw for sale in the shops of the town.

Kyala could not sit still for such prattle. She walked out into the moonlit barnyard and distracted herself by tossing stones onto the roof of the goat shed.

Later she tried to talk to her cousin alone, but his reticence was hard to overcome. "You should've seen the cottages," he muttered before shuffling off to his bed.

That night Kyala woke time and again from vague, threatening dreams. She could never recall their contents, only the feelings of dread that accompanied them. But in the darkness she asked herself questions she could not answer. Was this a demon or a mortal beast that had come to torment the town? And if it was mortal, could a Vigen lure it to its doom? But she did not know for certain that there was a beast.

Kyala woke another time and found the others already clearing bedding from the floor; she smelled bread baking. Looking up, she saw Balin's broad face, her lips set in a look of concern.

"Mother, I don't know what to make of it," Kyala said quietly as she rose. "The fishermen will blame me for this new problem. They'll say it's because of Pelask's curse."

"They blame a landsman for every herring that slips from their nets."

"But now it's not just any landsman. I'm the one chosen as the focus of every ill thought. And maybe what they say is true."

"Kyala, do you listen to seamen's superstitions?" Balin put a comforting hand on her daughter's arm. "The foolishness will pass. For now, be thankful we're welcome here, out of sight of the troublemakers."

"And what if the coastal towns are in danger? Watnojat wouldn't hide like a mouse, hoping the cat's teeth will drop out from old age."

"Daughter, I don't understand you."

"The duty of a Vigen is to drive off beasts, whether they come from the forest or the sea."

Balin's mouth opened, but for a moment she did not speak. "Is this what the old man taught you?"

Kyala lowered her gaze. "He never . . ." she confessed. "Never mentioned the sea."

"Then . . ."

"But why not? Why should the talismans protect us only from land creatures?"

Balin shook her head just as the front door was thrown open to admit the morning light. Kyala glimpsed on her mother's forehead, dimmed little by years, the circular mark of honor for service at Ormek's temple. Balin had served the Bright One in her own way, yet sometimes Kyala wondered if her mother remembered her old obligations.

"The flamens!" Kyala shouted with sudden inspiration. "I'll go to the temple and ask their advice."

"About talismans?"

"About the beast. Is it real or some drunkard's tale? Is it mortal or demon? They should know."

"I lived with them for five years," Balin answered in a quiet voice. "They don't know everything."

"But I've no one else to ask. I *must* go."

Her mother's frown deepened. "Strangers aren't welcome at the shrine. You'll be challenged at the lower gate . . . and the flamens may not talk to you at all."

"I can try. If I tell them about the Lame Ones . . ."

"Ormek's forgiveness! If you talk about Lame Ones, who knows what those temperamental priests will do."

"Mother . . ."

"I see you don't want to listen." She sighed and turned her face to the doorway. "If you must go," she said quietly, "then I'd best come with you. At least I can get us past the gatekeepers."

Kyala began to smile. "Today?"

"Are you in such a hurry to find new woes for yourself?" Balin stared at her daughter and at last her expression softened. "All right," she said. "I'll ask Ridrune to lend us a cart."

Bleary-eyed, Bremig held a chisel to the weather rod he was pretending to shape. Wek had wandered into the yard, making the carver's sham all the more difficult. The boy's face expressed concerns that Bremig could only guess at. But he hoped they had nothing to do with Kyala's escape. As far as the carver knew, his own absence last night had gone unnoticed.

Wek wandered closer, and Bremig began to perspire despite the morning cool. Why should he fret under the youngster's gaze? But he gave up working, slid the chisel into his pocket, and stared at his approaching brother.

"They've gone to cut black walnut," said Wek in a nervous whisper when he reached Bremig's side.

"*Walnut?* For a boat?" When his brother nodded, the carver shook his head in disbelief. The boat of black walnut was the stuff of legends, spoken of only in tremulous voices. Such a craft offered the promise of a desperate purging that might free the coast from Etma's wrath. But what of the risks? Would even his foolhardy cousins dare them?

"Aunt's takin' me away. To leave me with 'er sister 'til the trouble's over."

"If they mean to try it, then we should all go—as far inland as we can travel." Bremig frowned as he recalled the old tales. Which of his cousins, he wondered, would swing an ax against the most cursed of woods? Bremig scoffed at most of the ancient beliefs, but the idea of the sacrificial boat made him shiver. Even worse was the knowledge that he must surely have a part in its construction.

A tear slid down Wek's face and he leaned his head against his brother's shirt. "We're leavin' now," the child said miserably. "I hate the place we're goin'."

"You've never been there."

"Good reason to hate it."

Bremig couldn't counter that argument. He put an arm around the boy and recalled that Varva's sister lived a half-day's ride east. "But go anyway. I'll catch up with you as soon as I can. We'll fish in a lake. Have you ever done that?"

His brother did not answer.

"You'll like it. No waves and no demons, either," he said affectionately. "Now hurry! Off to where you're supposed to be."

Wek wiped his face on his palm, but another tear was coming. He turned abruptly and ran back toward the house.

Bremig unclamped the weather rod and flung it across the yard. *Black walnut!* He looked at his hands, knowing they soon would be stained from the dark sap of the wood. The usual prow-piece would not do for this boat. He'd be asked to carve something he had never seen, a mockery of a figurehead to goad the demon to her utmost wrath.

And he would comply. Perhaps as his last commission he would carve that absurd face, that contorted image to purge Etma's bloodlust. The work would provide a grim satisfaction.

CHAPTER 3

RIDRUNE succumbed to Balin's pleas. After the morning chores were finished, he lent her a cart with his strapping son Varn as driver. Kyala would have preferred taking the reins herself. Did her uncle think she was incapable of handling a pair, when she had driven four ponies halfway to the Teeth of Dawn? No, Kyala suspected that Ridrune, in sending Varn, was protecting his wagon as much as looking out for the welfare of his sister's kin.

During the journey, she sat listlessly by the driver while Balin sat on his opposite side. Though she and her mother had discussed the matter earlier, Kyala wanted to hear more about the habits and dispositions of Ormek's priests. But with Varn's large bulk between them and the cart rattling mercilessly, she could not initiate a conversation. And so they continued westward without speaking, then turned north to approach the coast via a lightly used road.

The noon sun was behind them when Kyala glimpsed the great crag, Lifegiver's Reach, rising from the surrounding green forest. At the peak, a tabletop of weathered stone leaned out over the sea, its beacon of Ormek's Fire invisible in daylight; there appeared no sign of human habitation. But as they neared the base, Balin pointed up and her daughter thought she saw the walls and roof of the shrine. It was built from the gray rock of the pinnacle, and only by squinting could Kyala see an unnatural straightness to its lines.

The road began to climb, and Varn rested the ponies at a spring that trickled from a mossy stone. Continuing, the travelers crisscrossed the face of the Reach twice more before meeting a gate of stout iron that blocked the path. At the top of each vertical bar sat a metal disk, each slightly different from its neighbors in the pattern of rays and dimples. Though the framework showed rust and age, the disks gleamed as if freshly polished.

No gatekeeper appeared, and Varn looked to Balin for instructions. Kyala hopped down to investigate, putting her face to the cold, rough bars and peering into an adjacent hut, the only structure in sight. A brown-robed figure was standing with his back toward her and his head bowed.

She was about to call to him when her mother arrived and touched a finger to her daughter's lips. "Honorable gatekeeper," Balin said softly.

The figure turned, and Kyala glimpsed a hollow-cheeked face. The man held in his hands a wooden wheel that nearly rivaled the one that Bremig had given her. Despite the disturbance, he continued his recitations while he fingered the notches of the wheel's rim. Balin said nothing more until he was done.

The man cleared his throat and came slowly out of the shelter. Balin touched a forefinger to her brow, and he seemed to take note of the symbol etched there. He frowned, licked his lips, and finally spoke. "Your service was long ago, lady. You have no reason to come here now."

"We've urgent news for Flamen Skendron."

The gatekeeper shook his head. "The First Flamen's health is poor."

"Nonetheless, he'll want to hear us."

"Tell me what you must say to him." He glanced once at Kyala, then fixed his gaze again on her mother.

"I cannot. Etma is stirring. Be content to know that much. The rest he must hear for himself."

"Etma?" At the mention of the demon, the gatekeeper clutched the circle to his chest. He turned first to the left and then to the right, as if seeking advice from unseen companions. "I would send you away," he said at last, "were it not for your mark of service." He put aside his disk and raised a long-handled wooden hammer to a gong. He struck three blows; the clangs echoed from the cliffs above. Then he pulled back a bar and let the gate swing open.

The way was too narrow for the cart, so Varn was obliged to leave his rig outside the gate. He tethered the ponies to a stone trough that had been chipped from the base of an outcropping.

"Only one of you may go up," the gatekeeper said. He offered them a crude bench. Kyala and her mother exchanged glances, but neither sat.

Balin's lips were pressed tight. At last she let her breath out in a long sigh. "Tell him you're Balin's daughter," she said softly to Kyala. "He'll remember me." Her complexion seemed to redden, and the young woman wondered if it was some trick of the afternoon light. "Tell him I'm waiting down here," Balin continued in a confidential tone. "And if he won't see you," she whispered, "I'll tell the gatekeeper enough to put a smirk on every face in the shrine."

Kyala's eyebrows rose as she tried to assimilate her mother's revelation. Balin had always been vague about her years of temple service. Kyala had heard more than one story about lonely flamens and the young women who served in the shrine, but had never thought to connect such tales with her own mother. She tried to control a smile that tugged at her mouth.

Soon a brown-robed courier arrived down the upper path. He was Kyala's height but quite stout, and he was sweating profusely from his hurried descent. When he learned that the daughter was his charge, he waved impatiently for her to follow him. At once he began to retrace his steps, treading barefoot on the rocky trail with no sign of discomfort. Despite the advantage of her sturdy boots, Kyala found herself breathing heavily to keep up with him.

The climb was steep and rapid. The trees gave way to scraggly bushes, and then to barren rock. On the ribbed and fractured crag face there were only cairns to mark the way. Above Kyala rose the shrine, a building larger than any she had ever seen. At first it seemed carved from the crag itself, but as they drew nearer she saw that cut stones had been tightly fitted together so that the gaps were almost invisible. The walls rose as high as three cottages piled one on top of the other. Faces of Ormek, large and small, new and seemingly ancient icons, had been incised into the outside surfaces.

An unexpected bleating came from the side of the path. Kyala turned in time to see a sheep being led into a low building that was attached to the main structure. "Our dinner, may the Bright One be thanked," her guide explained softly. A man wearing tight leggings and a bloodstained apron hurried in after the animal.

The visitors approached a vast courtyard that was partially roofed with dry branches. In the center, where there was no cover, lay a huge stone Sun disk half in shadow, half in the afternoon light. Kyala peered into the shaded surroundings and glimpsed what appeared to be a garden of mosses. Her guide held out his arm, barring her way until she removed her boots and stockings. Upon entering, she saw barefooted temple servants sprinkling water from buckets to keep the greenery damp. Others were kneeling to scrutinize each patch of moss and delicately cut away tiny strands of brown. A woodland fragrance lingered here despite the barren surroundings.

Crossing the bright patch on bare feet, Kyala felt the touch of sun-heated stone. She followed her guide, bypassing the moist beds and the disk with its inlaid rays that glistened like glass. At the far side of the courtyard they reached a smaller, solidly roofed chamber where the floor was cool and smooth. Here stood a middle-aged flamen in a butter-colored robe that hung to his knees. His legs were stockinged in yellow wool. He wore round-toed slippers of thin leather and held a walking stick capped by a bronze ball.

"Tem Flamen." The brown-robed escort bowed his head to stare intently at his toes. The flamen scowled at Kyala, who was looking him in the face, and she did her best to imitate her guide's gesture of respect.

"This is not the season for new servants," the priest said impatiently. "Why do you bring this uninvited stranger?"

"Tem Flamen. She bears news of concern to us."

"We have our own sources of news. Better take her back, before Skendron sees her."

"Skendron? But I thought . . ."

"He's out of bed today. Been hobbling all over the temple giving orders."

"Then woe to us all," the courier whispered. "But the First Flamen is in fact the one she seeks. I've been asked to take her to his chamber."

The yellow-robed priest turned to Kyala with renewed curiosity. "You *want* to see Skendron? Tell me why you think he'll admit you."

She felt obliged to explain. "My mother is Balin of Darst," she said hurriedly, her voice catching in her throat. "I was hoping . . . he might remember her and do me the favor of listening." She dared raise her eyes, and noted that the flamen's frown had softened slightly.

"Balin," he said as he rubbed his bare chin and scrutinized the young woman. "I know the name. That was long ago. And if my memory's right, you don't look a hair like her."

Kyala had heard similar comments so often that the repetition made her ball her fists in frustration. But she managed to answer calmly, "My father was tall and thin, more like me. But I have my mother's ears."

"Mother's ears!" He raised his chin and cackled. "I'll tell Skendron that. If he'll see you, I've nothing more to say about it." The priest turned and walked slowly into the long sanctuary, his staff tapping the floor at every step.

The First Flamen received Kyala in the privacy of his personal quarters. The room was high-ceilinged, the walls hung with faded tapestries. The air carried foreign scents of incense and herbal potions. Skendron sat on a padded chair with a brown blanket wrapped about his legs, his hands resting in his lap. What showed of his garb appeared similar to the yellow robe of the other flamen, and in addition he wore a tall, stiff hat with a sloping peak.

Kyala studied his lined face, the prominent chin and flattened nose. What might he have looked like years before? she wondered. Could her mother have found this priest handsome? Suddenly she saw another face, one she had been trying to forget. Bremig! In his younger days, this man had surely resembled her wood-carver. The priest lifted his hand and beckoned her with a long forefinger.

"You claim to be Balin's daughter," he said in a whiny voice, "but you're nothing like her."

"If you doubt me, my mother is waiting with the gatekeeper."

"Is she?" For a moment he seemed lost in thought. "Well," he said. "I can't walk down there. No. And I daresay she won't be coming up." Again he fell silent, shifting his legs beneath the blanket. "Better tell me what you came for. Something about Etma, is it?"

"Do you know about Pelask's curse?"

The old one frowned. "You come from Darst? Yes. Some half-witted fisherman asked Etma's aid. All because of a glassmaker."

"I was that Vigen's apprentice."

"*Was?* Oh, yes."

"He's with Ormek. I should be Vigen in his stead."

"You . . . ?" Skendron laughed once and then began to cough. When the coughing continued, he slapped his hand against the arm of the chair, the robe falling back to reveal his skeletal shoulder. Kyala looked about frantically for aid, but suddenly the fit was over. "So you've come," he continued, his mirthful expression gone, "to practice your art, have you? Come to rid us of the sea beast?"

"With the Bright One's help. But I know nothing of this creature."

"Is it the demon herself, you'll ask me next, or just some drunkard's dream? I think neither."

"Then . . ."

Skendron's frown deepened. "The sightings are reliable. We've had one from our own lookout." He nodded toward a small, high window that faced the afternoon sun. "Whether Etma is involved makes no difference. People will blame her in any case, and look to Ormek for deliverance. And if Ormek fails them, what will happen to their faith? The cursed demon worship will make further strides, and all our good works will be lost."

"Then we must try talismans. With colored glass, every beast of the forest has been tamed. Even Lame Ones."

The flamen nodded grimly. "Every *forest* beast. So I've been told. As for this one, we'll have to see."

"I've saved my pigments," she began. "I can . . ."

An angry flourish of the priest's hand silenced her. "You? Don't *you* do anything."

"But you said . . ."

"Yes, I agreed that a Vigen might help us. Let him dangle his beads, and learn if they can prevail. But we've already sent for our glassmaker, a man of some experience."

Kyala's mouth fell open, and she stepped back in surprise. Another Vigen? She had not known that any others could be found in this part of the Mejdom. "But . . ." Her thoughts were tangled. She wanted to explain about her gift, but did not know how to begin. Would a priest of Ormek believe that the Bright One had singled *her* out? "If the beast is strong-willed," she started, "the talismans may fail. If the color match is not perfect, they may also prove powerless. But even in such cases, with Ormek's favor . . ."

"Enough!" Skendron waved his hand in dismissal. "Our Vigen might need some assistance. What he'll think of taking on a girl I can't say, but I'm willing to make him the offer. Now, you go back where you came from and wait for word."

Kyala did not move.

"Go." He waved his hand again. She was trembling, but stood her ground. She was ready to risk the one lever that might move him.

"Did you forget that my mother is Balin of Darst?" she asked fiercely.

Skendron began to cough again, but regained control a moment later. "I hear a threat in your voice. Is that how you address the First Flamen of the Shrine?" He paused and reached for a silvery goblet, sipped slowly, then licked his reddened lips. "I recall well enough the name of your mother."

Belligerence, Kyala realized, would not help. She lowered her gaze as she had for the priest at the courtyard. "Then I ask you, Tem Flamen, for the Bright One's sake, to let me remain until your Vigen arrives."

The priest raised his head with a sigh and stared up at the gilded ceiling. "Stay, then. It matters little to me. But you'll have to earn your keep. And I promise nothing when the glassmaker comes."

With a smile of gratitude, she hurried from Skendron's presence and back into the courier's charge. "I must go down to the gatehouse and then return," she said. The brown-robe poked his head into Skendron's room, conferred briefly, then led her silently back along the path.

Varn was already fussing about his cart, but Balin still sat on the gatekeeper's bench. Kyala threw her arms about her mother. "He remembered," she said, holding back tears she could not understand. Was she glad of her victory or distraught at leaving her family again? She had been home so briefly. "I'll stay here," she whispered. "They've sent for another glassmaker. I can . . . work with him." Balin shook her head with evident anguish, but said nothing to deter her daughter's plans.

Shortly, Kyala found herself in the smoky kitchen, where her first chore was carrying split logs to the huge fireplace. The others who bustled in and out were a varied lot. She quickly learned that the brown-robes were under-flamens, men who might eventually rise to the yellow garb of their superiors. Much of the work was done by servitors such as Balin had been, gray-garbed youths whose hair was cut close to the scalp. These men and women would give their years, depart, and never return.

A third group contained, among others, the butcher who was now carving up the sheep she had heard bleating earlier. These villagers were paid wages from the flamens' coffers and were permitted to visit their families twice a month. They took no religious oaths and wore what clothing they pleased. But they were not allowed within the walls of the temple itself.

Kyala's first confidant was a coarse-looking girl named Meep who had been earning wages there for nearly four years. "It's the winter here that's the worst," Meep admitted as Kyala dropped at the hearthside what she hoped was the final armload of wood. "The wind whistles through every crack. Snow coats the floors. The buckets ice over if you leave 'em standing long."

Their conversation was cut short by orders from the chief cook. Meep and Kyala, each carrying two empty pails, trudged down a long trail to a well sunk deep into the hill. Kyala was grateful that she'd recovered her boots. Meep's raggedy footgear seemed to offer poor protection from the gravel underfoot. "But you know," said Meep, "I'd be worse off workin' down there. Can you see me fetchin' ale at the inn—every dirty farmer with his hands all over me? At least the priests are decent about it. Give me little things when I'm kind to 'em."

Kyala had half a mind to ask if Meep had been called by Skendron. He must be past that now, she thought. And perhaps she did not really want to know, just as she hoped never to learn the name of a wife Bremig might take.

During the meal, the hired servants remained in the kitchen while the gray-robed youths carried bowls and platters to the dining hall. Most of the staff were idle, waiting hungrily while the cookfire cast their shadows against the high walls. First the flamens were served, then the underflamens and then the lay servants. Only when Ormek's blessed had sated themselves were the others allowed to dine. Kyala found herself quickly growing annoyed with the shrine's hierarchy. The hired ones sniggered at Ormek's faithful, with their airs of holiness and their private weaknesses. Kyala understood these ill feelings, but tried not to share them.

Later, Meep showed Balin's daughter to an outbuilding where crowded sleeping quarters lay—rooms with straw-covered floors and greasy blankets. But Kyala had no thoughts of sleep. She crept outside into the cool air of the summer night. The cry of crickets rose from the forest below, and she saw here and there the flash of a firefly. By moonlight, she made her way about the perimeter of the low building until she could view the Beacon—a huge oil-fired lamp whose flame was protected by windows of rock crystal.

Here was her first close glimpse of Ormek's fire, lit from the sun itself by a process that the priests kept secret. From this place flame was carried to each sacred lamp in the small shrines of the surrounding country. From one such lamp had the torches for her mentor's pyre been lit. The sight of the

Beacon brought gooseflesh to her arms, and she stood staring at it until the brightness hurt her eyes.

"Cattle-brain! You'll fall to your death." The flame's afterimage blinded her even when she turned away. She recognized the voice as Meep's. "You're two steps from the brink."

Kyala knew that the Beacon sat at the tabletop's edge, but in standing beside the building had thought herself safe. "I can't see," she cried as fear suddenly set her heart pounding. She swung her hand wildly and touched a warm arm. The bluish ghost of the lamp danced in front of her as she allowed herself to be led back to safety.

Before dawn, Kyala was roused from her bed of straw to return to the kitchen's drudgery. With the last stars still visible, she groggily made her way to the woodpile. Afterward, when daylight had broken, there were buckets to be filled and others to be emptied. Soon she became familiar with the narrow path to the cliff's edge, where refuse was tipped out into the sea far below. The dumping point, a spur that jutted from the cliffside, stank of spilled slops. Gulls stood in rows along the brink, waiting to swoop for discarded tidbits.

After a hasty meal, the kitchen crew marched down to the gate in ragged procession. Two wagons stood laden with supplies at the top of the road. Kyala and Meep were soon wrestling with a sack of flour, grunting and swearing each time the awkward load slipped to the ground. Back and forth they went, lugging cured fish one time, hams another, until the goods were all neatly stacked or shelved in the storehouse.

In the early afternoon, a woodcutter reached the gate. Kyala and five others dragged a handcart up and down the rough path, slowly replenishing the pile of logs near the kitchen. She had lost count of the number of trips when a commotion snapped her out of her daze. Excited voices came from the shrine as she neared the crest of the trail. Kyala caught a glimpse of yellow robes on the Beacon's terrace; as she moved by, the high walls cut off her view. She wanted to drop her task, but her fellow workers plodded on.

As soon as they reached their destination, Kyala released her towrope and raced toward the seaward side of the building. Ignoring the cries calling her back, she found a vantage point that allowed a good view of the terrace. The flamens and their attendants were peering out to sea, gesturing and shouting, but their words were a jumble. Though she also stood at the edge of a steep cliff, the parapet blocked whatever they were watching.

Turning quickly, she hurried toward the dumping place, almost running full tilt into Meep along the way. The girl tugged at her sleeve, and tried unsuccessfully to drag her back to her labors. "Wait," cried Kyala. "I've got to look out. You can hold my legs." She took Meep's hand and reached the trail that led to the spur.

Gulls fluttered and hopped aside for her. From here Kyala could see past the jutting terrace into the choppy sea beyond. "Hold tight!" she shouted as she dropped to her belly and squirmed forward for a better view. She followed the outstretched arm of the nearest flamen and squinted into the brightness. Something was down there in the water—surely not a boat.

All she could make out was an irregular shape, rust-colored, glistening, that rose and fell in the surf. Then she noticed about the mottled hump the bobbing of bloodred sacs. The bladders were evidently part of the thing, keeping it afloat, but what limbs propelled it she could not discern. The mass was surely moving . . . toward Darst, she thought with a chill. Soon it was so small that she could see no details at all.

Meep tugged insistently, and Kyala allowed herself to be pulled back. "You can look now," Kyala offered, but the girl shook her head. What more was there to do? The thing was gone. With a weary sigh, the would-be Vigen returned to her dreary task.

On the way down the trail, Kyala mentioned the beast, but the others in the work crew showed no curiosity. The inhabitants were safe here, high above the waves, she thought. But these people had families in the villages below. She could not understand their indifference. "The Bright One'll take care of us," one youth suggested. "Nothing we can do."

The day passed, and then another. Balin's daughter spent the whole of one morning splitting logs, for she had foolishly revealed her skills with an ax. There were free moments, however. Whenever she could, Kyala slipped away to scan the sea from her lookout.

She saw nothing in the water, not even a fishing boat. Her patience was exhausted. She wanted to hear news, but no rumor of the beast's whereabouts entered the kitchen gossip. There was talk of Skendron's ill temper and of a mishandled ceremony at the altar. And one woman bore a bruise on her face that she refused to explain.

Kyala could stand no more of this life. She resolved to force her way into the First Flamen's presence and learn what had happened to his summoned Vigen. That night, when the meal was over and the attendants were too sleepy to block her path, she would confront the priest again. But as she was about to sit down to the kitchen servants' meal, a brown-robe came in and called her name. "You're wanted in Skendron's quarters," he said brusquely. "Take off your boots and come with me."

CHAPTER 4

IT was early morning, and Bremig felt the breeze through his loose sweater as he walked along the shoreline. So far as he could tell, not a single boat had dared set out today, though the water showed barely a ripple and the sky was clear. He gazed at the clutch of islands, the "hen's eggs" that lay at the mouth of Darst's cove, and then back along the shore. Not even the usual scavengers were out today. He could have his pick of the tide's leavings.

Behind him, his bay roan snorted softly and he turned to watch her nibbling at a bit of seaweed. She shook her dappled muzzle, directing his attention to a large pink shell of a sea snail. This one was new to him, and he studied its elegant spiral before dropping it into his pouch. The textures of shells had long fascinated the carver; he sometimes tried to imitate their flutings and striations in his work. Provided he stayed close to traditional patterns, his customers made no complaints. But he recalled how one time a seaman, irate over Bremig's design, had broken a weather rod in two and then refused to pay for it. The memory of the man's fit of temper made Bremig laugh aloud.

His feeling of amusement did not last. No matter what he thought about, the so-called Scourge of Darst was constantly lurking in his mind. Already it was known up and down the coast. Should it surface now, he thought, it might have an easy meal of wood-carver.

He had hoped to escape his gloom, but the ride and beach walk were proving ineffective. Since leaving Kyala, he had slept badly, if at all. There was a task ahead of him—one he found increasingly unwelcome—and he had not even sharpened his tools.

The carver continued along a sandy stretch where crabs slid into finger holes as he approached. A gull lay dead, and he wrinkled his nose as its foul air reached him. Flies buzzing about his legs, he kicked the fallen bird from his path. He came on another odd shell, but this time did not keep it. Turning with a sigh, he whistled for his mare.

Later Bremig stood in his shop, staring moodily at the pile of his personal carvings. Even these no longer gave him pleasure. He hefted a Sun disk and noticed careless cuts he had not seen before. He would not want anyone to see such work.

As he considered destroying the piece, Bremig heard voices calling to him from the yard. Hastily he threw a covering over his works, clapped the dust from his hands, and stepped out into the morning air. The two men waiting each carried a large ax, and from the glint of light on the blades he knew the tools had just been honed. He could guess what his cousins wanted.

Draalego, Pelask's eldest son, was the taller of the pair. He had the humped nose and florid complexion of his father, and the arm muscles revealed by his sleeveless jerkin told of years of toil in the boats. Another cousin, Sipt, large-eared and vacant of expression, leaned on the handle of the second ax. Bremig approached them cautiously and waited for someone to speak.

"Planks are almost ready," said Draalego, nodding in the direction of the boatyard. "You'd better get started on your piece."

The carver looked at the ground and clenched his teeth.

He had made a point of staying clear of the yard while the walnut boards were cut and shaped and taken to the boiling trough. But he knew that the carpenters had left no wood for his work. "I was promised a good block," he said without enthusiasm. "So far I've not even seen shavings."

Sipt smiled cruelly and lifted his tool. "Goin' cuttin' right now. You come with us. Pick your own trunk. Then you'll quit complainin'."

Draalego beckoned, swinging his long arm as he turned. The carver had no choice but to follow him to the waiting wagon.

Riding through Darst, Bremig noticed that the traffic was lighter than usual. He suspected that fear of the beast was keeping people at home. But he found himself envying the few townsfolk he saw. Here, he glimpsed a cobbler discussing a boot with a customer at his doorstep. On the corner, a weaver's shop stood open, showing a bright pattern on the loom. To be a landsman, with a shop opening onto a busy thoroughfare, was a dream the carver had never dared pursue.

Bremig felt the wagon lurch and noticed a few pedestrians scrambling from the path of Draalego's ponies. His cousin was driving recklessly, perhaps for the pleasure of baiting the townspeople. That fishermen were unpopular in these streets the carver had long known, but today the intense stares of hatred made him wish he could conceal his face.

To his further discomfort, the route passed the charred remains where Watnojat had once kept shop. Turning his eyes in another direction, Bremig struggled with his memories of Kyala. No, he would not think of her now. He had promised himself as much. . . . The wagon bounced to the end of the street and aimed toward the outskirts of Darst.

They crossed rolling country, fields of ripening wheat and pastures where sheep grazed quietly. Draalego's gaze was constantly on the hills. After a time he veered into a narrow track that led to a high-roofed barn. A man in a straw hat was tossing slops into a pigpen. He turned and frowned at the visitors, pushed back his hat, and looked up at them with narrowed eyes.

"Yours?" asked Draalego with a sweep of his arm.

The farmer nodded. Behind him, under the eaves, hung a row of Ormek's disks that stirred gently with the wind.

"Lot of work. You could use some help here."

"I've got help," he answered testily.

"But the hands can't do *everything*." Pelask's son lifted the ax from the bottom of the wagon. "Why, I'll bet you've got work up there in the walnuts." He pointed to where the trees straggled up a hillside.

"Trees take care of themselves," the farmer answered in a louder voice. "Not much to do. Little pruning sometimes, but not now."

"I can see trouble from here," Draalego insisted. "Too crowded. Needs more than pruning. Take one out and the others'll thank you."

"Good producers," said the farmer. Now he was almost shouting, and his face was turned to the barn. A row of round air holes on the wall, Bremig thought, would carry his voice inside. "Maybe the tree at the top's a little off," the man conceded. "Lightning struck, years ago. Never came back fully, but still a fine tree."

Lightning! Bremig felt his cousins' excitement rise at the man's revelation. What could be more cursed than a tree that had actually drawn lightning?

"We'll cut that one for you," said Pelask's son with a grin. "Do you a favor. We'll just take the trunk for payment." He raised the ax further, and the farmer stepped back without taking his eyes from the blade.

At that moment, a stocky man with tangled hair emerged from the barn. He carried a two-tined pitchfork over his shoulder and a long, heavy pole in his opposite hand. Draalego glanced once at the interloper, put down his ax, and climbed to the rear of the wagon. "Got a barrel of dried cod here," he said hastily. "Trade it for your tree. Come up and have a look." He pulled out a couple of leathery fish and waved them in front of the two landsmen.

The man with the pitchfork glanced at the other, who shrugged. Pursing his lips with annoyance, the farmer mounted the wagon and gazed into Draalego's barrel. Bremig wished only to be done with this odious chore. If the trade was accepted, it would mean he would be finished that much sooner. But the farmer sniffed at the dried fish once and then looked again at his trees.

"Etma's rising," said Draalego in a menacing tone. "Sea's not so far from here, you know." He pointed at the low hills to the west. "Do you feel safe when the wind's howlin' and the gulls are flockin' in your fields? Have you ever seen a waterspout?" He raised his finger higher, pointing halfway up the sky and squinting as if he could see a cataclysm coming. "A spout that crashes down and washes all this away . . ."

The farmer looked dubiously at the barrel again. "Maybe I can swap this for a couple of goats," he muttered to himself. He glanced at his burly farmhand, whose brow was wrinkled in thought. Suddenly the farmer straightened up. "Leave me the codfish and also one of those axes when you're done. Then we'll be even."

Draalego hissed through his teeth, gave the barrel a kick, and then slapped the cover back onto it. He pushed the keg carelessly to the back of the wagon and into the arms of the heavyset man. The farmer climbed down, leaving Draalego free to drive to the tree-covered hill.

Bremig was last to walk to the top. He stood back, staring at the fire-scarred trunk and the mismatched limbs. The tree forked, as if it were a man with two arms raised—one healthy, the other scarred and lifeless. The blackened side of the fork was clearly dead, but long leaves and round seedpods hung from branches on the opposite side. The trunk leaned slightly downhill, and Draalego seemed to have no doubts as to which way it would fall. He swung a straight stroke that bit deeply into bark and sapwood. The blow made Bremig start as if his own flesh had been cut. After not many more such blows, the black walnut toppled, sending twigs bouncing and snapping in all directions.

The wagon groaned under the weight of the logs. The tree had far more wood than Bremig needed, but his cousin had been charged with resupplying the boatwrights as well. The ponies strained, and Draalego showed little patience with his beasts. Despite his whip, the ride home went slowly. Passing through curious knots of onlookers, they descended from town to the crowded boatyard.

The commotion alone told Bremig that no ordinary work was being done; boat-builders did not tolerate onlookers or distractions. But this craft was to be unique. Instead of pleasing Etma, it must incite her wrath. The demon's ire, it was said, would focus on one hateful object so that all others might be spared. To this end, every rule must be broken.

He saw, as they entered the yard, how the usual precautions and superstitions had been turned inside out. Where dogs were normally banned, a dozen curs had been tethered. Where children were forbidden, a noisy group now frolicked, taunting the dogs. The din of children's voices along with the yapping drowned out any sounds of construction.

After watering his cousin's long-suffering grays, Bremig paused to study the progress of the work. Ribbands were in place about the mold, and the completed keel now pointed at the sky. Several strakes, in overlapping courses of planking, were finished but for a few final nails. Men wearing gloves against the heat were carrying more dark planks from the boiling trough, and he watched as two boatwrights bent a supple board to the frame.

A few steps away, a length of sailcloth had been spread on the ground. A toothless old man sat smiling beside it, beckoning all passersby to tread with their grimy boots on the fabric. Meanwhile, a young girl was gashing the cloth with a crooked knife.

"Carver! Mark this where you want it cut." Bremig felt a hand on his shoulder. He was spun around and led to where the new log of walnut lay.

He noticed that someone had already hacked away the charred portion and found solid wood beneath. Bremig had never examined an exposed section of walnut before. The dark grain intrigued him, yet he felt apprehensive because of the tree's repute.

"You'll want this part," said the carpenter. "But keep away from it when there's a storm blowing." He laughed coldly and handed Bremig a knife. The carver touched the blade to the wood reluctantly, as if expecting to feel a remnant of the lightning's long-spent power. When no spark jumped to his fingers, he quickly scored the surface, then left the sawyers to their work.

Now he could muster no more excuses. Tomorrow he would begin a difficult task, and so today he must sharpen his chisels and gouges. The afternoon was half gone by the time he returned to his shop and checked the condition of his tools. Most needed only a modest honing, but several were nicked and would require Arod's grinding wheel. With a surprising eagerness for the smith's company, Bremig set out for town.

There he found the forge cold and Arod sitting glumly at the rear of his shop. "Why waste charcoal when there's no work?" the smith grumbled. "I haven't seen a customer all day. The fishermen have empty purses, and the farmers don't want to come to town."

"You may think yourself better off idle when you hear what I have waiting for me," Bremig countered. "Black walnut. A lightning-struck piece. They want me to carve it."

Arod scratched at his blond beard. "I've heard a few stories about that wood."

"Then here's another, and a true one. My cousins are building a boat with walnut planking."

The smith gave a hollow laugh. "Why bother with such trouble? Just tie a lightning rod to an ordinary mast and smear the decks with pitch. What easier way is there to curse a vessel?"

Bremig did not reply, but began to unwrap his packet of tools. Discussing seamen's superstitions with a landsman, he knew, was unlikely to improve their friendship.

"I see you're planning to go through with it," said Arod. He rose with a sigh, walked to the grindstone, and began to crank.

The carver picked out a broad chisel, examined the distorted edge in the light from the side window, then held it to the rotating wheel at the small angle of its bevel. The noise made him grit his teeth. He felt the metal heating, then stopped to cool the tip in a water bucket before continuing.

Arod paused also and let the heavy wheel spin freely. "What do they expect when that boat's done? Coax down a storm to blow us all to sea?"

"It's supposed . . . to make Etma angry," Bremig said reluctantly.

"So?"

He bowed to Arod's insistence. What did it matter? "She throws all her fury at the boat—waves, wind, beast, everything. Beast most of all. That's what my cousins are hoping. When she's done, her wrath is spent. Then she leaves us alone."

"Do the townspeople know your friends' plan?"

Bremig shook his head. "What would they do if they found out?"

"Burn the thing now, if they have any sense. Never let it touch water. But I won't tell 'em." Arod spun the wheel again, and the carver finished grinding his chisel.

"You don't swallow that story," Arod said when the shop

was quiet again. "If you believed any of it, you'd be three days' ride inland by now."

"How do you decide that, my sooty friend?"

"Because you're the one who cheated Etma of her due. Don't you think she wants Kyala?"

"I don't pretend to know the ways of demons," Bremig answered darkly. "And don't you forget your part in it. For which I'm grateful, by the way. Regardless."

"Regardless? Ah, then there's more to this than I've heard yet." The smith's sly smile disquieted the carver. "I've seen anxious suitors before, but none who roused me with a commotion like yours. And you never came back to explain yourself."

"Balin's daughter is not for me," he said brusquely, squinting at another chisel. This one was badly nicked and would take more grinding than the first.

"Not for you?" the smith asked in a rising voice. "If you believe a woman's first refusal, then you'd better get used to cold beds."

Bremig did not meet his gaze, and finally Arod spun the grindstone once more. The spray of sparks gave the carver a brief respite from the smith's prying. The noise covered his pain, and he nearly allowed the metal to overheat. There was a soft hiss as he doused the blade.

"I hadn't the wit to tell her I like burnt soup," the carver blurted out. "That's what I should have said. I eat dried fish right out of the barrel and I patch my own clothes."

"Now we're getting somewhere."

"Are we?" The carver checked the blade and gestured for the wheel again.

"Finish this up and then we'll have a talk," Arod said firmly. "About women."

Bremig glared at the smith, but there was no hiding his inexperience. "She's not like the others," he said softly, and then he made sparks rain.

* * *

The walnut block was clamped to a stump and waiting. Bremig stripped away the remnants of bark, then chose an adze to rough out the shape. It was a poor log for carving—dry and dead on one side, still oozing sap on the other. Ordinarily he would not touch such wood, for the shrinkage and cracking as it seasoned would ruin his work. But this piece was not meant to last.

The color was of pale earth, with portions that hinted at violet. Every glance at the fine grain increased his interest, and his carver's instincts began to fight his distaste for the task. His earlier, crude plans began to change. The structure of the wood was unlike any he had shaped. What might he make of this?

He had learned his art by following tradition, imitating works done by others. An old craftsman had instructed him for a while, but there had been no formal apprenticeship. He had no examples for the face suited to a black walnut vessel, only the descriptions from ancient tales.

A grinning face with gaps between the teeth. A nose with nine nostrils, for Etma hates the number nine. Ears like ale cups. A chin with warts of a toad.

That was the prescription. He could do whatever he wanted so long as he kept to those rules. And though the new notion he had was cruel, it suited his mood. Arod, he suspected, would not understand. Not after the advice he had given. But surely Draalego would be pleased.

If Kyala was to blame, then why not let her own countenance goad Etma to a frenzy? Even with gaps between her teeth, nine nostrils, and ale-cup ears, he could make her recognizable. The caricature would amuse him, whereas the original had, so far, only brought him misery.

Bremig donned his tool apron and studied his walnut block with new enthusiasm. Yes. He could see her already in the dark grain. He lifted the mallet and made a decisive cut.

CHAPTER 5

KYALA was taken to Skendron's quarters, where he sat as she had seen him last, his blanket wrapped around him, his tall hat falling forward. Beside the flamen stood a broad-shouldered but otherwise smallish man who peered at her with undisguised curiosity.

"Here is your Vigen," said Skendron to Kyala with a toss of his head. "Modwetten. You should know the name. From time to time, he's been of help to us."

Now it was her turn to be curious. In her brief apprenticeship she had known but two Vigens—one a man she had admired with passion, the other a tyrant who had misused his art. And what could she make of this one? He had a high, sloping forehead, short gray hair and beard, and a pinched, mirthless face that reminded her of an innkeeper checking his accounts. He wore loose woven trousers and a sleeveless jerkin of cowhide that showed powerful biceps for a man of his size.

Modwetten. She scowled as she wrestled with the name. Perhaps she had heard of this glassmaker but hadn't realized that he lived within two days' journey of the temple. Modwetten . . . of Longval. She could associate nothing with him other than the name of his village.

"He admits he has little use for you," continued Skendron, "but we've come to an agreement nonetheless. You do what you can to help him, and then you go home."

"Little use?" Kyala could hold her temper no longer. "Will he cast the beads himself? Or does he have a doltish apprentice waiting to pump his bellows?"

The glassmaker appeared amused at her outburst. "I'm not like your former master," he said with a condescending smile. "I don't carry kiln stones around and set up shop in decrepit stables."

She frowned and waited for his explanation.

"I've heard of your Watnojat's exploits," the Vigen continued. "After all, he passed through Eastplain. The two of you stopped there for the night. I've heard the full account, for Eastplain's a town I visit now and then."

"Then tell me," she insisted. "You who know so much about me. Tell how you plan to cast your talismans."

The Vigen shook his head as if in exasperation at her stupidity. "Why cast new ones? I've with me all the beads I'll need. There are only so many colors . . ."

"But the match must be true!"

"And it will be. To *one* of my beads. We'll find out which one when we've lured the thing to our bait."

Kyala sucked in her breath, then glanced back at Skendron. The priest seemed unperturbed by this glassmaker's absurd claims. How could the man have so many talismans that he would not need another? Surely his confidence was not based on any experience. "Then when do we stalk our prey?" she said at last.

"Why waste time?" replied the Vigen. "We have men of the shrine who've offered to help, and I've brought weapons. Tomorrow we'll set our trap and be done with it."

Skendron coughed. "And keep the whole business to ourselves," the priest added. "Until it's finished. If we succeed, then we can claim a victory for Ormek. If we fail . . ."

The glassmaker grinned confidently. "Why talk of defeat? Ormek will triumph quickly enough."

"Tomorrow, then." Kyala turned and hurried from the room before she could berate the glassmaker for his foolishness. In the kitchen she found the others finishing their late meal, the soup pot nearly empty. She banged the caldron angrily while ladling out her meager portion.

In the morning, Kyala followed an odd procession down to the gate. The way was led by three servitors who had exchanged their gray robes for common jerkins and trousers. There must be nothing about this expedition, Skendron had insisted, that would show a connection with the shrine. And indeed, the group appeared to be made up of travelers from the countryside.

The three young men, with their short hair and shaven faces, might almost be taken as brothers. They were of differing heights, but all of slim build. Their names were Harb, Wasker, and Pech, and beyond that Kyala knew nothing about them.

Outside the gate stood the glassmaker's rig, his two ponies already in harness. The three youths climbed up to ride the wagon's bed, finding room amidst the long, wrapped bundles. The Vigen, having carried from the shrine a large carved chest, slid his treasure box beneath the driver's seat. Kyala was certain this casket held his store of talismans. She imagined how he had slept, curled up on a pallet with his arms protecting the contents. When she sat down beside him, she seemed to feel the power of the glass rising to warm her.

They descended the steep road quickly, and soon reached a neighboring farm. Here the Vigen made a detour, for his preparations were not yet complete. The first call proved unsuccessful, the farmer's wife turning him away at once. But at his second stop, after some haggling, Modwetten purchased a scrawny billy goat. Bleating furiously, the poor creature was hoisted into the wagon and tied to a ring. The three youths scrambled to sit in the opposite corner, well out of range of horns and sharp hoofs.

Following a track that the glassmaker seemed to recognize, they rolled through a gully, emerging between low hills at a deserted section of coast. "This is our spot," Modwetten announced calmly. "Here we'll set our bait." Kyala studied the scene, noting how a short curve of beach gave way on her right to the first of several bluffs. On the left, the beach was broken by low, dark rocks that jutted into the water. By stepping from one to the other, she thought one might advance a good twenty paces seaward.

Leaving his weapons for the young men to unpack, the Vigen ordered Kyala to light his two lanterns. This was the first sign of good sense she had seen from him. The beads needed Ormek's power—His heat and light. To rely on sunlight alone was risky. A lamp gave added protection, for touching a bead directly to the heat could subdue the most stubborn of creatures.

Needing shelter from the brisk land breeze, she climbed into the rear of the wagon before striking the flint. The goat swung his head at her, and she bleated back at him. The tinder caught and she quickly lit a taper, ignited the lamps, then left the animal to its lonely final moments.

The glassmaker had barely started unpacking his talismans when she set the lamps down beside him. Then she glanced into the open box and gasped at the display of riches. The reflected daylight made her blink in dazzlement. Once before, she had seen so many beads in one place, but never with such variety. One strand held deer eyes of various shades, the umbers changing gradually into deeper browns. On another tether, golden eyes for mature bobcats were strung with charms of darker hue for their young. Kyala marveled at one set after another—wild pig, bear, fox. How many years, she wondered, had gone into their preparation? And where had he found the scarce pigments in such quantities?

"I don't recognize these," she confessed as she picked out a dark strand with hints of deep violet.

"A rare breed of elk," answered the Vigen smugly. "Everything's here. Every variation that an animal's been known to show."

"So far," said Kyala under her breath. But she could not fault the glassmaker's work.

Soon the beads were laid out on the wagon's bench and footplanks. The order he chose followed roughly that of the glassmakers' mixing board, altered to take account of the variations from string to string. Reds, browns, golds—all were here. "Now we lack only our quarry," he said, and for the first time Kyala heard a hint of fear in his voice. He shaded his eyes and gazed at the waves. The sky was beginning to cloud over.

"Help me with the goat," the Vigen ordered suddenly. She went back to untie the rope's end, and the creature obligingly jumped down. Seeing a chance for escape, it plunged toward higher ground. Kyala lost her balance and tumbled, but kept her hold on the rope.

Modwetten cursed the creature's forebears while Kyala managed to right herself. The goat was twisting its head wildly, fighting the cord that burned her palms. It took her strength and the Vigen's together to drag the struggling animal to shore and then up onto the first low rock. The footing was slippery, waves lapping at their boots and then falling back to reveal shiny mussel clumps.

The bleating was piteous and the going painfully slow. When they were halfway across the jagged stepping-stones, Modwetten turned on the animal and seized its horns with one meaty hand. Pulling a knife from his belt, he sliced open the soft, white throat. Blood spurted in quick pulses, and the goat sagged to its knees. "I want it farther out," the Vigen insisted, dragging on the line.

There was no more fight in the creature. It left a trail of blood and hair on the rocks as they pulled the twitching burden to the final outcropping. Here they wedged the bleeding body into a gap, forcing it under a lip so that the waves could not easily loosen it. "Now we'll need patience," Modwetten said with a sigh.

Kyala looked back once at the body of the pitiful creature. It was thoroughly soaked now. A thin stream of blood colored the water that rose and fell about the matted pelt. "Careful!" Modwetten caught her as she nearly tumbled into the surf. Embarrassed that she should care more for a goat's fate than for that of the coastal settlements, she hurried back to the beach.

Morning passed into afternoon, and the clouds grew thicker. The youths took watches on top of the bluff, reporting nothing in the water. Their periodic shouts were monotonously the same. Modwetten lingered by his talismans, and Kyala's sole task was to keep the lanterns supplied with oil.

When the first raindrops hit, the glassmaker seemed not to notice them. Then, when the downpour threatened to douse his lamps, he gave orders to hang a shelter. The youth named Harb helped Kyala raise a canopy of cloth over the wagon. The Vigen, now beneath a makeshift roof, stayed in front while the others huddled under the rear of the leaky tent. Only Wasker, the one on watch, bore the full drenching of the storm.

Having spent a day with her companions, Kyala by now had found distinguishing features among them. Harb possessed a mole on his cheek and another at the side of his mouth. Wasker's front tooth was broken. Pech's left eyebrow grew bushier than the other. All three men were laconic, having spent several years in the near-silence of the shrine. She heard no complaints from Harb or Pech about the rain, and Wasker's calls spoke only of empty waves.

Night approached, and Wasker came in from his fruitless vigil. "Can't see past the rocks now," he complained, his drenched clothing sticking to his body. He took off the shirt and hung it from a nail. Kyala would have liked a fire, but despaired of finding any dry wood nearby. She remained under the canopy, staring toward the body of the goat until she could no longer discern the rocks at all.

After a time, Modwetten thrust one of his lamps at Kyala and suggested that she break out his provisions. "We'll be spending the night here," he announced. Her cold fingers moving stiffly, she found a smoked haunch of mutton, hard bread, and cheese amongst his bundles.

That night, the task of the "watch" was to listen, for nothing beyond shore could be seen in the gloom. The glassmaker huddled with the others in the wagon and did not speak. Later, Kyala noticed a light bobbing on the land side. Voices approached from the direction of the road and soon two visitors on horseback stood beside the crude shelter.

The men dismounted. Modwetten moved forward to converse in private, but even so, some of the words reached Balin's daughter. When she heard Watnojat's name mentioned, her curiosity drew her closer. "Maybe that big pyre was the start of our woes," said one voice. "The Old Vigen's burning on the high hill. It wasn't the common practice at Darst."

Pyre? What an odd subject to raise now, Kyala thought. Her cheeks began to sting, but she could not stop listening.

"Land breeze sprang up early that night," said another voice. "A stiff one, too. We've three reliable accounts."

"Pay attention, glassmaker," said the other. "To the wind and the size of the blaze. The smoke may have drifted a full day's sail from land. For all we know, smoke never reached that far before."

"And that's what drew the beast coastward?" The Vigen clucked his tongue. "The smell from the pyre?"

"This is our consensus. Would you rather follow reason, or do you prefer the tales of fishermen?"

Kyala clenched her fists. She had recognized one voice as that of an under-flamen from the Reach. What was the purpose of his new accusation? she wanted to know. First, the fishermen had blamed this beast on Pelask's curse. Tonight, the priests were pointing at Watnojat's pyre. In either case, Kyala herself was the chief culprit, and now landsmen would join seamen in despising her. For a while she could think of nothing else.

More muttering followed from the visitors as the talk shifted to other matters. At the end, a hasty agreement was made, something about a load of firewood, and then the two men rode away. The glassmaker returned, glancing at Kyala so fixedly that she pressed her back into the slats of the wagon. Wasn't it obvious that she'd been listening? But he turned to the others and spoke with surprising good cheer. "Tomorrow we try new bait," he announced. "Now all but the man on watch should try to sleep."

Bremig kicked angrily at the pile of chips and shavings that surrounded his workplace. Once again he studied the prow-piece that had taken shape beneath his hands. Why was he holding a chisel now, he asked himself, when all that remained to do was fine smoothing? A well-wrought face had emerged from the block, though not the face he'd planned. And now he found the image impossible to change. He untied his apron and flung his tools down in disgust.

The chisels were not at fault. But how could he explain his loss of control? "There *is* a curse in this walnut," he said aloud as he stalked into the cottage. He had no other answer.

He found his mother, Hekina, spinning wool, her head nodding dreamily with each turn of the wheel. His sister-in-law, Varva, was kneading a ball of dough on a trencher. Aside from the two women, the room was empty. Bremig sat on a stool and put his head in his hands.

"They're waiting for you," said Varva. "Give them what they want, and let them finish their silliness."

"I am tired of giving them what they want." He raised his long arms and pounded his fists on the table. Hekina did not look at him but went on spinning.

"What else can you do?" Varva gave the dough a final

pat, then covered it with a cloth and moved the plank near the morning's dying embers. "Why be stubborn, when it's not so hard to be agreeable?"

"I've been carving for their ugly cult all my life," he answered bitterly. "Now I can't manage my fingers. No matter how I try, my hands seem bent on betrayal."

Varva gave him a skeptical look. "I've heard walnut is a difficult wood."

"I should give you a chisel and let you learn for yourself."

She put a gentle hand on his arm. "Why don't you let me see what you've done."

With a despairing groan, Bremig stood up and strode back to the yard. The carving stared at him, its mocking countenance proof that he'd lost control of his skills. The prescribed features were present—nine nostrils and all. But the rest was not what he'd imagined. The face was unfamiliar, with an air of mystery that he could only attribute to the oval eyes and the exaggerated curve of the cheek, to the high forehead and the swanlike neck. For all his efforts, he knew he could not change that unintended image.

"I get tingly looking at it," said Varva, "but what does that matter? You've followed all the rules I know." She began to tick them off on her fingers, reciting softly until the list was done. "Cups for ears . . . a warty chin. All there. And it looks finished, too. What do you have to complain about?"

"But . . ." How could he explain his problem? Only if she knew what he'd intended could she see the difficulty, and he had made no sketches. He watched her return to the cottage and then turned again to the wood. If Varva thought the piece acceptable, then perhaps his cousins would make no complaint.

He forced himself to don his apron. She was right, of course; the figure was nearly complete if he accepted its current appearance. He had only some fine scraping, and then he could forget about walnut . . .

When he could work no longer, he retreated into his shop and closed the door. With a purpose he was slowly comprehending, he took out the cash box that he had long kept hidden behind a pile of scraps. Though he was not always paid in coin for his work, he'd amassed a modest sum. For the first time since purchasing his mare, he took an interest in the contents of that box.

Draalego and Juukal came later, their excited voices carrying into the shop. The carver did not emerge at once. From their comments they seemed satisfied with the carving, so why should he say otherwise? Finally, he poked his head out the doorway. "Take it away," he said. "And leave me some peace."

His cousin insisted that he accompany them to the boatyard, saying that final instructions were needed for the fitting. First the two bent to lift the work, but as soon as they touched it they pulled back. Draalego gave Bremig a puzzled look. "I feel the curse already," he muttered. Wiping his hands carefully on his jerkin, he reached again to grip the carved head. The strain in his face suggested that he was laboring under more than the wood's weight, but he and Juukal managed to lug the piece to the yard.

There Bremig saw the doomed craft almost ready, resting on her keel now, supported by timbers on either side. The lines of the high stern and prow had been oddly distorted, so that the boat looked awkward, not even seaworthy. A mast of knotty wood had been raised in her middle, and a youth was furling the grimy, tattered sail. Bremig grimaced at the sight, unable to decide whether the overall effect was laughable or sinister.

The fishermen set down the carving with evident relief, and both men wiped their hands vigorously. "We'll be finished tomorrow—ready to launch her," said Draalego. "All we need now is the crew."

"We'll find 'er," replied Juukal with an unpleasant smirk.

Pelask's son grunted. "Tomorrow I go huntin' her myself."

Bremig's eyes narrowed, the import of these remarks only now reaching him. "What are you saying?"

"We need the vixen, Balin's daughter." Juukal gave the carver a questioning glance. "She's got to be in the boat."

"In it?" He stared stupidly at his brother. Had he forgotten such an elementary point, or had he never been told? To his knowledge the craft had to sail with a cargo of corn husks and apple cores. There was nothing in the legends about a passenger.

Juukal poked him in the ribs with his knuckles. "Maybe you can help us," he said. "Now that you're done whittling. What do you say?"

Bremig looked once at his brother's raised eyebrows, pushed him aside, and walked slowly back toward his shop. His head was ringing with blows, though behind him the carpenters stood silent. *Put her in the boat?* The notion was preposterous, lacking even a basis in the seamen's foul traditions. And they wanted him to help find her, as well!

Bremig kicked aside the shop door. His decision was already made. He gathered the finest of his personal carvings, what tools he could carry, a few supplies for a journey. One final time he surveyed the shop and yard, then hurried to the stable to ready his mare.

He understood little of life beyond the confines of Darst's harbor. Now he must leave all that was familiar to him, and much that was dear, to search for a place in the landsmen's world. Over the years he had borne his discontent silently, never daring to seek an alternative. But now that he'd chosen his course, he could not linger.

Relieved that the men were still at the boatyard, he walked the path to the cottage and stepped into the room that smelled of baking loaves. "The work is done," he whispered to Varva. "Accepted and in place. And I am through with them. Whatever else they need for their demon will not come from these fingers." His brother's wife looked at him first in astonishment, and then, at last, with understanding. His mother pressed his hand, began to move her lips in prayer. Then she seemed to realize that he was truly going, and he was grateful she did not cry out.

Nervously, he stole from the yard, at a loss for what to say if Juukal should catch him. The mare sped through town by way of Widow's Knoll, and he paused at the top to check if anyone was following. From this height he could see all the streets of Darst and down into the harbor, as well. The fishermen were busy, and there was no sign of pursuit.

Nonetheless, he continued on the road that led *away* from his first destination. He doubled back at a crossroads, then hid in a copse until dark. Juukal had sensed something, he thought. Bremig would not make his brother's task any easier.

The carver had ridden to the farm once by moonlight, and this night managed to reach it again despite the clouds. Dogs set up a howling as he neared the main door of the house. There was no need to see her, he told himself; a message would suffice. Someone would emerge, and he would simply leave his warning. His heart raced as light showed at the jamb.

But it was the old farmer, Kyala's uncle, who came out. For a moment the carver could not speak his words. The uncle seemed to recognize him, and returned to call Balin.

The mother's face was intent with worry as she heard Bremig's news. "She's gone to the shrine," Balin said. "To Ormek's temple on the Reach. If she stays there, she'll be safe from your demon-worshippers."

"Will she stay?" He needed only that reassurance. One word, and then he could ride off, first to visit Wek, then to begin his new life. "Has she sense to keep hidden?"

"She's going to follow that sea beast. I'm sure of it."

Balin caught a sliding tear with her thumb. "Nothing will keep her from the shore."

"Nothing?" One word, and the wrong one. Yet he could not say he was disappointed. "Then they'll find her," he said to himself. "Unless I do first." To the mother he shouted a few words of consolation. "I'll help if I can," he promised. A drizzle started as he turned from the yard. Facing westward, his mare trotted briskly on the seaward track. Droplets blew against his face and dripped from his chin. Wek would have to wait, he thought unhappily. *But I'll find her first.*

When Kyala woke, the drumming of the rain had ended. A faint light showed on the horizon as Harb, reaching into the wagon, shook her again and then beckoned. She crawled past the sleepers and was alone on the empty beach.

The light grew, and she noticed how the tide had pulled back to leave the cluster of rocks well out of water. Curious, she followed them down the exposed strand. Where was the bait? She saw no hint of rough whiteness where the goat's body had been wedged. Cautiously, she peered closer, trying to make certain she had found the place. Where she stood, the tops of the rocks came level with her shoulders. Their undersides were thickly crusted, and the smell of drying mollusks did not appeal to her.

The goat was gone. Feeling a stab of fear, she hurried back up the steep grade. From within the wagon, she heard the others stirring. The glassmaker stumbled groggily into the open and seemed unperturbed by her news. He did not even bother to check for himself, but sent her up the bluff to watch the sea.

It was from this vantage point, when her attention strayed, that Kyala spotted a heavily laden dray rolling down the narrow track to the beach. She saw Modwetten rousing the three youths, and suddenly understood what had come of last night's conversation. The under-flamen had sent a load of firewood . . . and something else. She scuttled down the slope and discovered a dead calf atop the pile of split logs. From the looks of the creature, she thought it had been stillborn.

Modwetten insisted that the "pyre" be built high on the bluff. He climbed first up the steep side, then supervised the stacking of wood until the entire load stood before him. Wasker and Pech, with unconcealed repugnance, pulled the stiff animal up the rise.

And so that morning a fire burned above the beach, commending to Ormek a creature that had never known His warmth. Kyala stood at a lower elevation, staring to sea and wondering. After a night of doubts, she now found comfort in the priests' theory. If indeed the pyre's smoke, and not a demon, had brought the beast landward, then in all likelihood the thing was mortal. This was the question that Skendron had evaded, and now she had some inkling of the answer.

But proof was yet to come.

CHAPTER 6

HALFWAY up the bluff, Kyala stood on a ledge watching strands of kelp bob in the waves. Above her, the clifftop fire had almost burned out, its smoke dispersed by the morning breeze.

On the beach below, the Vigen waited beside his talismans, lifting now and again a brilliant strand. Splashes of color, reflections from the glass, shimmered on the weathered planks of the wagon. Meanwhile, evidently bored by the long inactivity, Harb and Pech sat on the stepping-stone rocks watching the tide come slowly up under them. Wasker strolled the margin, bending occasionally to pick up a shell. The sun was heading toward noon.

A pair of gulls swooped over the water, then turned to investigate the wagon on the shore. One dropped beside Modwetten and he brushed it aside with the back of his hand. Suddenly the two birds shrieked in unison and fled the wagon, winging hurriedly over Kyala's head. For a moment she thought that the Vigen had used a talisman to drive them off.

Then she glanced back down at the incoming tide and saw a huge shape churning in the water. The exposed bulk was the size of an ox, its color the rust of long-weathered iron. Surrounding the center, as if attached to parts still submerged, floated bloodred sacs in a rough circle. These bladders she had glimpsed from the Reach, but now she lacked the high crag's protection. Kyala could not find her voice. She pointed at the thing, managed a hoarse call. Modwetten did not raise his head. A long appendage broke the surface, and then another swung up. These pink limbs were slender, except where they broadened at the meaty tips. The ends were covered with bowllike suckers and bristled with toothy spikes.

The creature held its course, and Kyala did not dare move. She wanted only to know its eye color, and the beast, swimming directly toward her, seemed bent on making that task easy. Again she shouted, this time rousing the Vigen from his lethargy. By then, Harb and Pech had also spotted the creature; hurriedly they took up their weapons. Wasker, raising a bow, began to shoot arrows that fell into the sea far short of his target.

Suddenly a tentacle rose directly in front of the archer. Kyala could not believe the distance between the main body of the creature and the fleshy tip of its appendage. She screamed a warning, but before Wasker could react, a single swift blow knocked him down. He struggled to his knees and was felled again, sprawling with his legs in the surf. Pech tried to pull him to safety by his arms, but the body was suddenly ripped away. Kyala cried out as Wasker vanished into the waves.

There was nothing she could do for the youth. And Modwetten, despite his treasure of beads, would be helpless until someone learned the color of the creature's eyes. So Kyala doggedly stayed at her post, watching what she took to be the head of the beast as it closed with the base of the bluff. She clutched a poor handhold and leaned out, waiting for the lumpy mass to turn. Where were the eyes? She saw only a humped form whose texture resembled the carapace of an enormous crab.

And then, from beneath the water, the true head reared up. All this time, she had been watching the beast's back!

Now she saw a banded reptilian muzzle, crowned by a mass of suckered arms that writhed in all directions. Above the squirming limbs the eyes were hooded, but as she watched, a fold of skin opened to reveal a searing orb of violet. About the dark pupil, overlaying the deeper hue, danced a fiery sparkle of crimson. There was nothing like this in her memory, and Kyala's skill at recalling colors had never failed.

"We're lost," she cried as a tentacle began to explore the bluff's face. It uncurled toward her and she veered away, then stumbled down the path. As she ran, she shouted for the Vigen to make his escape. "The coloring's like nothing you've seen," she called. "Get away *now*, while the thing's distracted."

Suddenly she lost her footing, tumbled over the steep edge, and slid down the gritty slope the last of the distance to the beach. She struggled to control the fall, scraping her palms raw. "Go!" she shouted again as she tried to ignore the pain.

Nobody heeded her warning. Pech stood holding a spear, but the limbs had moved out of his range. Harb watched with evident disbelief as the creature probed the cinders atop the bluff, then began pulling the calf's charred remains into the water. Blackened bones spilled down the slope and into the beaked maw.

Beak? Kyala looked again, for the creature appeared to have *two* mouths, the one in the scaly snout now idle while the other fed. The head turned its gaze toward the beach while the feeding continued. And Modwetten remained dumbfounded, staring at his collection of beads. By this time, she thought, he had surely witnessed the beast's awesome eye.

Kyala rushed up to him and hastily pawed through the talismans to be certain there were none that might serve. Without hope she handed the Vigen a reddish wild pig's eye. "For what?" he asked, but despairingly he touched the bead to the hot cover of the lamp.

"There's none closer," she whispered. Had the match been true, the beast would have thrashed in agony. It took no notice at all, but continued devouring the bits of burnt meat. Lit coals rained, hissing and smoking as they fell.

And suddenly there was a shriek of pain behind Kyala. She turned to see Pech, his shirt torn off and his back bleeding in long stripes. He rushed away down the beach, a few steps ahead of the spiky tentacle that had scourged him. Then Kyala saw the water boil as the bulky mass of the beast began to throb. She shook her head, refusing to accept what she saw. The creature was breaking apart!

The snake's fanged snout slid away from the crablike body, taking with it the crown of suckered arms. The crab stayed afloat, its sacs bobbing on the waves. Kyala stared in wonder at the two creatures, then realized that the process of separation was not yet complete. Free of the carapace, the remaining part began to split again. The mass of limbs, with its long, trailing body, peeled off the reptile's banded head. A moment later, she watched a huge sea snake swim free, while the squidlike companion that had ridden its back returned to the bluff.

Three creatures! *Three sets of eyes*! Kyala knew then that the violet orb she'd seen belonged to the Squid. The reptile's eyes, which had been hidden below the mass of arms, were now below water and lost to view. But the snake had not vanished, for its churning made a long track of froth on the surface as it swam to follow Pech's flight. The youth veered inland, and the pursuing snake slithered up onto the beach. Its body was supple, with the girth of a sturdy oak. Bands of blue and gray alternated down its length, and barbed spines stood up along a line from its neck to its oarlike tail. Showing surprising speed, it squirmed toward the dunes that Pech had crossed.

While the Squid returned to plundering the pyre, the Crab swung toward Kyala and dragged itself partway onto the strand. This creature was spidery in shape, with armored legs and a twitching barbed tail that was darker than the rest, almost black. It had only one pincer, huge and constantly clacking open and shut as the rest of its bulk heaved from the surf. Now the float-sacs hung loosely at its sides and leafy strands of kelp dangled from its shell. The creature rose on all eight legs and began to swing the great claw. Kyala darted out of reach as the pincer smacked the wagon's rear wheel.

What of *this* beast's eyes? She fastened her attention on the twitching eyestalks—tubes that concealed the colors she must see. The stalks would not hold still for her. The claw struck the wagon again, splintering planks, and she was unable to get closer. Then the creature pushed past the wagon, battering the undercarriage with a twitch of its tail, forcing her to flee. The glassmaker was already in retreat, and she saw him backing against the face of the bluff, his cheeks bloodless with fear, his hand still holding the powerless charm.

Kyala saw no choice but to follow Pech's escape route. Whether the beast was three distinct creatures, or one of three parts, mattered not, she realized. She must learn each one's colors if she was ever to prevail. But the Crab was unapproachable now, and Pech might need her help.

The ponies, tethered in a stand of beach grass, were frantically trying to break loose. Kyala hurried past them and found the furrow left by the passing Sea-snake. Farther inland the growth thickened; thorny wild roses and scraggly brush lay ahead.

The narrow path of destruction had cut through the thin topsoil to the pale sand below. Bushes lay uprooted and broken. And then Pech's wail made the hairs bristle behind her neck. She leaped from the beast's track and circled around toward the source of the cry.

What she saw made her weep. Pech's head was in the Sea-snake's mouth, his battered body no longer struggling as the jaws widened to swallow him. She watched his legs vanishing into the craggy mouth and tried to overcome her revulsion. There was no time to mourn; she had to think only of getting closer. But, for a moment, all she could do was cover her eyes and shudder.

Keeping downwind of the creature, and using the sparse growth for cover, she crawled forward on her belly. The body pulsed and contracted as the thing swallowed, the spines rising and falling rhythmically. The creature carried a stench of dead fish that threatened to make her ill. But the eyes . . . she had yet to see them.

The translucent lids were fluttering, teasing her. Through these foggy panes she could not read color. Then one membrane slid away fully and she was stunned by a frigid whiteness, a coldness deeper than northern winter. In the eye's middle, a black slit glistened, but the iris was the blue-white of glacial ice. She filled herself for an instant with the color, so that the memory would linger for months and years. But in that moment, the eye saw her.

Ahead lay a stand of conifers whose branches leaned landward and hugged the ground, their trunks so tightly spaced that she could barely squeeze past them. Might they slow the thing, she wondered, or at least cover her flight? She slipped under the twisted branches and between the distorted boles, snapping dead twigs as she went. Higher up, the trees were bare and black, victims of a burn. She staggered into a dry gully and followed it to the top of a rise.

Pausing to catch her breath, she heard a distant rustling of branches. Then she saw that her pursuer had turned and was heading back to water, returning along the track it had made through the thorns. The Snake seemed slower now, perhaps because of its heavy meal. For the moment she was safe.

But two youths were gone for certain, and she knew nothing of how Harb and Modwetten had fared. Crossing the face of the hill, she came down onto the wagon track to find the ponies vanished and the beach empty. Ponies . . . Had they escaped or been devoured? She studied the sand, dreading what grisly scene she might discover, but found no sign of the animals.

In the eerie silence, she did not dare cry out. She turned to the bluff, and there saw a hint of movement. Back from the flattened peak where the fire had been, she thought a figure lay. Nervously she crossed the open stretch of beach.

The wagon had been smashed, beads spilled from the tilting bench onto sand. Valuable as they were, she did not stop to retrieve the Vigen's talismans. In a moment she gained the bottom of the steep bluff trail.

Now she could no longer see her objective—the sprawled figure. She tried to climb silently, but her labored breathing echoed in her ears. Then from above came a terrible scraping sound. Perspiring with fear, she abandoned the rough trail for an even steeper route that led away from the noise. As soon as she neared the heights she saw its source—a great limb flailing, probing the top of the cliff.

Then she spotted Modwetten's dark trousers. He was trying to belly-crawl backward, his gaze never leaving the overhead tentacle, but he was making slow progress. The creature's search appeared methodical, and the Vigen had little time.

Kyala worked her way behind him, crept close, and whispered a warning. She grasped the small man's ankles, and pulled him toward safety with a quick jerk. "On your feet now," she hissed, but he lay trembling with his face to the ground. She flattened herself as the tentacle swept by, then gave another tug.

"I saw its eye," Modwetten groaned. "The color of demon blood. Talismans can't touch it."

"There are three beasts," she answered testily as she dragged him again, not halting until she reached the first line of vegetation. "The eyes are different on each. Did you see them all?"

He turned his dusty face. "I . . . I saw the demon's orb, no other."

"I saw the blue-whites of the Sea-snake. What of the third beast?"

"Third? I saw no other." He covered his face with shaking hands.

"The one that smashed the wagon. The Spider-crab."

Modwetten's head fell limp, and he gave no answer. But she needed to know what lay at the ends of the eyestalks, and thought she might yet have a chance.

Modwetten seemed out of danger for the moment. Kyala left him in the brush, moved along the cliff halfway back to the road cut, then crawled forward along the ridge to view the shore. The Squid still swam below. But where were its two companions?

Scanning the waves, she noticed a small bump that made her heart quiver. But when she blinked it was gone. Descrying no other movement, she feared for the one remaining youth. Had Harb too been lost?

As soon as the Squid tired of its search, she expected all three creatures would depart. But what if some new bait appeared? She wondered if she might draw the Crab back to shore. Canted, but still burning, a lantern clung to the wagon's ruined bench.

She slipped down the back of the bluff, reached the track, then hastened to the cart. The talismans, useless as they were now, could not be abandoned. She grabbed up the beads on their strands and stuffed them into the casket. The wagon's supplies she tossed aside, keeping only the haunch of mutton within. Then she drenched the boards about the meat with lamp oil and tipped the lantern's flame to ignite a blaze.

The wagon was old and dry. The wood caught quickly. She dragged Modwetten's casket away from the blaze, then turned to climb again to watch what this new fire might bring. Suddenly a great claw reached out to block her way.

The Crab! For an instant she thought the beast was coming from the water, but then she saw her mistake. It was approaching from the inland side, and Kyala could not skirt its path. Its bulk lay in the road's notch, while the pincer cut off her route up the bluff. The creature plunged toward her, leaving but one way open.

There was no time to skirt the burning wagon. She ducked under and squeezed through. Ashes singed her face, but she reached the edge of the tide. Behind her she heard the cracking of timbers as the beast smashed past the ruins of the cart.

Kyala could not swim, but she knew the depth of the water here. She plunged into the cold surf, making for the rocks that now showed only their tips. The sea sucked at her ankles and her feet felt shod in stone. She turned for an instant to see her pursuer push the flaming boards aside. The creature crawled forward, following her into the waves.

She struggled against the surging water, using her hands to propel her as her body grew buoyant. The salt stung viciously where her palms were abraded. The chilly sea broke over her head and she spat in panic after tasting the sour tang. Behind cover of the rocks she might find safety . . . if she could better control her direction.

By kicking and thrashing, she reached the outermost stepping-stone. There, out of breath, she clutched a ragged horn of rock, fearing what might happen if she lost her grip. The current first wrenched her toward open water, then tried to crush her against the outcropping. Hand over hand, she pulled herself around to the shelter of the far side.

She heard shouting from the beach, and thought that Harb had survived after all. He would be a fool to come after her. She hoped he would make his own escape.

The rocks might save her. She pulled herself forward, thinking she could reach shore while the Crab still searched for her amid the waves. The water was deeper on this side. Her feet touched bottom once, but suddenly she lost her footing. Her grip slid from the stone, and she could not hold back a cry as the ocean pulled her away. The current had her in tow now, and she gagged on seawater.

Her head came up again. She coughed uncontrollably. Beside her in the water came a frantic splashing. She struck out with bruised hands, though she could not see her assailant. Something gripped her shoulders.

Wildly she turned, but the thing in the water beside her was not a claw. She clutched at the arm that was trying to help her. Legs moved beneath her own. Somehow she was making headway to shore.

Halfway in, she managed a look at her rescuer's face, and at that moment she knew she was doomed. For she'd heard forbidden tales of Etma's deceit, of how she sent beasts to destroy men. And a common trick was the spinning of a final delusion in which the victim saw a friend or loved one in place of the attacker. How else to explain Bremig's presence here?

Yet, when he pulled her to shore and carried her up the beach, she could not doubt that he was real. She glanced back once more. The beast had rounded the rocks, and she saw its armored head rise up, its mouth parts flapping. Bremig tried to drag her on, but she broke free and dared return to the surf. The eyestalks, aimed directly at her, halted their restless twitching. Her chance had come.

The color was gray, a silvery hue with a dull, malevolent sheen. These were like insect eyes, of many facets and impossible to fathom. Could glass have power, she wondered, against a beast so different from any she had known? Before she could think further the Crab launched itself toward shore. Again the carver grabbed her arm, and this time she scrambled after him, heading for the shelter of the trees.

For a time Kyala lay panting on the ground, still trying to cough seawater from her lungs. She was unhurt, she realized, shaken, chilled, and soaked, but otherwise well. Rolling to her side, she looked up at the bedraggled carver, his face bristling with unshaven beard. Why, she wondered, had he come? "The things . . . I told you at the farm," she said hoarsely, "were cruel but true. You should have . . . believed me."

The carver cleared his throat. "I came only to give you a warning. Should I have shouted my message at the waves?"

Trembling still, she glanced down at her drenched clothing. "You can see how I listen to warnings."

His breath hissed between his teeth. "Then I've ridden all night just for one last look at you."

Kyala turned from him and spoke in a quiet voice. "After what I said to you, you should have left me to drown."

"I can fling you back," he offered. She was silent, and he continued in an exasperated tone. "Then listen to my advice. Stay away from the coast. Go where nobody knows you."

"But . . ." Puzzled, she turned back to stare at him.

"My cousins built a boat of black walnut," he said, scowling. "They want to put you in their cursed craft and send it to Etma, hoping the demon will purge her wrath and all will be well again."

She pushed the drenched hair back from her forehead. "I want nothing to do with boats. I even get sick on river rafts."

"Then heed my warning. The men'll be searching for you . . ."

"I have work here." She glared at him, then felt her body betraying her words. Suddenly she was sobbing, and she felt him trying to comfort her. Pressing her face to his soggy jerkin, she let the tears run their course.

"There's no more I can do for you," he said at last, his tone softer now. "And I have matters of my own to settle. I've left Darst . . . for good."

"Left?" To Kyala, this news was unexpectedly harsh. "You need to be free of those fishermen," she conceded. "I can see your reasons."

"And you?" he asked. "Will you continue to fight sea beasts with your colored glass? I saw no signs of victory."

"This time we didn't have the right beads. But now I know how to make them." She studied again his narrow face, still wet from seawater that dripped from his hair. Was it possible she wouldn't glimpse that face again? But such matters must now be put aside. "I've seen all three eyes," she explained, trying to speak with more confidence than she felt. "I can cast talismans that will stop these creatures. What I need are the materials and a workplace."

He shook his head sadly. "You know about your shop?"

She nodded."But there's another Vigen who can help me. The flamens called him here from Longval." She rose to one knee, then stood and clutched a sapling for support. Her legs were steadier than she'd expected. "We've got to find him. I think he's safe. He and I together can destroy these beasts." She reached down to help Bremig to his feet.

The carver sighed. "Am I to be part of this, then?"

"Help us get moving toward Longval. That's the only aid I'll ask of you."

He frowned, and she thought he might refuse her.

"The place is inland . . ."

"Then maybe you'll have sense to stay there awhile." He stood and stretched his legs. "I'll do what I can for you," he added quickly. "But then I'll be off . . . to set myself up as a landsman's wood-carver. I hope to have my brother Wek as apprentice."

Kyala nodded. How could she fault him for turning his skills to good use? She would have preferred knowing he would stay in Darst, but there was no time for regret. She leaned forward to peer through the branches and choose her direction. The first task was to find Modwetten, and she did not wish to approach the shore again.

Kyala ached in her limbs, and the water's chill had not dispelled. Though she craved the day's warmth, she clung to shadows as long as possible. It was necessary to cross the road cut, and she waited for some time before making the headlong run. Bremig was hard behind her as she climbed to where the glassmaker still lay.

The Vigen's eyelids fluttered when she approached, and he turned his head weakly. "Is it gone?" he whispered. There were no tentacles waving overhead. She crept to the bluff's edge and peered down. A huge rusty bulk was moving toward open sea, and she assumed that the sea beast's parts had reunited. On the beach lay only charred and splintered boards where the wagon had been.

"It's leaving," she said as she hurried back. "But what about Harb? The others are gone for certain, but . . ."

"Harb?"

"The boy with moles." She pointed to her cheek and above her lip.

"Gone too," he said with certainty. "Demon-squid took him. Poor fella." Modwetten closed his eyelids and his head fell limp. Kyala dropped to her knees, put her ear to his lips, and heard steady breathing.

"We'll need another cart," she told Bremig. "To get us to Longval. But maybe the ponies weren't hurt; maybe they just ran off. Two grays. Do you think you could look for them?"

"Grays? I can try."

"They were tethered near the road," she shouted after him as he headed back down the slope.

She was shivering in the wet garments. As soon as Bremig was gone, she stripped off her wet boots and clothing and spread them out to dry near the top of the bluff. Her skin was puckered and red, but as soon as the sun's warmth touched her she began to feel better.

The beast was no longer visible, and she knew she still had a small task below. The Vigen had lost his wagon, yet he possessed things of far greater value. Nervously eyeing the sea, she made her descent.

What remained to salvage? Reaching shore again, she

found an ax unbroken. A few arrows lay on the sand. And the casket of beads, holding the work of lifetimes, lay where she had left it. She gathered the surviving supplies and tools in a heap, then hurried back to the sleeping Vigen. His breathing was still regular. She hoped he needed only rest to recover.

Leaving him in shadow, she stretched herself out in Ormek's light, spreading her slender legs to welcome the warmth. The chill was gone now, and each moment she felt her strength returning. Never before had she enjoyed such comfort, letting the sun's rays touch every part of her.

Tugging at her thoughts were the horrors she had just seen, but she refused to let them break through. Ormek's power would prevail soon, she told herself. The beast could not last against Him. Raising her face to His gentle fires, she hoped that Bremig's search would not go too quickly.

CHAPTER 7

GROGGILY, Bremig set out on Kyala's errand, sliding down to the dirt track below the bluff. He had not slept the previous night, riding steadily from farm to shrine and then to this desolate coast. The recent events—the struggle in the water, the rush to find shelter above the beach, already seemed unreal in his memory.

That he had clutched her cold and quaking body to his own he could not deny. Perhaps he had given her some comfort just by his presence. But until she finished her self-imposed task, her "Vigen's duty," he would be no more to her than a convenient stranger.

And what if she succeeded in this battle? He shook his head, not willing to hope for such a chance. Days ago, he had resigned himself to losing her.

He rubbed his eyes and tried to focus on the tasks at hand. Before he could help Kyala he needed to find his own mare. At the end of his ride the animal had caught the sea beast's scent and had nearly thrown him in her frenzy. He'd let her free when he leaped into the water. How far she'd run, he could not guess.

Bending to inspect the sandy road, Bremig made out the mare's retreating footprints. He turned with a sigh, expecting a long trek. But soon, to his surprise, he saw where the horse had slowed her crazed flight, the prints shallower and closer together. He began to whistle a tune of two notes.

Continuing along the path, he whistled again, and soon heard an answering whinny. Rounding a bend, he found the roan cropping coarse seaside grass at the road's edge. He hugged her neck, reached into the saddlebag for a bit of sweet cake he'd brought for her. He had eaten nothing himself since the previous noon, but felt no hunger.

Having located his animal, he pondered the fate of Kyala's grays. He'd seen something of the land about the beach, and realized that any route other than that of this road would prove difficult for the ponies. Also, he'd noticed smaller hoofprints pointing in both directions. Perhaps the grays had returned this way as well. Swinging up into the saddle, he continued to follow the track.

Only now did he realize how saddle-sore he'd become. Though he rode the mare often, it was always on leisurely jaunts along the coast. Now he felt the results of his night of hard riding, the bruises and chafed skin. At least, he thought, the pain would keep him awake.

Approaching the main road, he pondered which way to turn. There was no chance of recognizing tracks in this well-used path. To his left lay forests, the Reach, and finally Asep River. To his right lay fenced meadows whose unmown grasses would surely tempt the animals. That seemed the natural direction to try.

A farmhouse lay not far along the road. He spotted no one about the house or barn, but in a nearby field found two men fixing a fallen rail fence. They did not look up when his mare's shadow fell over them. One man was digging a new post hole, and remained silent until his excavation was done. "I suppose you want to sell me that lame mare," he said when the post was finally lowered into place. He had not even glanced at the roan.

"Sell? I came only to ask after two missing grays."

"Ah, you can get those from the peddler who was here a

while back. Red-haired fellow. His ponies were lame, too. Must have been, by the fool's price he was asking."

"And how do I find this rascal?"

The digger shrugged, used his thumb to wipe sweat from his dusty brow. "He'll be trying the farms along here one by one. Unless he gets all the way into Norplain. If he does, you won't catch him."

Bremig hurried back to the road. He passed a second farm, and there heard a similar story. And as he approached the third, he spotted two gray ponies trailing behind a dilapidated peddler's cart.

A single tired horse was pulling, while the grays, tethered behind, easily kept pace. Bremig rode abreast of the rig and looked down at a squat man, round of face, heavily tanned, his whiskers and hair red and unruly. The driver's welcoming smile faded at once. "Fine day," he said hastily. "Ormek's best."

"I've lost two grays," replied the carver soberly. "I heard someone was trying to sell them."

The driver looked unhappily back at the animals trailing him. "Couldn't be. I found this pair runnin' loose, and now I'm lookin' for the owner. I expect there'll be some reward."

"I can have a chat with the magistrate in Norplain," countered Bremig. He assumed the local penalty for thieving was suitably severe.

"No need. No need. Why, I don't even deserve a reward. All I did was save these two from breakin' their legs in some ditch. And I watered 'em and gave 'em grain. Any stranger would do that."

Bremig had to laugh. "Then you deserve something for your trouble."

The driver halted and looked up expectantly. Bremig reached for his pouch of coins but did not open it. For a moment, he studied the peddler's rig and wondered if it would serve Kyala's purpose. In the back lay a bundle of dirty cloth, a few battered pots, and a small barrel.

"I happen to need a cart to go with these ponies," said the carver cautiously. "Your rig looks ready to collapse, but I haven't far to go in it."

The peddler stiffened. "You could ride all the way to see the Mej in this. Home again, too, and never have a worry."

"Let's come to an agreement, then. I say nothing about how you got the ponies. You sell me the cart." Bremig wondered what such a sad rig was worth in coin. He named a sum that he hoped was fair.

The red-haired man frowned. "Can't sell it. I'd lose my livelihood. What'll I do when the money's gone?"

Bremig had plenty of coppers. He upped his offer, but the driver was unmoved. The bargaining at a standstill, the two men sat staring at one another. "Here's an answer," the peddler suggested. "Let me drive you where you want to go. We'll use one of your fine ponies and give my nag a rest. Get there twice as fast that way."

The carver's eyelids were heavy. The plan seemed sensible, though he hesitated to trust the scoundrel. He tried to think of alternatives, imagining himself riding into Norplain. But he had no experience dealing with country people. And perhaps to *buy* a serviceable rig would take more money than he had.

"Are you willing to go as far as Longval?" the carver asked.

"As surely as they call me Hapko!"

"Then turn your cart, peddler!" Bremig motioned for Hapko to follow him, but soon his misgivings began to grow. The carver kept glancing back, afraid the man might disappear if he had the chance, taking the ponies with him. Each time Bremig looked, however, the driver gave him a cheerful wave. They reached the side track and soon halted at the wood-strewn shore.

The carver insisted that Hapko accompany him up the bluff. At the crest, however, he wished he had left the man below. For he found Kyala asleep next to her clothes, and he could only stare at her slim waist and girlish breasts. Then he turned to glare at Hapko beside him. Seeing the peddler's rapt expression, Bremig elbowed him in the chest and sent him tumbling halfway back to the beach.

The commotion woke Kyala. She reached for her linen undershirt, and the carver could not take his eyes from her. He felt less a rush of desire than a muted longing, a half-forgotten dream.

The shape of a woman's body was no mystery to him. His family shared a washhouse with four others, and he commonly happened on a cousin or a wife in a state of partial undress. In truth, he sometimes planned such "accidents," and the musty smell of the washhouse was now linked in his mind with frustrated hungers.

Kyala was unlike the women he'd observed, more delicate and subtle in her femininity. Her slender arms and legs were well muscled, and he recalled her strength in the water. She seemed not to care that he watched her as she pulled the stained shirt over her head, covering not only her fair features but the glossy bead that hung from her neck. As she picked up her goatskin trousers, he forced himself to turn away. The peddler was dusting himself off below, staring up at Bremig as if wondering what was expected of him.

"Nice-looking daughter you have," said Hapko wistfully.

Bremig frowned but did not correct the man. "I'll tell you when to come up," he said. Then when he saw, from the corner of his eye, that she was dressed, he asked what she knew of the Vigen's condition.

"I've been asleep," she confessed. He hastily explained how he'd met Hapko, and what the peddler had suggested. Motioning for the red-haired man to ascend again, Bremig told him to keep his distance as he and Kyala approached the sleeping glassmaker. It would be best, Bremig thought, that Hapko not know too much about Modwetten.

The carver strode ahead to where Kyala's friend lay with his mouth open in a snore and his arm thrown over his eyes.

Bremig stood so he could watch both Vigen and the peddler, for the latter, he feared, might yet be tempted to flee.

Kyala roused the Vigen, who sat up dreamily. "Where are those boys?" he asked her, his eyelids fluttering. "There were three of 'em, weren't there?" Then his mouth fell open, and he shook his head slowly from side to side.

"You remember now?" she asked softly.

Modwetten licked his dry lips. His eyes opened fully, and he cleared his throat. "I watched," he said hoarsely. "I watched and could do nothing."

"We must cast beads," Kyala said firmly. "One for each part of the beast. I know the colors we need."

"Beads?" He rubbed at his beard and pursed his lips. "You want to use my shop, don't you? You think you can make better talismans than mine." His voice trailed off.

"We have to do it," she insisted. "How else can we stop the thing?"

"But I had them all. All the talismans."

"Should we go back to the flamens and tell them how your charms fared?"

Modwetten blinked. He looked at his dusty hands, turning them from back to palm. "I've made more talismans in my lifetime than even the famous Kolpern."

"That may be, but we still need three new ones." She leaned over to help him to his feet, but he pushed her away and stood of his own accord. Bremig found the Vigen uncommonly small of stature, yet the broad shoulders gave him a look of power. And the Vigen's squint-eyed face, despite a dazed appearance, suggested a harsh shrewdness in his nature.

"Get the wagon ready," Modwetten said wearily. Then he seemed to realize his mistake. "Do we even *have* a wagon?"

Kyala glanced at Bremig, who quickly beckoned for the peddler. Hapko strode forward, and after a brief discussion and some haggling, Modwetten accepted his proposal.

Loading the Vigen's belongings onto the cart went

quickly. Now that Modwetten had recovered his wits, Bremig noted how he began to take charge. The glassmaker sat stiffly on the driver's bench while Hapko freed the tired horse and put a pony in the traces. When the Vigen told Kyala to ride in back with the bundles, Bremig watched her face redden in anger.

But she did not comply at once. As the carver stared with frustration, uncertain how to ask for some final words with her, she put her hand gently on his arm and drew him aside. "Don't fret about us," she said.

"The peddler worries me," he answered softly. "He'll be happy to take everything you have."

"I'll watch him." She held up her chin and gave such a fierce stare that he began to laugh. She broke into a grin also, and the mirth made it easier for him to finish what he had to tell her. This new notion had crept up on him, making itself clear only in the past few moments.

"I'm going back to Darst," he told her. "I need to find out their plans. My cousin Draalego's the worst of the troublemakers, and I won't rest until I know what he's up to."

Now she grew serious again. "Draalego . . . Pelask's son?"

The carver nodded. "I doubt his friends will ride as far as Longval to look for you. But when you're done with your glassmaking, how will you reach the coast again? They may still be searching these parts."

"We'll get past them. Somehow." She glanced at the ground and kicked a stone with her boot.

"I'll slip back into Darst. That's the most useful thing I can do now. Then I'll come tell you what I've learned." He had added the last part so quickly and naturally that he thought she couldn't object.

In fact, she merely smiled and gave his arm a quick squeeze. Then she raced back to the cart, climbed in behind, and raised a clatter with Hapko's pots until she could make herself comfortable. Aglow with his victory, Bremig stood motionless until they were out of sight.

He would see her again at Longval. He need think ahead no further than that.

Kyala peered back at Bremig until the cart rounded a bend. What a shy but persistent suitor he was proving to be! She no longer had the will to discourage him, yet his promises worried her. He would surely be in danger if his return to Darst was discovered. She only hoped he could move quickly, for she knew she would welcome seeing his brooding mouth and solemn gray-green eyes again.

And what of her own journey? The Vigen's home lay to the east, on a road that ran roughly midway between Asep River and the Buttresses. To get there, unfortunately, meant traversing a section of the dangerous Asep Forest. As she sat in the rumbling cart, watching pastures of the coastal road drift by, memories of a recent ordeal in the woody paths came back to her.

It was true that she had met the Lame Ones in a different quarter of the forest. And certainly those two-legged beasts now were all dead. Travel through the region remained risky, however, and she was glad of the Vigen's vast store of beads.

What they needed along with his talismans was a lantern, but the glassmaker's had been smashed. She turned to the peddler's belongings, pulled a hide cover from his barrel, and looked in at the contents. An old sooty lamp came to hand along with a flask of oil. Rummaging further, she found his fire-striking kit in a greasy little pouch. These supplies gave her some comfort. She would not enter the forest without the protection of a flame.

A small settlement stood on the forest road. Evening was coming on, and the Vigen was wise enough to order a halt for the night. A half-dozen rough log buildings sat astride the rutted track, and behind them lay the first tall stands of ash, branches heavily shading the path.

An inn of sorts did business here. In a tiny, dank room, a handful of travelers huddled about crude tables. The Vigen was obliged to buy Hapko's meal and bed, but Kyala handed coppers from her own purse to the bull-necked proprietor. While the glassmaker complained about watery ale, she slipped out to have a private talk with the stableboy.

The animals had no proper stalls, but were merely tied to a rail that ran the length of the shed. A skinny youth whose head barely reached her shoulders stood tossing rope rings at a stake in the ground. Behind him, dropped carelessly with its tines in the air, lay a wooden pitchfork.

She showed the boy a small coin, and his eyebrows rose. "If either man comes for the ponies, I want you to wake me," she told him.

He laughed and snatched the coin. "Play me a round of quoits, and I'll do it," he said, showing his overlapping front teeth.

She picked up a handful of rings. The game was not new to her, and in fact she was skilled at it. They alternated throws. Soon the youth began to scowl. "You cheat," he said. "Stand back where you're supposed to be." She moved well behind him, and still could beat his tosses.

Dusk had fallen and the peg was difficult to see. Rather than make the boy angry, she purposely threw wide and allowed him to win. "Play again tomorrow," he insisted when the game was over. He tried to slip his hand around her waist, but she slapped it playfully.

"Tomorrow. If there's time."

The travelers all slept on pallets in the room that still stank of ale and stew. Kyala chose a place by the door, so that anyone coming out would have to pass her. She did not know whether it was Hapko or Modwetten she trusted less. If the glassmaker could avoid it, she did not think he'd face the beasts again.

When the light woke her, she jumped up in alarm. But the two men still lay sleeping, the peddler snoring softly. She brushed off straw from the bursting pallet, then stepped outside for a breath of untainted air.

She found the youth dozing in back of Hapko's wagon. He had done that much to keep faith with her, so she owed him a return favor. She filled a bucket with cold well water and dribbled it onto his face until his lids popped open. He groaned, turned over on his hard bed, and was asleep again in an instant. She sprinkled water onto his neck. "You wanted another game," she said, laughing.

This time she stood behind him again, but threw no quoits wide. She trounced him several times, then told him he needed more practice. As she sauntered back to the inn, she heard a scraping noise behind her and turned just in time to dodge a shovelful of horse apples.

Inside, she found only cold bread and a bit of cheese for repast. Hapko seemed eager to get moving, but the Vigen chewed his crusts thoughtfully while he stood with his precious casket at his feet. When they finally pulled out onto the road, a scraggly-bearded drayman hailed them. Kyala recognized his broad-brimmed, floppy hat from the inn, but hadn't gotten a look at his face in the dark room. Now he seemed a cheerful sort, with a large mouth and warty complexion. The glassmaker shrugged at his suggestion that they travel together, but Hapko found the offer welcome. The drayman cracked his whip and led the way.

The road was reasonably flat for a time, emerging now and again into clearings. Even in the shaded sections, patches of sunlight reached the trail. Kyala found the woods far less forbidding that morning than she had at the previous dusk. Nonetheless, she kept thinking about Hapko's lantern.

They stopped to water the horses at a pebbled stream that crossed the road. Kyala noticed Modwetten reaching into his box. He kept the lid down, presumably to conceal its contents from the other men. She assumed he could sense the colors with his fingertips, for that skill was basic to the Vigen's art. Suddenly he seemed to find what he wanted, extracting a short strand of beads and hurriedly slipping it into a belt pouch.

The glassmaker glanced about and saw her watching him. "There's talk of cave lions," he whispered. The drayman was busy with his team, and Hapko was out of sight. "Say nothing," the Vigen cautioned. "But keep the peddler's lantern burning."

With that warning, what had appeared a pleasant scene took on an ominous air. Kyala noticed footprints by the edge of the stream that might have come from the dangerous predators. The flesh of ponies and horses, she had heard, served as the cave lions' preferred diet. Reaching into the barrel again, she took out the greasy pouch.

She would have liked to stretch her legs after the long morning ride. When her task was done, she had but a few moments to dash into the woods and relieve herself. Returning, she saw Hapko bringing the spare animals back to be tied to the cart. He seemed briefly puzzled to see the burning lamp, but then nodded his head in apparent understanding. Travelers who could afford them, he must know, were wise to carry talismans on this road.

After the brief rest, the track rose to more densely wooded country. Here the occasional splash of daylight was rare, and the road lay deep in gloom. The animals became skittish, reacting nervously when a twig snapped or a few dry leaves dropped. The drayman was a few wagon lengths ahead, his load of barrels bouncing and squeaking at each small bump in the road.

Suddenly Kyala saw two dark shapes bound across the trail in front of the drayman. A roar sounded on the closer side, and a large she-bear came lumbering toward his loaded wagon. The cubs had crossed first, Kyala realized, and then the driver had cut them off from their mother. His frenzied ponies made directly for the woods, and snagged the rig in the first line of trees.

The bear seemed furious at the intrusion. She reared onto her hind legs, showing foreclaws like curved needles, while Hapko fought to control his own cart's pony. Modwetten, having in his belt pouch only the cat eyes, threw open the lid of his box and scrabbled for others. The scent of the creature was overwhelming, and Kyala could barely hold the lamp steady for her fear. Thinking the Vigen would not find the beads in time, she clutched with one hand the side of the weaving cart.

The drayman tried to hold off the coarse-furred bear, cracking his whip at her while reaching for a more useful weapon. The Vigen jumped up with a strand of beads, grabbed the lantern from Kyala, and let its wavering light fall on the glossy talismans. *He found them!* she thought as she held on even tighter. Hapko's pony, trying to skirt the frenzied bear, slammed the peddler's cart into a trunk on the opposite side of the road.

The Vigen lost his balance, and the strand of talismans as well. But he did not drop the lamp. Kyala leaped down to retrieve the fallen charms. "Move off!" commanded Modwetten to the bear as soon as he had the talismans in hand again. When the beast ignored him, he approached her on foot and brought the beads closer to the lamp, charging them with this source of Ormek's power. The drayman was using a spear to fend off the creature, but suddenly, in apparent reaction to the glass, the bear turned in fury to Modwetten.

"Go!" the Vigen shouted. "Away! Into the woods!" Kyala could see only the open jaws, the heavy canine teeth. Swinging a great paw, the creature swatted the glassmaker to the ground and then she fell on top of him. The lantern dropped, and lay still burning. While the men tried to dislodge the beast with their weapons, Kyala risked the punishing claws. She dodged in after the lantern, singeing her fingers as she snatched it to safety. She needed also the strand of glass, and had to pry that from Modwetten's limp fingers. The rank smell of the animal made her choke for breath.

She must try the charms again. Panting, she held the glossy beads to the light, and then she understood why they had failed. In the Vigen's haste, he had taken the wrong strand from his box! Or perhaps, even worse, the bear eyes had been lost in the rubble at the beach and he'd been forced to pick a substitute. Yet she had seen these beads evoke *some* reaction from the bear, so the colorings were not far off the mark.

The beast, now distracted from Modwetten, was roaring furiously as Hapko prodded it with an ax handle and the drayman tried to get in with his spear. In a moment it would fell them both, she knew. There was no time to search for better charms.

Would Ormek help her now, as He had done several times before? The match was not perfect, but the glass might serve. "Run away!" she shouted to the animal as she brought the talismans near the heat. The bear, tossing its head, ignored her as it had Modwetten. The lamp was too weak to succeed with this poor match, Kyala realized. She needed the Bright One's favor as well.

She thought of the moment not long before when His warmth had touched her. She pictured the glowing sky and the wonder of the sun at noon. "Run!" she called again, this time daring to touch the string of beads to the hot metal of the lamp. By herself, this was the utmost power she could command. But a few times before, such modest heat had drawn to her Ormek's vast strength. Would His fury return? There was only an answering jerk of the creature's head.

The beast knocked the ax from Hapko's grip, and at that moment Kyala saw her foolish pride. She could not come close to Ormek by merely enjoying His rays on her skin. No, she must fill herself with the Lifegiver's image, allowing His glory to obliterate all else. She must forget the world beyond, submerging herself in the Lifegiver's strength and beauty.

"Ormek!" she cried, and at last the feeling of His power began to flow. Focusing all her attention on the Bright One, she marveled as His wonders grew within her. But she could not delay. Not certain she was ready for the task, she again touched the beads to the heat, and this time a glow erupted; a blaze seemed to spring up before her. The flames spanned the width of the road, and for a moment she could see nothing beyond the fire.

Then she made out the beast rising on hind legs, its white claws slashing at the frightening power that surrounded it. The creature fell to all fours again, turned to the forest with a moan and a toss of its head. With a last whine of pain, the she-bear lumbered after her cubs and was gone.

The two men stared in disbelief after the departed animal, and then they rushed to Modwetten. Kyala brought the lamp, lifted it to shine on his bloodied face. The glassmaker spat dirt from his mouth and sat up angrily. He seemed unaware for the moment of the slashes to his shoulder that had shredded part of his jerkin. But when he wiped away the grit, only his upper lip was bleeding freely. There were scratches on his arm and shoulder, but none appeared deep.

"The talisman should have worked the first time," he said petulantly. He tore the strand from Kyala's fingers, but when he saw it in the light he dropped the beads in fury, turning to glare at her with narrowed eyes.

"The coloring was close . . ." she said softly, not needing to explain his error. "It was Ormek's favor that overcame the mismatch."

"Favor? I need no fanciful tales from you," retorted Modwetten. "The beast was angry, strong-willed, difficult to handle. That's why a close match failed. After it calmed down a bit, the bead could act."

"But the lamp flared up . . . the brightness grew." She glanced from Modwetten's accusing face to those of the other men. Did the Vigen think she was trying to disgrace him with her claims? "Didn't you see . . . ?" she asked the drayman.

"I saw the bear run off. That's all I cared about." The man's teeth were chattering.

"And you?" She stared at the peddler. He too denied seeing any light other than the lamp's usual flame.

Kyala knew it was pointless to explain further. Even her mentor had not known Ormek in her special way, had not been allowed to see into His heart. But Watnojat had accepted her experiences, and had said she possessed a remarkable gift. She did not think Modwetten would ever be so gracious.

Turning from the men, she found a log to sit on by the roadside. There she closed her eyes, still feeling the remnants of the power that had touched her. Ormek had shared with her His glory, but who would ever know of it? Bremig would believe her, she thought. Of all men still living, perhaps only he.

When she was ready to face the others again, she saw that the horses and ponies had been untangled and the rigs brought back onto the road. The glassmaker had found his spilled casket, and was hurriedly shoving the beads back inside. Hapko noticed what he was doing and called nervously to the drayman. The two exchanged frightened glances at the sight of so much colored glass. Suddenly both were pointing and shouting, "Vigen, Vigen," with evident distress.

Modwetten banged shut the lid, but the damage was done. Both men cupped their hands firmly about their eyes, and the peddler appeared to be shivering. "Now we've lost any chance for a quiet journey," the glassmaker said bitingly.

Kyala had seen such behavior before. In her travels with Watnojat there were many towns where ignorant people feared Vigens. To use colored glass against a *person* was contrary to Ormek's law, and a grave offense. Nonetheless, in places where no glassmaker had established his trustworthiness, the fears persisted. *Never show a Vigen your eyes*, was a common maxim.

"Don't you think he's had a good look already?" she asked Hapko, who peered at her through splayed fingers. "Not that it matters to him. He knows his obligations."

"Maybe he didn't see, and maybe he forgot," said the red-haired peddler. "Why should I risk it?" Grudgingly he went back to his work, but kept his face turned away from Modwetten. The drayman managed to get his wagon rolling first, and hurried off without waiting for the cart. Kyala was astonished that he feared a Vigen more than the dangers of the forest.

CHAPTER 8

WHEN Kyala was gone, Bremig turned wearily to his mare. As he'd promised, he would return to Darst. But with Draalego's friends roaming the countryside, he did not care to travel by daylight. "You need a rest," he said to the horse. "We both do." He wandered a short distance inland, found a shady copse with a pond, and slept until dusk.

He took his time traveling, hoping that the town would be quiet when he arrived. Slipping into Arod's back alley around midnight, he tapped softly on the door. The smith called out sleepily, and Bremig whispered a reply. At last the door opened to show Arod standing barefoot, clad in his nightdress and holding a candle.

"You shouldn't be here," the smith hissed, beckoning the visitor to hurry inside. "There's talk. Some think you know where Kyala is."

"She's where they won't find her. For a while, at least."

"Maybe it won't matter soon." The room was dark but for Arod's candle. He padded toward a bench near the cold hearth and sat down.

Bremig followed but did not sit. "Explain yourself," he demanded.

"Your fishermen are fighting among themselves now. Draalego's faction wants her in the boat. But so far they don't have her."

"Thanks to Ormek . . ."

The smith started at that remark, and he eyed the carver curiously for a moment. "Perhaps. But the beast attacked here just after sunset. Three more cottages down, and two lives lost."

Bremig bowed his head in sorrow as he listened to the details. He knew the displaced families and one of the dead men.

"A noisy group came to my shop afterward," the smith continued, "and they bought up every weapon I had. They were talking about defying Draalego's orders and launching the boat tonight."

"Without Kyala . . ."

"They said the craft alone would be enough. And I'll tell you this much. There's a storm waiting out there somewhere. I can feel it." He rubbed one arm, and Bremig recalled mention of an old fracture. Arod claimed to sense weather changes, and from the carver's experience he was generally accurate.

"I'll be glad if they do it," said Bremig. "If the boat's gone, they won't bother her anymore."

Arod frowned. "They sent a rider after Draalego. If that mule-head gets back in time, there'll surely be a fight. Whatever happens, you'd best stay clear of it."

Bremig looked around the shadowy room. He saw shapes of cooking pots, a heap of soapstone bowls, and, in the corner, a pallet where one of Arod's sons lay asleep. "I can't stay *here*. Too risky for you."

"Then go inland. You're a landsman now, from your talk. Behave like one."

Bremig smiled weakly. "I'm not a landsman yet." He faced the door, but an insistent thought made him turn back to the smith. "Where did you say he was?"

"Draalego? What are you thinking?" The carver gave no answer, and Arod sighed. "South coast. Down toward Hesh. That's all I know."

"Then maybe," Bremig said cautiously. "Maybe I can meet him before he gets here. Give the others a chance to get rid of that boat."

"You think you can stop him?" Arod clucked his tongue.

"I can try. . ." As a youngster, Bremig had been thrashed by his bullying cousin so often that the sight of the man still made him shiver. "Surely, I can slow him down."

"Bare-handed?" The smith frowned. "At least take this." He lifted something from a hook on the wall, then turned to offer the carver a sheathed hunter's knife. Bremig stared at the bone-hilted weapon, not wanting to glimpse the blade beneath the leather. He had never needed such a thing. "Take it," Arod insisted. "Your cousin carries a fiercer tooth."

Uneasily, Bremig held out his hand. He tied the sheath to his belt, then said his farewells to the smith. Stepping into the breezy night, he felt the unaccustomed weapon dangling against his hip. Perhaps he would grow used to it.

He mounted the horse and paused to consider his direction. Before he sought his cousin, he must take a quick detour. Choosing little-used alleys, he rode stealthily to the shore, then followed the water's edge. The wind was gusting seaward, and Bremig smelled the oncoming storm.

Then he saw torches across the short stretch of beach that separated him from the boatyard. He heard voices raised in anger, arguing, but couldn't make out the words. The walnut boat was surrounded, and while he watched, the men about it heaved the craft closer to the surf. The men holding torches were trying to halt the launching, but at this moment seemed outnumbered.

What a strange sight this boat made, Bremig thought, with its crooked mast and its ill-formed prow and stern. In front, where no man stood, the torchlight played on the grimacing prow-piece. So alien were its features that Bremig could scarcely believe he had shaped the thing. He noticed how the quarreling seamen avoided touching or even looking at the carving.

And what would be the outcome of their disagreement? he wondered. Without Draalego to lead them, his cousin's faction wouldn't stand against the majority. But Pelask's son was on his way, and might yet force his will on the divided throng. Hastily, the carver turned, heading for the coastal road to Hesh.

His plans remained uncertain. To the carver's knowledge, Draalego was no horseman, and so he expected his cousin to be driving a cart. When the fisherman approached, he intended to hail him, and after that there was no telling what might happen. Bremig knew well the brute strength of his cousin; he could not hope to fight him. Perhaps he could damage the rig, cut the traces, free the ponies. He ran his fingers over the sheath, halted briefly, and drew Arod's knife. The moon was nearly full, and the blade glinted in its pale light.

And as he rode on, his plans became increasingly fanciful. Dig a trench across the road at a dark turning? He had no shovel. Light a fire to block the path and frighten the ponies? He carried no flints. With his head full of such absurd schemes, he halted again.

Alone on the road, his doubts were many. Perhaps Arod had been mistaken. Possibly Draalego had taken some other route. It might be better to return to Darst and try to meet up with his cousin there. But as he argued with himself, he heard sounds of a rider approaching.

There was no cover beside the track. Bremig moved to the side to let the other pass with moonlight against his face. *Draalego?* The man rode by so swiftly that the carver was not certain. And where could the fisherman have gotten such a fast horse? He shouted his cousin's name.

The rider slowed. Bremig turned to catch up with him.

"Is that you, carver?" came the familiar voice. "What word from the boatyard?"

Bremig saw the torches in his mind, but could not answer. Now he was riding beside his cousin, and his hands were trembling.

"Got no time," shouted Draalego. "You have news, let me hear it."

Bremig ransacked his thoughts for a way to delay him. He smelled his cousin's acrid sweat, stronger even than the horses' odors. "Kyala," he managed to say. "Do you want her?"

"So Juukal was right?"

"Juukal? He has nothing to do with it."

"Do you know where to find her. Yes or no?"

"How soon do you want her? If you need her tonight . . ." His hand gripped the knife, and he thought he might lean down now and cut one of Draalego's saddle girths.

"Tonight? Plow-brain! I've something else to deal with first."

"But I've heard rumors." The horses were side by side. Bremig stretched his arm to reach across . . .

"Tomorrow you come talk to me. And have your answers quick and ready, or I'll beat them out of you."

"But your saddle! Cousin, wait!" With the blade concealed in his hand, Bremig lunged, but already Draalego had spurred his horse. In a moment, Pelask's son was galloping away, leaving the carver alone on the road. His face burned with shame at his failure, but he flung himself into pursuit.

Bremig could not catch his cousin, but the fisherman's lead grew only slowly along the coastal road. The carver followed through Darst's streets as Draalego rode full tilt for the harbor. The torches had moved to the water's edge, and another was afloat, casting reflections on the waves. The boat was already launched.

Pelask's son raced directly to the noisy crowd and jumped from his horse. Bremig took a roundabout approach, reaching shore at a short distance from the others. Torchlight fell on the arriving fisherman, and the onlookers muttered his name. Some tried to push him back, but a few blows from his fists cleared a path.

Draalego had come too late but Bremig could scarcely

take credit for that. The boat was moving out, its sail set, its helm lashed in place. A torch blazed in the bow, light playing through the peculiar rents in the sail. The prow-piece was pointed to sea, and the quickening breeze was drawing the boat in that direction.

Draalego grabbed a brand from one of his friends and sprinted toward the dock. No other boats were in sight, and Bremig assumed that all had been moved out of reach of the expected cataclysm. Pelask's son angrily tossed the light into the water, then pulled off his boots and trousers and dove into the brine.

The wind was gusting more heavily, and Bremig gave the man little hope of catching the cursed craft. But he saw that he could make Draalego's chance even slimmer. The fisherman, in his anger, had started his swim from the dock. Bremig could cut him off.

Forgetting his thoughts of concealment, the carver kicked off his boots and plunged through the cluster of onlookers and into the choppy surf. He barely felt the cold as he swam to meet his cousin.

"Out of my way!" spat the oncoming fisherman.

From the shore came shouts of encouragement, and the carver stroked all the harder. Ahead, the torch-lit craft continued to pull away.

Bremig was on a course the fisherman could not evade without losing the walnut boat. On land, the man was a dangerous brawler, but how well could he fight in the water? The carver plunged forward and grabbed for his cousin, catching an arm. A fist came up to batter his face. He fell back, then kicked mightily as he reached for his cousin's legs.

He caught an ankle and would not let go. Draalego turned on him viciously, beating him about the head and kneeing him in the ribs. Bremig was choking on swallowed water, but ducked under to reduce the impact of the blows. He felt his fingers being pried loose and bent back. The pain and cold broke his grip.

Again Bremig propelled himself forward, and this time he managed to latch on to his cousin's thigh. Draalego was thrashing at him, fists and feet everywhere; the carver felt a deep blow to his stomach. For terrifying moments he could not breathe. The current sucked him under.

At last he recovered sufficiently to paddle against the water. He broke the surface, drew in a vastly painful breath. Pelask's son was gone. Bremig looked about and realized that his cousin was now beyond his reach. As for himself, the carver wondered if he could regain the shore.

Wheezing, he drifted, hoping to recover some strength. When he glanced seaward, it appeared that Draalego would have to chase the boat all the way out to the islands. That would be some consolation, but not worth drowning for. He tried a few weak strokes, then rested once more. His head dipped under.

Coming up for air, he heard a thunderclap and then saw the first flash of lightning. On shore, the hazy shapes of onlookers were running for shelter. Did they believe, he wondered, that the boat had drawn this storm? Whatever the cause of their panic, they evidently cared nothing for his fate.

The waves broke over him repeatedly as he stroked, and the current tugged him outward. Sometimes he couldn't tell if he was making progress. A few onlookers remained, but none showed any willingness to help him. He had tried to stop his cousin, a move that must have pleased many in the crowd, yet now all they would do was watch his suffering.

Thunder boomed again, and a heavy downpour started. He glanced once more at the beach and saw two figures moving toward him. Aid . . . was it finally forthcoming? Suddenly a board with a line attached flew from shore and splashed down within reach. He grabbed the float with both hands and let himself be pulled in.

Someone threw him a blanket, and a gust of wind whipped it about his face. Still out of breath, he could barely stand up, and now he was shivering badly. And what of his cousin? Looking toward the islands, he no longer caught a glimmer of the boat's torch. Draalego was out there somewhere, and if Bremig had seen the last of him, he would not be sorry.

"Get to cover!" shouted one of his rescuers, trying to pull him away from shore.

"My horse!" The carver had tied her to a bush farther down the beach. "My boots!"

"We've got 'em," said the other.

The rain was soaking through the blanket. Rivulets poured down his cheeks. With a final seaward glance, he staggered toward higher ground.

They found shelter in a narrow outbuilding well up the slope, Bremig's bay mare and three men crowding in with two ponies already stabled there. The carver fell shivering into a pile of straw, and pulled down a dry horse blanket to replace his sodden one. He saw light flicker as one of his rescuers adjusted a guttering lantern. Bremig's panting slowed, but still he was racked by occasional shivers.

The smoky flame sprang up strongly, and the carver could see the faces of his benefactors. He did not know these young men, but was certain they bore no love for his cousin. When he felt able to speak, he learned that their families had moved inland, while they remained behind to help with the walnut boat. They seemed to hold no grudges, nor did they point any blame. To them, the sea and its creatures were merely unpredictable.

"Let this be the end of it," one muttered as he rubbed his hands and peered out through a crack in the boards. "Etma, do your worst."

With the storm whistling about the building, nobody could think of sleep. One youth pulled out a *patna* pouch. Still wrapped in his blanket, Bremig was drawn into a game he generally avoided. He felt warmer now, in the close air of the stable, and needed to keep his mind from his near-drowning.

The manner of play was simple. The holder shook the pouch, while the others wagered on the outcome he called for. Then the holder slid his finger from an opening, and a pebble—dark or light—dropped into his palm.

Aware that such pouches were often stuffed with more stones of one shade than another, Bremig paid attention to how the owner placed his bets. He did not believe, as did many, that by talking to the pouch with the proper endearments one could charm the chosen pebble out.

"Dark as a dead man's eyes," chanted the shorter youngster as he placed his small copper on the wagering board. "Dark as the inside of a whale's belly." This particular patter had some success, and soon there was no one willing to bet against it.

"Let me try," insisted the taller youth. Bremig stood up to stretch his legs. He had heard no thunder for some time, and the wind seemed to be slackening. Where, he wondered, was the purging apocalypse that the boat's launchers had expected?

"White as a frozen mast," intoned the new holder of the pouch. "White as the feathers on a gull."

The carver opened the door a crack. Had Etma already vented her wrath? One part of him believed the old tales, though he scoffed at most seamen's superstitions.

Fishermen and landsmen agreed that Etma once had been Ormek's wife. Reigning together, the two had created all living things. But the seamen claimed that He'd cast her down without cause, and that now she roamed the oceans, driving storm and wave to suit her whims. The landsmen believed that she had planned to usurp His power, and for that reason was deposed from the sky. Their acount, far more comforting than the seamen's, had her powerless, chained to the sandy bottom, condemned to perpetual gloom.

"White as a frozen mast . . ."

The carver turned to his companions. "Storm's dropping," he said. "I don't hear the rain anymore."

"Are you sure?" The youths scooped up their coppers, along with a few of Bremig's, and hurried outside. To everyone's astonishment, the sky had cleared and the stars were glistening. Curious, the pair headed back to the beach to search for signs of the missing fisherman. Bremig hung back. He was in no hurry to meet his cousin.

Draalego was dead, he tried to assure himself. Still suffering from the cold and wet, the carver returned to the stable and lay down in a heap of straw. He closed his eyes, and was suddenly back in the water, coughing and thrashing. This time he was sinking helplessly, his arms rigid with cold. He woke with a cry, and realized he had slept but a moment. Again he fell into dreams, and this time it was a clamor of voices that roused him.

Outside, dawn was just breaking. He heard cottage doors opening and saw a crowd moving toward the water. Pulling on damp boots, he hurried after them. About him sounded cries of astonishment, and he could see for himself that the walnut boat was coming home. Sail furled, it made for shore slowly, propelled by two makeshift oars. And the cruel grin of the oarsman could be seen even from that distance.

Despite his fear of his cousin, Bremig raced after the others and stood with them by the shore. "I told you it wouldn't do by itself," Draalego shouted to them across the surf. "Now we're going to find the vixen and finish this thing right."

The carver could not move. He still had Arod's knife, which was suffering, no doubt, from its salt bath but still would serve. If he stood at the landing spot, and waited until his cousin turned to him . . . If he struck a surprise blow . . .

Perspiration dripped coldly down his ribs as the boat glided in. Then he was running, away from the harbor, away from Pelask's son.

CHAPTER 9

STARING moodily into the forest, Kyala rode again in back of the wagon. Modwetten was driving now, while Hapko steadfastly kept his face turned from the Vigen. The young woman would have liked to shake both men, knocking their skulls together until their senses were restored.

Which of the two was the greater fool? she asked herself. Hapko's behavior was merely annoying. But the glassmaker's refusal to understand her gift might soon prove a costly error. She kicked the wagon's panels and wished she were kicking Modwetten's ribs.

At last she leaned back and tried to make herself more comfortable. Give him time, she thought. Maybe he would recall the details of the attack—if not by choice, then in his dreams. Then he would know that the she-bear had *not* calmed down as he suggested, and that Kyala had dispatched it in the heat of its fury.

The rig rattled under her, the jarring growing worse as they left the high forest. The leaf canopy thinned, and broad patches of daylight appeared. Soon the travelers emerged into a swampy region where brambles edged onto the road.

By the time evening neared, they were crossing open country. Kyala thought the Vigen would not stop, for he drove on through moonrise. But soon she saw his head drooping, and when they reached an old barn marked with lanterns he turned from the road.

"Keep quiet here," Modwetten hissed to the peddler. "Not a word from you about Vigens." Hapko showed him the back of his head.

The barn was no more than a shelter for travelers. A boy charged a small fee for entrance, and the "guests" had free choice of bundles of straw for their beds. Outside the wide doorway, a tinker was roasting a plump fowl over a campfire, and for a coin he agreed to share his meal with the Vigen's party. They sat on logs, Hapko choosing a place far from the firelight.

Recalling the drayman's hasty exit, Kyala decided to sleep on the wagon. The glassmaker shrugged, took his casket, and found a place in a corner of the barn to bed down. Kyala's straw stank of sweat and tobacco, and the air was filled with banter from *patna* games. But her eyelids fell shut, and she did not open them until the movement of the wagon shook her awake.

Startled, she sat up and saw Modwetten holding the reins. As the pony trotted ahead, she heard Hapko behind her shouting, "Vigen thief! Vigen thief!" There were other cries, and the men in the barn were covering their faces. Kyala tried to piece together what had happened, but all she could think was that Hapko had betrayed them. Catching up with the wagon as it rolled past the big doors, the peddler managed to clamber aboard.

"I warned you to watch your tongue," said Modwetten viciously. "A Vigen could break his oath for a bullhead like you."

Hapko whimpered, his eyes already shielded. He said no more, and they drove steadily eastward toward the first redness of dawn. All morning the peddler sat on the edge of the bench, as if ready to jump off at the least provocation. But his livelihood was in the glassmaker's hands, and Kyala believed he would wait until he could wrest back his cart and nag.

In early afternoon they reached a broad valley flanked by meandering hills on either side. Here the haying had begun already; lines of men were scything the tall grass. The road crossed a riverbed that was almost dry, then continued through a cluster of weathered timber buildings. "Longval," the Vigen announced as they passed a smithy. "We're almost home."

He turned at a crossroads, leaving the dusty village behind. Close to the foot of the southern row of hills, he turned again, taking a track that was overgrown with weeds. A skinny, spotted dog greeted the travelers with a meager yelp.

The house was a simple affair of rough-hewn planks, with a sod roof and a few tiny windows. Several outbuildings were equally modest, and Kyala wondered which might be his workshop. A small, squat structure behind the barn boasted a fieldstone chimney, and there, she supposed, Modwetten's kiln must lie.

The Vigen's barn leaned ominously, and she wondered what a brisk wind might do to it. As they entered the open doorway, a man Modwetten's size, but heavily whiskered, emerged from the shadows. "Back already?" he said with no enthusiasm.

"Help me unload," replied the glassmaker. The ponies were led off to be fed, and Hapko hastily harnessed his own horse to the wagon. As soon as Modwetten removed the last of his belongings, the peddler snapped his whip. He nearly ran down Kyala in his eagerness to be gone.

"He didn't even wait for his money," said Modwetten with unconcealed satisfaction.

"Why should he be so frightened?" Kyala demanded. "I've seen one bad Vigen. But the others are honorable . . . or so I've been told."

"Do you think it's that simple—a choice between mutton or mush?" The glassmaker picked up his casket and headed, with a scowl, for the door. "Your Watnojat should have taught you some truths of this world."

"He said I must use judgment," she answered with a toss of her head, following him into the unkempt yard.

"Judgment, yes. And that's precisely what you lack. How can you expect otherwise at your age?" Setting down the box at the door of the chimneyed building, he produced a short wooden key from his belt. The door swung open after some jiggling of the lock, and Kyala looked into the dark interior. The air smelled heavily of wood ash, but she could discern nothing in the gloom.

Modwetten pulled the casket inside, then unhooked flaps of hide that covered his glass windowpanes. The room flooded with light. In comparison with the rest of the farmstead, Kyala found the shop's interior to be surprisingly neat. The bellows, mounted on a simple frame, had a rope and pulleys for easy pumping. The modest kiln was of trimmed fieldstones, tightly fitted together and well caulked. On the opposite wall, Modwetten unhooked another hide, this one behind his shelf of vials. Light poured through the row of panes, igniting his store of colored glass and sending bright hues dancing across the plank floor.

Kyala's mouth fell open. His supply of these scarce pigments far exceeded her own, and his manner of displaying them made the treasure all the more impressive. Tentatively, she lifted one squat vial and shook the glass fragments within. The color was a milky blue, of little use for animal talismans . . .

"I know what you're thinking, my high-minded apprentice." Modwetten plucked the container from her fingers and replaced it on his shelf. "But you know, I'm sure, the honest uses of such glass."

Kyala nodded. A living person's eye bead had but one application—in the case of extreme illness. With such a talisman the Vigen helped the healer, and remarkable cures were sometimes worked. Beyond that, a bead cast during someone's lifetime might be retained by his loved ones, for a Vigen who held such a bead could later call on the departed one's spirit.

"So," she said. "You have some business with healers. A worthy use of your talent. And I suppose you call spirits from time to time."

"Few spirits," he answered dryly. "And now that you're satisfied as to my virtue, you'd better go in the house and see what we have to eat. My brother's not one to keep the larder stocked."

"But we've work here. I want to start mixing the pigments . . ."

"As if you were making some talisman for foxes?"

"I saw the beast's eyes. I can match the colors from memory."

"And if your match isn't true? Must I risk my reputation on your untried skills?" Modwetten pursed his lips. "Even if your work is accurate, I doubt this beast can be touched by an ordinary bead."

"Then what . . ."

He smiled coldly. "What we need is a *bead-of-all-colors*. I've never made one, but I know the details of the technique."

Kyala stared at the Vigen with amazement, half wondering if she had misheard. A bead-of-all-colors was a thing of legend, a single talisman that could sway any man or creature. The famous Kolpern, it was said, had cast such a bead and then destroyed it. But no glassmaker in this age believed such a thing could be created.

"So you doubt me, my apprentice? Go into the house now and do as I said. Tomorrow we'll begin our new talisman."

In the face of Modwetten's confidence, Kyala could only turn away. She had risked the fangs of the Sea-snake and the Crab's huge claw just to glimpse their eyes. And now the glassmaker claimed that her knowledge was unneeded! She could scarcely hold back the tears.

That night they ate hard biscuit and smoked meat. Patro, the Vigen's brother, dragged out a pallet, and she slept before the fireplace in the main house. In the morning she could not find Modwetten. The door to his shop was locked and the flaps inside now covered the windows again. Carrying her search into the barn, she noticed a pony missing, as well. Patro was hunched down, milking the single cow, and Kyala had difficulty getting him to talk to her.

"He's gone," said the white-bearded brother at last. "Gone on his business. That's all I know." He could not tell her when the glassmaker would return.

Had he ridden after materials for his impossible charm? she wondered. Perhaps he sought a special clay for the mold, or a rare fuel for the fire. If he needed new mineral pigments, however, he might take months searching, might never return at all.

In the afternoon, fuming with impatience, Kyala found a saddle for the other pony and rode back into Longval. She stopped at the smithy, and the sooty blacksmith laughed nervously when she asked after the glassmaker. "Haven't seen him for a year," the man told her while hammering at a harness fitting. "He sends his brother on his errands, I'm glad to say."

That evening, her plans decided, she shared a silent meal with Patro. She could not wait for Modwetten. She would cast the beads herself, in the colors she had witnessed, and then she would stalk the beast without him. "I'll need the key to his shop," Kyala said when the brother seemed ready to retire. "It's urgent. I'm assisting him, and we've talismans to make. In the morning, I have to begin."

"He's got the one key," answered Patro with a shrug. He left her alone by the cold hearth.

Bremig took the southern route to Longval, and thus was spared the hazardous forest trail. But Draalego's threat pursued him, and he checked the road at his back whenever he crested a hill. That he had proved himself both weak-willed and foolish he had no doubt. But he would not compound his failings by leading the fishermen to their quarry.

He avoided showing himself where he might be remembered, skirting the towns, seeking shelter from isolated farmers rather than at inns. Coming at night to a farmhouse door, he would keep his face in shadow while he bargained for a meal to be passed out to him. He slept in a stable, and was gone before dawn.

He had passed two nights since leaving Darst, and Longval was a half-day's ride farther. The road wound past the Buttresses, sheer walls of rock that climbed abruptly from the flatlands. So far as the carver knew, these heights had never been scaled. But tales abounded of riches atop the blunt peaks. He found himself staring at the stone towers and not watching the road.

A cart passed, and he caught a flash of familiar red whiskers. He wheeled and saw the driver whipping his horse furiously, but the peddler's rig could not outrun the roan mare. "What have you done with them?" Bremig demanded of Hapko when the man finally halted. His poor nag was winded, wheezing heavily.

"I've done nothin' to anyone," the peddler replied in anguished tones. "We'd a bargain, and I kept to it. But when'd you tell me the runt was a Vigen?"

Bremig shook his head in disgust. "What does his trade matter, so long as his money's good?"

"Fine for you to say. I'm still waitin' to be paid."

"You were trying to run from me. Is that how you collect your debts?" Bremig leaned down from the saddle and grabbed the peddler by his frizzy hair. "Is the girl all right?" he demanded, fixing the man with a fierce stare. "Swear an oath on the Bright One."

The peddler hesitated. "She was fine when I saw 'er. And the ol' Vigen is probably past botherin' women."

Angrily, Bremig released the man, then tossed him the

agreed-on price for his services. "If you know how to keep a secret, I have this for you, as well," he added suddenly.

The peddler looked up at the silver bit between Bremig's fingers.

"By the Bright One, I swear it," said Hapko quickly.

"Swear what?"

"Whatever you want."

"That you won't tell anyone where you've been or what folks you've seen."

"I swear it. Nothing. Not a word . . . By the Lifegiver's heat."

Bremig handed him the silver doubtfully and watched the peddler scrutinizing the piece. The greedy look in Hapko's eyes troubled him. "You break your oath, and we'll find you," the carver warned. "You'll learn for certain what a Vigen can do." Then, thinking that whatever else he said or did would make matters worse, he turned his mare eastward again.

After that, he found himself even more cautious than before. Wishing to avoid speaking to anyone who might remember him, he asked directions too seldom, took a wrong turn, and did not discover his error until midafternoon. He could not reach Longval before nightfall, he realized, and feared getting lost again should he push on in the dark. So it was not until early the next morning that he crossed the gully at Longval and paused to let his horse drink from the scanty flow.

Fortunately, the local smith was just opening his shop. "You looking for Modwetten?" he said incredulously. "That makes a second stranger wanting him—one yesterday and one today."

"Is he so hard to find?"

"Not many like his company." The smith scowled, then waved a large hand as he gave directions. Bremig hurried out, his heart already speeding in anticipation.

A loose pig trotted across the path that ran toward the dilapidated farmhouse. Nobody was in sight, but Bremig heard a rhythmic pounding and decided to follow the sound. Reaching a chimneyed shed, he found, to his surprise, Kyala banging with a log as if she meant to smash in the door. When she saw him riding in, she dropped the log and gaped at him with an expression of fury mixed with delight.

"The Vigen ran off," she shouted, flinging out her arms. "And left the shop locked. I'd like to use his head to break it down."

"It looks solid enough from here," Bremig said calmly. "Making a key might be an easier way to get in."

"Can you do that?" Some of the anger drained from her face.

"I've whittled more than a few." He dismounted, and she followed him as he bent to the keyhole. "Did you see what it looked like?"

She drew a shape with her finger against the panel. He nodded, walked to the woodpile that sat beside the shed, and began to poke through the kindling. An unexpected stick came to hand. He peeled some bark away, and then he was certain that this was black walnut. *Cursed wood*, he thought, and was about to fling it aside. But he paused, realizing he might have another use for the piece. Turning for a moment from Kyala's task, he tucked the stick into his saddlebag. Then he found a softer piece of kindling and took out his whittling knife.

"Like this?" he asked, holding the flat key out to her. It fit the hole, but would not turn. He made a small cut, and when that failed, made another. A few moments later, the bolt pulled in with a squeal.

Suddenly she was about his neck, hugging him so that he tumbled to the floor of the shop, rubbing his face with her hair. He laughed and tried to pull her closer, but she sprang up and began to uncover the windows.

Seeing the vials filled with pigments, Kyala's hopes rose. If Patro left her alone, she thought she could finish her task.

Glancing outside, she found no signs of either brother. "Let's bring in all the firewood we'll need," she told Bremig.

They hastily raided the woodpile, then barred the door behind them. If Patro wanted to stop them now, she thought, let *him* try to smash in the door. She brushed bits of bark and dust from her hands, then turned again to survey the rows of colorings. Now she must begin the mixing, a painstaking task.

And what of Bremig? She could not deny her elation at the carver's return. But whatever news he carried must wait. Reaching to the shelf above the workbench, she brought down the Vigen's mixing board, a plank marked off into many small squares. She placed it where sunlight spilled across the bench. This was to be her testing ground.

What if Bremig knew how few talismans she had actually made? Yet her mentor had told her that her color sense was extraordinary—even for a Vigen. Provided she could find the appropriate pigments, the mixing should go well. She stood before the rows of vials and pictured again the Squid's demonic eye. Still shuddering with the recollection, she lifted a bottle of crimson grains.

Each of these containers held fragments from a different glass. Modwetten, or one of his predecessors, had first combined sand, pot salt, and ground seashells with appropriate minerals, then fused the mixture in the kiln to produce a single-colored batch. Before her stood the results of countless labors and trials, for the control of the final hue was always a difficult task. The type of fuel, the tightness of the kiln, the purity of the materials, all affected the outcome. And some batches could not be reproduced, even by the Vigen who had made them.

Kyala possessed little experience in the casting of glass. Someday she hoped to have a shop and the time to pursue this arduous craft. But for now she must use the colorings that others had made.

She worked the wooden stopper out of the bottle and carefully shook out a few bright grains onto one square of the mixing board. Angry as she was with Modwetten, she would not waste his pigments. Turning again to the shelf, she carried first violets, then deep reds to the bench, until a dozen squares of the board held powders. "This will take time," she told Bremig, who had dropped onto a low stool and was whittling on a twig from the woodpile. She felt a vague apprehension about his presence, despite the fact that the basic principles of her craft were no secret. Without knowledge of the proportions and Fires, no outsider could hope to make glass. And without the rare color sense, creation of a workable talisman would be impossible. Nonetheless, Bremig's nearness troubled her.

She had no heart to send the carver outside. With a sigh, she returned her thoughts to the board, mixing the colorings in her mind as Watnojat had taught her. Once the grains of different batches were stirred together, the process could not be undone. The result must be clear to her before she picked up a single grain.

Using a tiny copper paddle, she dipped into each of the heaps she had poured. Her hands trembled as she gently stirred the combined fragments. Had she correctly foreseen the result, or merely wasted Modwetten's colorings? Suddenly she saw the frightening hue of the demon-eye emerge in the powder. But until the final fusing, she could not be certain.

At once she transferred her mixture to a thimblelike depression in a clay mold. There must also be a pupil, and she hunted again through the Vigen's shelves until she found the appropriate indigo. At last, she was finished with her first preparation.

Next came the mixing for the Sea-snake's eye. Fortunately, the Vigen had a good batch of milk glass and no shortage of brilliant blues. This second task went quickly, and she asked Bremig to start the fire in the kiln. It was the third bead that might give her trouble, she suspected, for the Spider-crab's eyes were akin to those of insects. A color match alone would not suffice. She must reproduce the metallic glint, the silvery gray with its harsh sheen.

She looked once more through the Vigen's stores and began to despair. Pulling one stopper after another to peer in at the contents, she found nothing suitable. Soon she began to view Modwetten's pursuit of the bead-of-all-colors as less than preposterous, perhaps even worthwhile. For matching the Crab's eye seemed impossible by ordinary means. Bremig had the fire going, and the small room was heating up. He'd become impatient, she noticed, for he'd abandoned his whittling and was poking about in a corner of the shop.

"Tell me if you find any hiding places," she said. "If there's a rare pigment somewhere, it may save us."

Bremig had his hands on something. She peered over his shoulder and watched him pull a board loose from the wall. "I remember you kept your valuables under the floor," he said with a grin. "And I think I've found your Vigen's secret cache."

Reaching inside, he began to pull out talismans, and they were all of blues and greens and grays. "Your glassmaker had hidden wealth," the carver exulted. But Kyala shook her head in dismay at this collection of human-eye beads. She could not believe that Modwetten possessed these for any noble purpose.

Raiding the compartment again, Bremig produced tiny vials of crushed glass in colors she could not identify. The powders shimmered with green iridescence, or the glitter of starlight. What other wonders and abominations lay hidden here? Pulling out one small container after another, at last he showed her a steely dust in a long, narrow tube. She held it to the light and studied the reflection from the grains. Yes, this would serve. But there was not much left of the pigment; she would consume at least half to make her bead.

For a moment she hesitated, not knowing the value of

what she must expend. She consoled herself with the certainty that Modwetten had an evil purpose for this glass. Why else would he conceal it with the other proofs of his guilt? So she poured the powder onto the mixing board, scrutinizing again the unique tint before adding smoke glass and a hint of gold.

The color was matched. Whether the sheen would be right, she could only guess. The mixing was done. The powders were ready in their molds, copper strips inserted so the beads later could be strung. Bremig opened the kiln's hinged iron door with a poker, and she pushed the clay mold inside.

Then the tedious work began, pumping the bellows and tending the fire. The air rushed into the kiln in great sighs. With the shop's door shut, there was only ventilation through a few air holes, and Bremig soon stripped to the waist, his face and chest awash with sweat.

While he rhythmically pulled the handle, the carver at last described his journey, and his face darkened. "The fisherfolk are in awe of Draalego now," he told her in conclusion. "You should have seen their faces when he rowed home in the boat. They think he's privy to Etma's secret thoughts."

"Because he came back safe from a common thunderstorm?" she complained. "If their beliefs are false, we need no demons to explain his escape."

"A fisherman has a different way of viewing things."

"Then, because he says so, they won't rest until they tie *me* into that boat."

"We won't let them catch you." Bremig frowned and started to pump harder. His agitation seemed to make his pumping irregular, and Kyala had to ask him to maintain a steady pace.

"We should leave as soon as this is done," he said. "They may find you even in Longval."

"How could they?"

Bremig's frown deepened. "Hapko!" he said, speaking the name like an epithet.

"And what's the likelihood that Hapko would ever speak to one of your roving fishermen?"

"I imagine," he said hoarsely, "that the peddler's asking in every tavern between here and the coast. Asking if someone wants to know about a Vigen. And I'm to blame for it."

"You! Why?"

"Because I took his oath. Paid him for silence." The carver shook his head mournfully. "Now he knows that talking's worth something. All he needs is to find the right buyer."

"He swore?"

"To Ormek, for what that's worth. I'd trust his oath on a hen's egg as easily."

Kyala laughed. "I didn't think the peddler such a dishonest fellow as you make him. But he was certainly afraid of Vigens."

"Maybe that fear will outweigh his greed." Bremig stopped to wipe sweat from his face, and Kyala took her turn at the bellows.

The heat grew so fierce that she dared open the shop door. Still, Patro did not appear; nor did his wandering brother. At last Kyala peered into the fiery kiln and observed that the powders had fused. "We can stop," she said wearily. "But we've got to let them cool slowly."

She allowed the fire to burn out, but forced herself to wait before opening the kiln door the width of a spike. Time passed, and she widened the gap. When the talismans finally were cool, daylight had almost gone.

Nervously, she removed the mold, took it outside, and studied the beads she had made. The Squid's eye was as close a match as she had hoped, a frightening orb of violet with the proper crimson highlights. Here was proof, she thought, that her mentor's confidence in her was justified. And the Sea-snake's talisman had captured its glacial stare, the piece chilling her as thoroughly as the original had done. Only the Crab's eye was wanting, for it showed a pinkish luster she had not planned.

Bremig also studied the beads, but he failed to see what troubled her. "It must have been the touch of gold I added," she said sadly. "Sometimes when you reheat glass, the color changes. A Vigen should discard such batches, but Modwetten was careless."

"Then we'll have to start over?"

The shop was in gloom. "I can't mix again until tomorrow. I saw the eye in daylight, and I must work in daylight."

"Then let's hope your Vigen stays away." He replaced all he had taken from the hidden compartment. She tidied the workbench, and they closed the shop door.

Kyala saw a light at the main house, but did not care to face Patro. Perched on a clean pile of hay in the barn, Bremig shared with her the bread and cheese he had bought that morning. To Kyala they tasted as good as the finest delicacies from her mother's table.

"We'll sleep here," she said, stretching out on the straw, feeling a comfortable weariness after the day of labor. When he slipped his arm around her, she made no complaint. His embrace made her pulse quicken, and an unaccustomed warmth began to grow. She thought of Jelor, and of the barn much like this one where they had often met . . .

But then she recalled one of her mentor's admonitions. "Not until the beads are finished," she whispered. Squeezing Bremig's hand once for assurance, she forced herself to roll away from him. She heard a long, indrawn breath, his only sign of disappointment. How could she explain this odd Vigen custom? But the carver asked for no details, and soon she knew by his breathing that he was asleep.

CHAPTER 10

KYALA did not sleep well. Each time she woke, she saw Modwetten's concealed talismans, the orbs of blues and greens that accused him of breaking Ormek's laws. If these beads had been cast by request, then they belonged with those who'd commissioned them. And if they'd been cast in secrecy, then the glassmaker was surely guilty.

Modwetten was no Hestafos, she thought, recalling the legendary miscreant who had destroyed his village. Nor was he another Untmur, who had held a whole town in thrall. This Vigen was more subtle in his ways than the others, yet he'd hinted that beads might be used against men for sound reasons. Convinced that he sometimes found such reasons, she began to fear for Bremig's safety.

Kyala had no worries for herself, for she was protected by the bead that dangled from her neck. This talisman of her own eye color warded off control by another Vigen's glass. But Bremig had no such protection. How vulnerable might he be, she thought, if Modwetten indeed produced a bead-of-all-colors?

Turning restless in the straw, her concerns shifted from one matter to another. What of the mismade talisman, she pondered, the one she must redo? She'd been fortunate for one day that Patro had not disturbed her. Perhaps he'd been preoccupied in the fields, but she could not expect this convenient inattenton to last. And she also recalled how Bremig's presence had weakened her concentration. Thinking she must finish the work alone, she slipped back into the shop before he woke. Though she had barely light enough to find the vials, she began to pour out colorings.

Kyala pulled the silvery pigment from its hiding place, this time knowing she must consume the last of it. And she hunted for a different gold, choosing an aged and near-empty bottle. Such a well-used batch she thought she could trust.

As Ormek's early rays reached the windowpanes, she realized that she must cast a second charm that day. The Crab's eye was her first task. But she also wanted one more talisman—a charm to match Bremig's gray-green eyes. Though this decision brought gooseflesh, she held to it, for she knew how vital to his safety such a bead might prove.

In the solitude of the shop, she took her time with the mixing. She would have no more chances to remake either talisman; she must leave this place as soon as the work was done. Kyala poked at the grains, squinting, studying, until her eyes were bleary and she could not doubt the correctness of her preparations. She readied the mold and built up the fire.

For some time the only sound was the wheezing of the bellows. When the shop door suddenly scraped open, she shuddered with surprise. In her absorption with the colorings, she'd forgotten to bar herself in! And now Patro stood watching her, his eyes blazing, his white whiskers bristling in all directions. "I thought he left this place locked up" was all he said. Leaving her gaping, he banged the door behind him and was gone.

Kyala waited for her pulse to slow before she touched the bellows' handle again. *The man merely shrugged.* All she could think was that Patro neither knew nor cared for his brother's craft. But Modwetten would come, perhaps within the day. And how would she explain the missing pigments?

She looked into the kiln in hopes that the fusing might be finished. Not much longer, she thought as she studied the two glossy orbs. The work was almost done, and this time she expected the Crab's eye would be correct.

She was grateful that the carver remained away, for the solitude had enabled her to focus on her task. Perhaps he had found business elsewhere; if so, she was glad. For there was another reason she did not want him in the shop . . .

When the beads began to cool, she left the overheated building to sit in the shadow of the barn. Now and again she returned to open the kiln door a bit wider. Each time she checked the glass, her optimism grew for these new charms. But as the morning wore on, she became fretful over the carver's continued absence. At last, as she was taking the talismans from the mold that lay on the workbench, she heard a rider coming. *Bremig!*

Without thinking, she poked his charm into a pocket of her breeches. The other bead she carried to the yard. "Does it match?" came the carver's voice as she held the new glass to the light. She studied the talisman and began to grin. There were no unwanted shadings now. The sheen, the menacing glint, was exactly what she had seen in the creature's eye.

And what of Bremig's talisman? she asked herself. Why was she not handing it to him, explaining its purpose? She could find excuses. Why worry him, when Modwetten might pose no threat at all? Only glassmakers, so far as she knew, wore their own talismans for protection. A man who feared losing his will to a glassmaker, after all, was unlikely to commission such a bead!

These answers did not settle her uneasiness, yet she kept the talisman pocketed. Perhaps later she would explain the matter. Meanwhile, she stepped forward to show him the silvery orb—the Spider-crab charm.

"It looks the same to me as the other," he said, scratching at the dark growth that had begun to thicken on his face.

"The reddish tint is missing. That makes the difference."

"I can't argue. You're the glassmaker." He smiled, then pulled from its scabbard at his hip an unfamiliar knife with a dark handle. "Look, Arod gave me this blade and I carved a new hilt for it." He nodded in the direction of the village. "The smith there helped me change it over."

She stared at the odd carvings, tiny fringed faces that reminded her of dream creatures.

"Black walnut is a strange wood," he said. "When I start to work it, the tools seem to take over my hands."

Kyala found the handle's images disquieting. Touching the wood, she felt an unfamiliar tingling beyond her sense of its dark color.

"I can't explain it," he continued as he sheathed the weapon. "When I first carved the figurehead for their cursed boat, I was angry with myself. But now that face haunts me. It comes from the same place as these." He rubbed his thumb over the fanciful visages on the hilt.

Kyala could say nothing to his discovery. If there was power in glass, she thought, then why not in wood? But what god or demon might be responsible for it she did not know. "My work here is done," she told him softly. "We should leave as quickly as we can."

Hurriedly they cleaned the shop, and then Bremig worked his key to lock up the place. Kyala went to saddle the pony again, and found Patro poking about the barn. "I've got to borrow this gray," she said to the brother. "Tell Modwetten to meet us at the coast if he casts his bead. We'll try again at the same spot."

Patro shrugged. "If he comes back, I'll tell 'im."

"And I'll replace the pigments I took," she added, though she knew she possessed nothing resembling the silvery powder. He would have to accept some other rare coloring —one from a batch that Watnojat had cast long ago.

Patro turned away with a grunt as Kyala rode out into the afternoon light. The pungent smell of new hay filled the air, and she imagined briefly that she was back at Ridrune's farm. Her mother and the rest of her family must still be there, hiding, afraid to go home. Now, with the three talismans ready, she could finally do something to help them.

"Which road?" she shouted to Bremig as she caught up with his roan mare.

"Not through Asep's Forest," he answered. Instead, he suggested a westerly route before turning north. Having doubled back several times, he claimed now to know the fastest way past the Buttresses. But they must go cautiously, bypassing villages whenever possible.

They crossed meadows when they could and tried to use the less popular roads. Even so, they passed occasional travelers. Several riders glanced at Kyala with open curiosity, and later she suffered a lengthy scrutiny when they approached a wagonload of harvesters. Five sweaty men turned their heads to follow her; she watched them with a sideways glance.

At nightfall they paused by an isolated farmhouse where the glow of lanterns moved about the yard. Kyala hung back in the shadows while the carver made his approach. The stocky farmer, however, turned out to be a curious soul. He lifted his light and stepped past Bremig to have a better look at her.

"You and the lad will have to wait a bit," he said pleasantly with a wave of his arm. "Go water your mounts, and we'll call you when the cookin's ready."

Kyala was not surprised to be taken for a boy by lamplight; this had happened before. Yet the large man seemed unduly curious about her.

Later, he showed them a narrow outbuilding equipped with pallets and blankets. The room was empty that night, the farmer said, because the hands who usually slept there were helping with his sister's haying. Kyala kept out of the light all the time he was talking, but the man's curiosity did not wane.

"Been traveling long?" he asked Bremig casually.

"A few days," the carver answered.

"Seen anything odd? I hear there's strange people on the roads."

"I saw a peddler in a green wagon," the carver said with a laugh.

"Stranger than that. Fishermen from the coast. Riding from one village to the next."

"Fishermen?" To Kyala's ears, Bremig's feigned surprise sounded hollow. She forced her feet to be still, though the urge to run was fierce.

"I was even told," the farmer continued, "that one of 'em's lost his wife."

"Wife?" Now the carver's shock was genuine, she thought. Perhaps he hadn't anticipated Draalego's cunning.

"They say she's got a temper like a cornered cat, and she's not much to look at, either." The farmer patted himself on the chest. "Not much here. You know what I mean. Funny thing, though, the fellow's so eager he's offering a purse full of coppers to get 'er back. How do you explain that?"

There was a pause. Kyala pressed herself against the rough wall, as if by so doing she might melt through it. "Some fishermen have odd tastes," the carver suggested with a catch in his voice.

"Must be. Must be. I almost took *you* for a fisherman. That's why I asked."

Bremig cleared his throat. "I'm a wood-carver," he said cautiously. "Here's a sample of my work, if you're interested." He drew the knife and offered the handle to the farmer. The other studied it under the lamplight, and Kyala watched a look of apprehension spread across his face.

"Not something I'd like to own," he said hastily. "But I

see you've a talent for whittling." With a last glance back at Kyala, he left the lantern, then strode away into the yard.

At once Bremig slid a stave across the inside of the door. "Draalego and I will have another thing to settle," he said bitterly.

"I think he and his friends must be covering the whole countryside," she answered in a weak voice. Her knees felt unsteady. She threw herself down on the pallet. *Purse full of coppers!* "His tales must be everywhere now. We can't stay here. I don't know where we can go."

Bremig drew his knife and studied the blade in the yellowish light. Kyala watched him with alarm. "What . . ."

"I put a keen edge on it today, and now I've a use for it. I'm going to make you look *more* like a boy." He knelt by her and grabbed a tuft of her hair. "If you sit up, it'll be easier."

She sighed and allowed him to start trimming. "They say I'm not much to look at anyway, so why should it matter?"

Bremig laughed. The blade was nearly silent, but she felt the tickle of hairs falling against her nape and cheek. "Shears would be better," he said, "though I've a good hand for this work. As for my cousin's opinions on women, I'd sooner ask a cow."

When he was finished, she reached up to feel the scruffy result. Maybe the shortened hair would deceive others, but this farmer's doubts could not be undone. Bremig opened the door and reported the yard empty. Watching the main house nervously, they saddled their mounts.

Reaching the road, they heard a rattle of carts and two deep voices singing. A pair of tinkers' wagons, the first one bearing a light, had just passed by. "They can lead the way for us," Bremig whispered. Kyala would have preferred to be already bedded down for the night. Cursing Draalego and all but one of his kin, she nodded and followed.

From their roisterous songs, Kyala judged that the tinkers had emptied an ale barrel between them. The two drove slowly, and she grew impatient with the pace. But Bremig persisted in trailing them until finally the carts pulled off the road. Then he motioned for her to wait while he advanced slowly.

She saw the men waving their arms drunkenly, but could not quite hear their conversation with Bremig. Soon the light went out, and she dared approach a bit closer. The quarter moon had risen, but she could make out little more than the shapes of the wagons.

Shortly Bremig beckoned her. As she advanced, she heard a chorus of snores from the wagons, then saw the carver holding up what looked to be blankets. Spreading one over the stubble of the field at the road's edge, he sat down and pulled off his boots. The night air was cool, and Kyala welcomed the chance for rest and a bit of warmth.

After seeing to the pony, she dropped down beside him and let him pull the other cover around them. The wool smelled of campfires and horses, but she was glad of the thin wrap. His hands touched her tentatively, gently, and despite her exhaustion she felt a stir of excitement. Now that the beads were finished, she could not bring herself to discourage him.

But then his fingers slackened and his breathing slowed. She whispered his name, and he did not answer. Smiling—for she understood his weariness—she let sleep take her.

When she woke at dawn, she could not recall having closed her eyes. The tinkers were still slumbering, and she was happy to leave them to their dreams. Now was the time to move quickly.

For a brief while the roads remained pleasantly quiet, but as the sun rose behind her, Kyala nervously watched the traffic build. *Market day?* Surely some nearby town was drawing many visitors. And Bremig could find no way around the crowds. Carts and wagons of all varieties were coming and going on every narrow track. She felt too many eyes watching her.

Approaching a busy crossroads, everyone had slowed to a walking pace. Ahead of Kyala crawled a cart piled high with crook-necked vegetables of yellow and green. Another wagon held dusty grain sacks. A trader in a straw hat was leading a string of ponies.

Kyala fixed her attention straight ahead, while watching as best she could for signs of interest from other travelers. Only one man glanced at her, a long-necked grandfather on foot who was driving five goats. He stared at her and would not turn away. She refused to meet his gaze, but finally he tapped her leg with his looped staff.

"Trading the pony?" he asked in a dry voice. "Decent-looking animal."

She shook her head, hoping he'd lose interest.

"Not trading?" he asked with a frown. She turned quickly away from his bony face. Something about his intent stare made her shudder. "Then you must have somethin' in those bags for the fair." He reached up unashamedly and began to probe her saddlebags.

"Nothing," she said with annoyance.

"Then you've no business here." He contemplated his statement awhile. Kyala kept her head steady, but shifted her gaze enough to see Bremig's reaction. His lips showed only mild annoyance.

"Stranger!" shouted the herdsman. "You're not from these parts. I say you come here from Darst."

She stiffened in the saddle. He repeated his conclusion even more loudly. Attempting to deepen her voice, she answered angrily, "I come from Longval, and what does that matter to you?"

"See!" he cried in triumph to the others in the road. "Bad temper, like the fishermen said. She must be the one they're lookin' for."

A few heads turned, the youths on two nearby horses mildly curious. The long-necked man tapped her again with his prod.

"I'm not one of your herd!" she retorted, reaching down to wrest the carved stick from his hand. She flung it over his head into a cluster of flowering weeds.

"She's the one, she's the one," the herdsman called excitedly, but he turned aside to search for his lost staff. His bleating goats flocked about his legs as he pushed through the overgrown plants. "She's the runaway wife those fishermen want."

Kyala caught Bremig's eye. "That way!" he said suddenly, pointing to a pasture that bordered on a quieter road. With farmwives and draymen staring at them, they jumped their mounts over a sagging section of fence, then hastened across the field. The new road was heading north, and seemed a fair route for now. She glanced back, spying no sign of pursuit. The ones who had heard the accusation were still trapped by the crowded crossroads, and no one was venturing to follow them across the field. "If they find a fast horse, they can catch us," she shouted after Bremig. Her pony was not up to heavy riding.

They reached higher country, where orchards stretched across the hillsides. "We can hide among the trees," she called.

Bremig nodded and led her up one of the rows, then over a ridge so that they were hidden from the road. On the branches the apples shone, and the rich scent reminded her how hungry she was. Coming to a place where the trees stood so close together that the boughs touched, the two halted and slipped to the ground. "Don't eat too many," Bremig warned as she reached for the ripest fruit she could find.

For a while she sat holding the apple, her back against the knobby trunk while she waited for her pulse to slow. At last she bit into the fruit and let the juices drip down her chin. She barely tasted what she was eating. "We can't keep running, dodging one way and then another," she said, her voice about to break. "How can we ever get close to the beast if we have to keep hiding from men?"

"What we need," Bremig said, "is Modwetten's bead-of-all-colors. We could use it against Draalego and his friends."

"Don't say that," she chided. But in truth, a similar notion had run through her own mind. What if she had a talisman to control Pelask's kin? Then she could get on with her task unhampered by their mulish plans.

But there was no point arguing the merits of such an idea. She had talismans with her, but none that could harm the fishermen. Even so, at least one might be of help.

She reached for the pouch that was securely fastened at her waist. Her fingers slipped inside, and she felt the beads hidden there. To charm a living man was a grave offense, but to call a departed spirit was permitted in times of urgency. And she carried with her always a special bead—she could feel the blue-gray color with her fingertips. This was the talisman that matched her mentor's eyes.

Watnojat had worn it for protection. With its aid, she had helped a healer restore him to life. And now she must use it for a task that she'd never before attempted. She must invoke the old Vigen's spirit and ask his advice.

Pulling out the glass piece, she studied it with great sadness. One did not trouble a spirit without good cause. Watnojat was with Ormek now, though the process of union with the Bright One took many years. As time passed, she knew, the calling would become increasingly difficult and the spirit ever more angry at any disturbance. But she could not guess how Watnojat would receive her pleas.

She took out the talisman and warmed it between her palms. The body's heat must flow into it first, and then the fluid of life must wet the glass. "Bremig, I'll need a knife," she said quietly when the bead had warmed. She took the walnut handle with reluctance, and held it only for a moment. She nicked the ball of her thumb, letting blood run onto the bead.

"This will sound strange to you," she warned the carver. You'll think I'm talking to myself." Then she addressed

Watnojat by the name she had used years before starting her apprenticeship. "Uncle!" she cried. "Uncle, please talk to me."

At first she heard nothing. Was it possible the spirit would not respond to such familiarities? "Tem Vigen," she cried, though she had never addressed him so respectfully in his lifetime. "Tem Watnojat, I need your advice."

The orchard was quiet but for the trilling of birds and the soft rustle of branches. But even those sounds suddenly faded, and Kyala could hear nothing at all. This was the necessary beginning—the onset of silence before one could hear a spirit's voice.

"Uncle?" Out of nothing came a hiss, and the hiss seemed to be making words.

"Uncle, is it you? Speak louder. Please." A peculiar sour taste grew on her tongue.

"You call me . . . so soon." The voice was a sigh of wind.

Her hand trembled and she almost dropped the talisman. "Is that truly you, Uncle?"

"Waste no words, Balin's daughter," came the throaty reply. "I cannot . . . stay long."

"The beast!" she shouted, roused by his warning. "It rallies Etma's followers and weakens Ormek's ranks. And now I can't fight it for Draalego's interference."

"Go after it . . ." The voice was fading.

"How, Uncle? Tell me!" She squeezed her thumb again to draw fresh blood. "The coast is watched. The beast must be lured. It all takes time."

"No time for bait. Find its . . . lair." Now the words were barely audible, and she thought she must surely lose him.

"How, Uncle? Hurry!"

Another windy sigh. "Cross Asep. Cross."

"The river! But where?" she squeezed the bead frantically.

"Overhang. North. Just past . . . river's mouth. Find it there."

"And what of Modwetten," she pleaded, hoping for a last bit of advice. "What of his bead-of-all-colors?"

"He must fail . . ." The words trailed off, and nothing would bring them back. Suddenly she heard the chatter of birds, harsh songs from the living world startling her with their intensity. The sour taste was gone, along with all other signs of the spirit's presence. She glanced up at the carver's puzzled face, knowing he had heard only her own part of the brief exchange.

"I reached him," she said, rubbing the bloodied glass with a feeling of wonderment, and only vaguely aware of the pain in her thumb. "I did reach him. He spoke to me." And then she tried to convey the little she had learned.

CHAPTER 11

"WE'LL find your creature's lair," Bremig promised when her explanations were done. "But we'd best stay hidden until dark." She watched him toying with a twig, his brow wrinkled, his eyes half closed, and she wondered at his thoughts. Did he believe the voice's advice, or was he merely placating her with his agreement? For now, the answer made no difference.

"Moonrise will be late," she said. "If we're going to ride, we'll want torches."

The carver snapped the twig and flung it aside. "Applewood won't do." He rose, seemingly with reluctance, and peered along the row of trees. "Maybe higher up. Come on. If we stay on this side of the ridge, we can't be seen from the road."

Leading their mounts, they walked warily, following the ridge's shoulder toward the crest of the hill. About halfway up, they came on a low shed, and Bremig raised his hand in warning. There was no sound but the chatter of birds, and no indication that the shelter was in use.

Advancing, Kyala noted that the two walls were simply branches thrust into the ground, angled toward each other to meet in a jagged peak. A sheepskin covered the entrance, and she pushed it aside to look in. At first, she saw nothing in the dim interior, but she sniffed at a pleasant odor of dried leaves. As her eyes became accustomed to the meager light, she noticed that the floor had a thick covering of leaves and fallen blossoms. Leaning in beside her, Bremig found a pruning saw near the entrance and pulled it out.

"Up there looks promising," he said, pointing to a small stand of pines at the edge of the orchard. Leaving the animals at the hut, they quickly reached the grove.

Fallen branches lay across an ancient log. Bremig lifted a thick pine limb and tried breaking off a protruding twig. "Still a bit green," he said. "It may do." With Kyala's help he cut several lengths, then carried them back to tie to his saddlebags.

"Now we'll just have to wait for dusk," he said as he carried the saw back to the shelter. But instead of merely dropping it inside, he bent down and crawled past the door flap. When he did not come out, Kyala pulled back the hide and met with an unexpected sight—the carver stretched out on the bed of leaves. He appeared comfortable, and there was ample room beside him.

The tilted walls left little headroom, but the carver had made his way in. Now he was staring at her, and his expression suggested nervous anticipation. Suddenly she knew his thoughts and could not hold back her smile.

One of them should stand watch, she knew, but then they could not be together. The rich smell of leaves was dizzying as she wriggled into the woody nest. The sound of his quickening breath made her own pulse start to throb.

He studied her in the dim light that filtered through gaps in the wall. Shyly he put his hand to her cheek, ran his thumb along her chin and down the delicate skin of her neck. Unable to contain herself, she threw her arms about him in a squeeze that made him groan. "Ah!" he sighed again and again. "Is it you, Kyala, and not some fancy of my tired eyes?"

He was so timid that she had to lead him, assuring him with whispers that he could unfasten her goatskins. As he stroked her, she thought of his long fingers holding the disk of Ormek on the day he'd come to her shop. Now those fingers ran over her skin as if she too were a delicate carving.

He caressed her cautiously, seemingly fearful of the result. Did he not know the difference between her cries of joy and the sounds of pain? She reassured him, encouraged him, taught him with her answering touches, allowed him to discover for himself the wonders he could work. It was not until dusk that he entered her, and the sweetness was almost unbearable. Upward he bore her, into a realm that she had forgotten or had never known.

She drifted back to a dark space where he pressed against her, his chest damp with sweat. She could still feel the vanished caresses and the warmth that had blossomed within her, but now she must turn her thoughts to the difficulties at hand. "We must go," she whispered, realizing that night had come. By touch, she located her clothing, brushed off adhering bits of debris, and managed to dress herself. She crawled out into the cool air and heard the pony nicker.

Behind her, she heard Bremig wrestling with his boots. At last he emerged, his feet shuffling along the ground as he made his way uncertainly. "I have your mare," she said, catching his hand and guiding it to the bridle. They followed the contour of the hill downward until Kyala glimpsed a flickering lantern.

The thoroughfare was busy with rigs returning from the market. Falling in after a farmer's wagon, the two travelers spared their torches. So long as the driver kept to the main path and paid them no heed, they had only to follow his light.

As the ride continued, Kyala's thoughts were a jumble of hopes and plans. She did not wish to peer too far into the future. While the sea beast plagued the coast, she told herself, nothing else must matter. But if she destroyed the pillager, would she return to Darst? Lacking both shop and kiln, her career as a glassmaker must begin from a heap of charred timbers.

And what of Bremig? He had seemingly dedicated himself to her cause, giving no argument when she disclosed their destination. How could he have such faith in Watnojat's words when she, who had heard them, still doubted? She shook her head, thinking that his assent had more to do with his feelings than with logic.

She struggled to clear her thoughts. It was best to focus on an immediate goal, she decided. The beast's lair lay on the far side of Asep River. How might she reach the site quickly? Bremig had told her that this road led north as far as the river.

She recalled Jannford, the closest crossing, and the memories of her last visit there made her shiver. The houses had been shuttered, the streets empty, as the residents took shelter from marauding Lame Ones. But now that the two-footed beasts were gone, Jannford should be a lively settlement again.

Brooding on the journey ahead, she barely noticed the villages they passed. When the farmer, their guide, finally turned, Bremig rode up and asked to light a torch from his lantern. The wood blazed nicely, and with the aid of the man's directions the two continued alone.

The night was clear, the stars crisp overhead. Kyala gazed upward, watching the eternal Vigen pursuing the Beast across the sky. The Star-Vigen would never rest, his prey always a few steps ahead of him. She wondered if the same were true of his earthly counterparts.

The moon rose as they traveled, and Kyala kept time by its progress across the sky. At last, Bremig called a halt at a stream. The animals were watered, then allowed to graze briefly. Soon Kyala saw signs of people stirring at the farms along the road—lanterns bobbing across dark yards. She envied the early wakers for the beds they had climbed out of.

It was midmorning when the travelers reached Asep's bank. The animals bent to drink, while Kyala rested against the trunk of an overhanging tree. She closed her eyes, and when she opened them saw a thick-lipped man in a straw hat watching her.

She turned to see Bremig asleep on his back, his bare toes and ankles dangling in the water. Then she glanced again at the stranger, who now waved the hat to cool his fleshy face. She realized that half the afternoon had passed while she dozed. "Empty country between here and any settlements," the man said. "Might not make it by dark."

Kyala was too groggy to think what he was hinting at. She noticed behind him a wagon festooned with blue and yellow ribbons. *Trader*, she thought. His kind roamed up and down the river's course, carrying goods from one village to the next.

"You look to be traveling light," the stranger commented. "Sure there's no way I can heip?"

She'd planned to stop at Jannford for supplies, but had expected to be there by nightfall. Now she must see what this wayfarer had to offer. "Our food's a bit low," she admitted, which was no lie, since they had none at all. "And a blanket might help," she added, remembering the evening's chill.

The trader grinned and led her to his wagon. She was glad that Bremig remained asleep, for she had seen how guileless he was in bargaining. The thick-lipped man displayed several packets of cheese, and she found fault with them all despite the rumblings of her stomach. At last she settled the provisions and moved on to negotiating for the blanket, finding she could get two carelessly woven coverlets for the cost of a single finer piece. Even so, barely enough remained in her purse to pay the man.

Bremig woke just as the trader's wagon rattled away. His eyes widened when she showed him the cold sausage and pale yellow cheese. A few paces behind them, a sparkling brook tumbled into the river. They sat at its bank eating hungrily, dipping water with cupped hands from the stream.

Despite the trader's warnings, they reached Jannford well before dusk. The man had deceived her about the distance, but she did not believe she'd gotten the worst of the bargaining. And now, in front of her stood a familiar cluster of houses, each on a raised stone foundation for protection against spring flooding. The road led toward the river, where the watercourse ran broad and shallow, poles marking the way across.

She was acquainted with the head man here—Lebbon. Though he did not dignify himself with the title of Magistrate, he took responsibility for the settlement's affairs. "This way," she told the carver, leading him to Lebbon's two-chimneyed house. Climbing the steps, they found his door open. She remembered the shop in front with its odors of furs and spices, its shelves piled with a jumble of goods.

The wiry proprietor emerged from the back room, and his jaw fell as he saw her. "So it's *you*," he said, pushing his beaverskin cap back on his head. "Didn't think you'd be passin' here so soon." Lebbon did not smile, but hurriedly shut and secured the door behind his two visitors. Then he stood looking at Kyala while he rubbed his short gray beard with the back of his hand. "I wish I could give you the greetin' you deserve. But . . ."

"I can guess," she said angrily. "The fishermen have been here. What story did they tell?"

He shook his head slowly. "Somethin' about a runaway wife. I didn't believe a word of it."

"And everyone in the village has heard of the reward by now."

"But who'd betray you? Not one of *my* folks."

"Then why bar the door?"

Lebbon frowned. "Too many strangers passin' this way. It's good for my business, but doesn't help my sleep any."

"You know about the sea beast?"

"Heard talk. You tell me what's true."

Kyala smiled grimly. "I've . . . heard its lair is half a morning's ride from here. But it's not likely to come upriver after you."

At that, the proprietor took two steps back toward the safety of his inner chamber. "You came for something," he said nervously. "Tell me what you need, but don't stay long. Go somewhere those pig-brained fishermen can't find you." He turned to stare at Bremig, who had remained quietly behind Kyala.

"This is my friend, a wood-carver by trade," she explained quickly. "We'll need weapons and a few other things. The creature won't be easy to kill."

"I may have somethin' for you," Lebbon said, suddenly regaining his trader's confidence. He moved a stepladder and climbed to one of his highest shelves. "Should never have taken this." He brought down a tarnished harpoon that showed wicked-looking barbs. "Thought I'd bring it to Darst and get rid of it there, but haven't had time."

"It needs a cord," said Bremig.

"A chain would be better," Kyala said. "The thickest that will slip through the hole."

Lebbon eyed her with puzzlement, then grumbled and bent to sort through a pile of rusting links. He found a chain that would fit, about ten paces long. "And a clamp," she added. The shopkeeper raised a clatter as he dumped out the contents of a keg, but he found what she needed.

"I've somethin' else for you," Lebbon suggested, returning to his ladder. "Don't know much about the beast you're after, but this might help." He pulled down a roll of heavy fishnet and dropped it across his counter.

Kyala glanced at the carver, who merely shrugged. "I'll take it," she decided. "And a poleax, a lantern, a haunch of smoked meat . . ."

"Slow down," said Lebbon. "I wasn't expectin' a list like that. We'd better talk terms first."

At once she reached for her bead pouch and extracted a wild dog's eye, which she could spare. She held it out in her palm, knowing that any trapper or hunter he dealt with would be eager for its protection.

"I don't know. . ."

"It's worth five times what you'll be giving me. You can throw in provisions, but that won't balance the score."

"Provisions?" The trader began to laugh, but was interrupted by a pounding on his door. "Come back in a while," he shouted irritably. "Can't you see I'm closed up?"

"Well?" Kyala set the bead on the narrow table, where it caught a band of sunlight from the high windows. The rich browns glistened and the proprietor's gaze remained on the glass. She lifted a length of Lebbon's chain with two hands and gave it a tentative yank. She was satisfied with its solid feel.

"I can take my business elsewhere," she suggested, though she and Lebbon both knew the weakness of her threat.

"A poleax . . ." the wiry man said with a sigh, picking up the talisman and putting it into his cash box. "I may have one here somewhere . . ."

At last, their burdens swinging from the saddles, the travelers approached the ford. A yawning toll-taker extracted a small coin for the privilege of crossing. Kyala was first into the moderate current, finding that the water barely reached the pony's knees.

Twilight had come by the time they gained the far bank, and Kyala suggested a halt for the night. Now they were safe, she said, at least from Pelask's kin. This north side of the river was the province of hunters and miners, and held no permanent settlements. The fishermen would not seek her here.

They built a small fire, and Bremig unpacked his lantern. "Let's save the oil for tomorrow," she said. But she took out her talismans against wild dogs, placing them near the fire to lessen the chance of attack.

That night the forest sounds seemed more menacing than any on the southern bank. Huddled in the blankets, Bremig fell instantly asleep. But Kyala had first to convince herself that she was hearing only harmless owls, crickets, bats. She built up the fire, laid out the rest of her animal talismans, then crawled back into the meager warmth of the covers. She was safe now from bears, cats, and wild pigs, but couldn't help wondering whether the Sea-snake and the Crab might roam this far inland. When the question kept troubling her, she also put out the icy talisman and the one of glinting gray.

Several times she woke and fed the fire. At last, impatient to get moving, she pushed Bremig out onto the cold ground. He woke and looked at her sheepishly. "Get up," she said, giving a gentle shake to his shoulders.

"I hadn't meant to fall asleep so quickly," he said.

"No time to think about that," she answered with a quick smile and a playful tug at his beard. Dawn had almost arrived.

By the time they finished a hurried meal, there was sufficient light to find the path. The trail followed the watercourse, and the river made a comforting sight compared with the dark tangle of forest on their other flank. The flood broadened as the travelers neared its mouth, soon dividing into smaller streams. Then the forest thinned and the land rose toward cliffs that overlooked the sea.

An excavation site caught Kyala's eye. A huge pile of tailings lay beside a ragged pit. Riding closer, she found the remains of a mining operation—a deep shaft partly filled with greenish water. "We might be able to use this," she said when Bremig caught up with her. "Drive the Crab into it. With those steep sides, it couldn't climb out."

"First we have to find your Crab," he countered.

She lingered for a moment, studying the scraggly bushes

and trees that sprouted from the sandy soil. Glancing up, she saw the bluffs ahead giving way to low hillocks that edged the coast.

She halted briefly at a notch that commanded a view of a broad sweep of beach. On the left spread the Asep's many-fingered delta; on the right lay a peaceful bay. And in front, a dark crag sat half submerged, its peak stained white by gulls. Between this tiny island and the base of the cliff, numerous smaller rocks jutted up from the water.

Below on her left, Kyala noticed that the cliff's face had been hollowed by waves, but she could not see how deep a cave had been cut. Was this the place Watnojat's spirit had spoken of? She hadn't quite convinced herself that she'd understood the old Vigen's words, yet here sat an overhang just north of Asep's mouth. "The lantern!" she whispered. And while Bremig dismounted to ready the light, she tied, with trembling fingers, the strand holding three new talismans firmly to her wrist.

They left the animals, taking with them only the lantern. Kyala picked a pathway down the gritty slope, trying to make no sound. Her foot slipped, and a cascade of pebbles clattered to the rocks below.

At once she halted, clutching at a snag. She listened, dreading a response, but all she heard was the slapping of waves and the louder thrumming of her blood. Glancing at the jagged island, she studied its whitened peak. Though the crag bore ample signs of their roosting, the gulls were now gone.

Once more she began to descend, each step confirming Watnojat's words. Water reached beneath the hollow as far as she could see. What better den for the creature? But the tide was dropping, and soon the cave would be dry.

Between cliff and island stood a rough bed of rocks. Through the waves she could discern the bottom, dark as the crag but shot through with long, pale streaks. The ribbons seemed to undulate as the brine flowed over them, and suddenly Kyala clapped her hand to her mouth.

Was she mistaken? She dared go no closer. Again she saw a surprising movement. Now the streaks were curling! One tip of a pink tentacle lifted out of the water. She turned so quickly that she nearly collided with Bremig on the path.

"It's down there," she hissed. "See for yourself." The wind shifted, bringing a suffocating odor of decay. A loud clacking echoed from beneath the cliff, and then the Seasnake's head appeared with its crown of Squid arms. Before she could react, the Crab's armored body scuttled forth, its two passengers riding the compartment as it crossed the rocky terrace, then veered into open water. The bright floatsacs were vanishing . . .

Gone! She had not even tested her talismans. "Tide's falling," Bremig whispered, pointing to the waves. "When the water's high again, it should be back."

"Then we'll wait. We can do nothing else." She climbed the slope, then sank, still trembling, to sit at the edge of the rise.

CHAPTER 12

BY the time noon arrived, the black rocks at the cave's mouth lay fully exposed. Kyala stared dully past them, knowing the beast would not return until the tide rose again. Bremig sat beside her, whittling at a twig, letting shavings drift to the beach below. She noticed that he did not use the walnut-handled knife for this work, as if saving Arod's gift for some more vital task.

Later he handed her bits of food from Lebbon's larder. She chewed without tasting, barely noticing what it was that she ate. "See! The waves are coming in," he noted, pointing to the wet forecourt that had earlier baked in the heat. She tried to rouse herself to full attention, but the constant watching had made her drowsy. Again and again her eyelids fell shut . . .

"Out there!" His hand on her shoulder startled her awake and she jumped up, still groggy, to squint into the glare. Following his finger, she spotted a rusty hump rising and falling with the waves.

Almost here. Her stomach fluttered as she turned to check that all was in readiness. The mare and pony would be safe —tethered back near the river trail. And Bremig had prepared the harpoon, looping a chain through its eye, concealing its barbs in the haunch of meat. Now she watched him sling the poleax over one shoulder, the harpoon over the other.

"Can you carry all that?" She stared at him with such astonishment that he broke into a smile.

"For a short way," he answered. "I'll start down, and you can meet me at the bottom." The chain dragged behind him in the dust.

"I'll be quick!" At once she turned to striking a blaze in the tinder she had readied. She lit a taper, but it would not hold steady for her as she poked it toward the oil-soaked wick. *The Lifegiver's heat and light*, she thought, when at last the lantern quickened.

Below, she saw Bremig making his slow descent, balancing the weapons with evident discomfort. Once more, she asked herself why he'd joined this undertaking, which to him must seem without hope. Did he believe that a handful of glass could defeat such a creature? He had never, so far as she knew, seen a talisman at work. Perhaps, she admitted to herself, his true purpose was only to drag her to safety should their efforts fail.

Bremig reached bottom while Kyala was but halfway down. Glancing out to sea again, she saw that the beast had changed course. It was skirting the small crag, making directly for the carver. Did he notice what was happening? He dropped the baited prong, swung the ax from his shoulder, and rested its head on the sand.

Panting, risking a tumble, Kyala raced down the path to join him. "It's coming this way," she shouted. Squinting into the light, she saw first only the Crab's back. Yet the beast had surely sensed Bremig's presence, for why else would it change course so abruptly? Still distant from shore, one of the Squid's great tentacles reared up. She could not command the beast at such a distance, but its limbs would soon reach land.

Hurriedly, she glanced at the talismans. As before, the Crab served as vessel, the other two riding within its shell.

She planned first to halt the crustacean, then to disable its passengers. But the beads were not yet tested.

She held the silvery Crab-eye near the lamp, her lips numb as the creature came closer to shore. Bremig stood warily with his ax raised, and she wished he would move farther back. She must halt the creature *now.* Could she even speak the necessary commands?

Her tongue seemed dead in her mouth, her throat clogged. Another tentacle flipped up, its bristly pad of suckers clearly visible. The Crab advanced steadily, bringing its companions ever nearer to shore. "Hold!" she cried, and the word came out so feebly that she shouted again into the waves. "Hold. Stay where you are!" Was the charm working? She screamed her demand once more. The eyestalks rose, dripping seawater, and began to twitch. The rusty pincer emerged from the surf, but came no closer. The legs halted, as if the beast had been shackled!

Kyala stared with amazement at the creature that stood in the shallows. It had ceased advancing! But this was too soon to claim victory, she knew. The tentacle continued to wave menacingly; the Squid was watching her with its frightening orb. Before it could strike, she brought the demon-eye close to the heat, ordering the beast to retract its long appendage. The tentacle quivered. She commanded again, and watched with satisfaction as the pale limb slowly withdrew. *A second bead tested!*

Then the Snake shot forward from its compartment, forcing Kyala and Bremig to scramble from its path. "Halt!" she insisted, but the reptile paid no heed. Had she made some error, she wondered? Hastily she checked the icy color of the glass.

Kyala's face burned when she saw the talisman. The match was true, but the bead was dangling from her wrist. It was powerless there! Hastily she caught the blue-white glass and brought it to the lantern's heat. Meanwhile, the Snake wriggled partway onto the beach, the Squid riding placidly on top. "Go back," she warned. "Back in the Crab's shell, and stay there."

She watched the beast struggle against her power, spasms pulsing from head to tail as it pressed forward again. This Snake must have the strongest will of the three, she thought, for it was resisting all her ordinary efforts. Now she must try a more fearsome example of Ormek's power.

"Stand clear," she warned Bremig as she retreated again in case the beast should thrash. Then she allowed the talisman to touch directly the heat of the lamp.

At once a fit shook the reptile. Its head beat the sand; the lipless mouth opened, spewing small bones and bits of flesh. And the Squid was tossed brutally, its arms and tentacles limp in the water. "Back!" she told the Snake again. When it ignored her, she let it feel the bead's full wrath once more. The surf frothed with its throes until she withdrew the talisman. When she gave her command a third time, the reptile returned at once to its resting place.

She had proved her beads! Now she knew that sea creatures were vulnerable to colored glass. But her task was far from over, for she must charm the Crab up the slope and force it into the abandoned digging.

Wielding the gray bead again, she stepped aside for the beast and waved Bremig even farther back. He took the weapons with him, and she hoped he would not need them. The Crab had become docile, scuttling to her order up onto the beach and then in a straight line for the base of the rise. The dangerous tail twitched several times, the only sign of belligerence.

Finally, she was driving it up toward the gap. "Climb!" she cried, and legs scrabbled sideways onto the crumbling slope. Tentacles trailed in the sand, leaving broad furrows as the Crab carried its companions higher.

Kyala picked out a moderate grade, but the Crab still had difficulty with its footing. Gravel and stone were loosened by its repeated scratchings; debris cascaded toward the beach. "Pull if you can," she shouted, switching her attention to the awesome Squid's eye. "Use those tentacles!"

With further prodding, she induced the Squid to aid the difficult ascent. Its short arms fastened on the shell, while its two long limbs swung toward the top of the slope. The forward tentacles probed for support, poking into crevices, grasping at roots. The Squid convulsed, and the entire body lurched higher.

"Again!" Kyala shouted, the roar of debris from the cliff face nearly overpowering her voice. The Squid strained once more, and the Crab was almost at the top. Then it was over the edge and out of sight.

Shouldering his loads, Bremig followed the scoured route. She rushed past him, climbing nimbly up the loose surface. "Wait!" he cried when she reached the peak, but she could not stop for him. Now it was only a short distance inland to the trap she had planned. She drove the creature toward it, following as it scrambled over occasional bushes and thorns.

But then, halfway to the old digging, the beast rebelled. It turned to face her, clacking its claw, fluttering its mouth parts. She must punish it, break the beast's will. Touching the gray bead to the searing metal, she sent the Crab into a terrible dance of pain, thrashing, striking the ground with its pincer. In the course of this struggle, the reptile emerged, colored bands shimmering, white fangs aglow.

The Snake slid free of the compartment, and she saw the long body of the Squid stretched out along its back. "I'll try the bait," shouted Bremig, and she turned briefly as he struggled over the rise. To the side of the Snake, a sharp nose of rock poked up from the sandy ground. He draped the long loop of chain around it, and when she spared him another glance he was fastening the ends with the clamp. Moments later, he tossed the meat toward the fanged maw.

Kyala let up on the Crab for a moment, hoping she had tamed it again. But despite her cruel attack, it still refused her demands. Instead of making for the pit, as she ordered, it swung its pincer at her head.

Retreating out of range, she saw Bremig heft the poleax, his attention on the stirring Squid. The reptile it rode was prodding the carver's bait with the end of its snout, and she wondered if it would be fooled by this trick. The slender tongue flicked out, retreated, touched the slab of meat. The jaws widened.

The Snake struck so quickly that she did not see its motion. The bait was exposed one moment, gone the next. The Snake kept swallowing, taking in half the harpoon's shaft. The head shook angrily as the creature realized its predicament.

But what of the Crab? Her control seemed almost gone. In desperation she tried once more touching the charm directly to the heat. This time the creature was not thrown into spasms, but continued its advance, legs moving with evident strain, tail raking the ground. The crustacean's will was beyond anything she had foreseen.

Now she was truly in need of Ormek's special favor. If she could channel His power, as she had done with the she-bear, then surely this creature would be vanquished. But today, she could not find Him within her. She tried to focus on His image, but felt nothing—no growing warmth, no connection with His glory. The gift she had proclaimed to Modwetten was gone!

Had the Lifegiver abandoned her, retracted his favor? She tried to bring herself to the state she had known before, but the images would not come. All she could do now was shout a warning to Bremig. "Save yourself. I can't hold this creature much longer."

"We're not beaten yet," he answered. "We've got the Snake." A harsh clanking of the chain confirmed his words. "And the Squid may dry up out of water."

"Right now, the Crab is the worst of the three," she said. "You run. I'll delay it as long as I can."

"We can both get down to the river. Look!" She dared not turn from the advancing pincer. "There's a path between two boulders," he said. "The Crab can't fit through, and by the time it gets past them we'll be gone."

Kyala was so filled with despair that she pretended not to hear him. Then a tentacle slithered toward her along the gritty ground. "What are you doing?" she shouted when the carver raced forward wielding the poleax. He swung viciously, but the beast pulled the limb aside. Moving closer with senseless bravado, he hacked at one of the shorter arms and succeeded in lopping off half the appendage. The Squid's body shuddered as yellowish fluid began to ooze from the wound.

"No more of that," pleaded Kyala. "Get to safety." But again Bremig swung. There were too many arms; he could not hew them all. "Pull back!" she ordered the Squid, testing to see if she still might sway this beast. Bremig stood in the thick of its tangle, and she dared not send the creature into spasms. Holding the bead as close to the heat as she dared, she spoke her demand again. "Pull away!"

Bremig groaned, and she realized that one vicious backlash had caught him. Despite the evident damage to his shoulder and upper arm, he swung the ax again. But then his left arm fell useless at his side. Kyala shouted futilely at the beast while Bremig dodged the next pair of limbs, finally staggering away in retreat. How could he do otherwise with his arm slashed and bleeding so that he could not lift the weapon? He dropped the ax and reached for her with his good arm as he made his escape.

"Enough," she cried. "Let Etma have me." But he was already propelling her between the rocks, his grip so fierce on her shoulder that she could not slow her steps. Behind her she heard the cracking of brush, and then a grating sound that made her gooseflesh rise. The Crab was beating against the obstacle, and until it swerved past the boulders she and the carver would be safe.

Panting heavily, they came down to the edge of the delta where the animals were tethered. Only then did she dare look closely at his wound—at the torn sleeve that was soaked with blood, the flesh scoured in streaks. Kyala was sobbing, and trying to catch her breath at the same time. Looking at his injury, she suddenly stiffened, knowing what she must do. With a great act of will, she drew his walnut-handled knife and cut away the ruins of his jerkin. Hurriedly, she sliced the cloth into strips and bound the wound. They mounted the animals and headed for the ford, Bremig slumping in the saddle, but managing not to fall.

Night had fallen when they reached Lebbon's house. The trader was less than eager to see them, but did not turn them away. "I don't understand these Vigen things," he muttered when he saw Bremig's arm. "What good's a talisman if it doesn't work every time? What if I trade that wild dog's eye of yours and the thing fails?"

"Your hunter won't meet a dog with the will of these sea beasts," Kyala said darkly. "There's never been a pack that could stand up to a such a talisman."

"Never? I'll be glad to let someone else test your claims." Then he began muttering to himself as he studied Bremig's wound by lamplight. "Got to clean and dress this right away," he said.

He left the room, returning with a bowl of milky fluid and several clean cloths. When he tried to wash the scraped flesh, Bremig howled with pain, then toppled from the stool.

The shopkeeper caught him, and with Kyala's help dragged him onto a pallet by the fire. "It'll be easier now," Lebbon said as he bent over the slumped carver. She turned away, not caring to see the harsh pink hue that the liquid in the bowl was taking on. "Should have a healer for this," he added, "but I'm the closest they've got around here. Plenty of trappers bring me their business." He gave a cold laugh. "Interestin' work if you don't mind a bit of blood."

Kyala found herself thinking of the talisman still hidden

in her pouch. What if Lebbon needed help to restore the carver? She had cast Bremig's bead with this thought in mind—that he might be wounded and need such aid. For to force a weak man to swallow medicines or drink was acceptable to Ormek, so long as the man's will to live remained strong. But what did she know of the Bright One now? Perhaps she could no longer wield any sort of charm.

Turning back to Lebbon, she watched him smear buttery salve on a long cloth strip, then wrap the arm and shoulder. "He's young and strong," said the trader. "You look worse off than he does. But I don't know what I can do for you."

"Nothing!" Filled with the misery of her defeat, she could face him no longer. She rushed to the front door, threw back the bars, climbed onto Modwetten's pony. A few torches blazed in the streets, and by their light she found her way to the river road. There she came on an abandoned cottage, choked with vines and weeds. Feeling her way, she entered between the roofless walls with the animal in tow. She took out the blankets and unsaddled the pony. Wrapped in the covers, she lay down in the rubble with her eyes full of tears . . .

"Kyala." The voice was barely a rustling of wind. "Kyala, you must listen."

She was dreaming, and in the dream a sour taste flooded her tongue.

"Balin's daughter . . . you must hear me." The voice was as quiet as a fox treading moss. But where was Watnojat's talisman in her dream? One must hold a bead to converse with spirits. All she had before her was a night sky full of stars.

"Your glass . . . was not at fault," the voice went on, incredibly faint, yet audible in the dead silence that surrounded it. "Your charms were well made."

"Uncle?" she cried. But his talisman lay in her pouch.

She was not even holding it, much less charging it with power.

"You must gain back Ormek," the spirit voice continued.

"I tried, Uncle. He would not come."

"Because . . . you have pushed him from your thoughts for another."

"But Uncle . . ."

"It is true. I see that Lanorik's son means more to you than the Bright One."

Kyala blinked, still not able to explain the voice. She wanted to reach into the pouch, to hold the Vigen's talisman in her palm, but her hands remained rigid. Whether she was asleep or awake she could not say; she could only look at the sky and answer. "Isn't it true, Uncle, that even Kolpern had a beloved?" she asked in despair, recalling a legendary Vigen.

"You are not the same as Kolpern."

"But why, Uncle?"

"The Lifegiver has chosen you for His reasons. I'm not privy to His thoughts."

"Then I must abandon Bremig?"

"Do what is needed, but bring the Bright One back into your soul."

Kyala was trembling, and not because of the night's chill. "Is there no other advice you can give?" She strained but heard nothing.

"Uncle?" Had he gone already? She still was surrounded by his silence.

"One word more, before I weaken," said the Vigen. "Go to the flamens. Talk to that faithless Skendron."

"Skendron? I've had enough of him already. All he cares for is his reputation."

"Tell the old fool . . ." The sound was fading, and she strained to catch the breathy whisper. "To give you the Gathering Stone. Learn to use it . . . may help you find Ormek again."

"But Uncle. I don't even know what the Gath . . ." She halted as the raucous sound of crickets flooded her hearing. The spirit taste was gone as quickly as it had come. She was fully awake, free to move, and she plunged her fingers into her pouch. Watnojat's bead was still there; she could feel its blue-gray hues. But he had spoken to her when the talisman merely lay close to her skin. How was that possible?

CHAPTER 13

CHILLY and shamefaced, Kyala rapped on Lebbon's door as first light broke. Eventually she heard footsteps and muttering within, followed by the scraping of the double bars. The trader gave her a dour stare. She said nothing as she hurried across his threshold.

"Your friend had a quiet night," Lebbon told her grumpily. "Slept lots better than I did."

She seated herself by the small fire. "I have . . . to talk to him."

"When he's up and strong enough. Right now he's still sleepin'."

"Then. Then maybe I'll just leave him a message."

"Run off without seein' him?" The wrinkles deepened on the trader's brow. "I don't understand you two. And with the troubles I've been hearin' about, you don't want to go ridin' alone."

"How can there be worse news than what I already know?"

"Fella came through yesterday talkin' about the Mej's men." When Kyala stared at him blankly, he continued. "They rode into Darst two days ago," he said. "Haven't been soldiers that far north in anyone's memory." He clucked and tugged at his beard. "Don't know what it means. The Mej must have thought we were bein' invaded."

"He should try killing the thing," she said without hope. "He has soldiers to spare."

"Ha. Won't waste 'em on *that*." Lebbon was thoughtful for a few moments. "Long as no foreigners are likely to march into his capital, he'll be content enough."

"So the men will ride home again, and leave us to be ravaged."

Lebbon clucked again. "Even the priests have lost their senses. What senses they had." He turned to the fire, where a small pot was steaming, and began to scoop porridge into a wooden bowl. "Join me?"

Kyala was about to turn him down, but her stomach's grumbling was insistent. She accepted the offered bowl, at first happy just for the warmth on her hands. "What's this about priests?" The trader evidently had heard quite a bit of talk.

"News from the Reach. They're sayin' that maybe Etma's in this after all. That maybe the demon sent your Scourge. Now how can they turn around like that, after all these years of sayin' Etma's chained in the deep?"

"Who told you the flamens' words?" She leaned forward, scowling with disbelief.

Lebbon shrugged. "Lots of people pass through here."

Ormek's priests acknowledge Etma's power? They'd be betraying their faith, she thought. But the trader's expression seemed so glum that she could not dismiss his tale.

"I'll find out for myself," she declared. "I have other business with those slippery priests."

"Goin' to the Reach, then?" He raised his shaggy eyebrows.

"Yes. Will you tell the carver?"

"You'd best tell him yourself. I'm a trader, not a go-between." Lebbon took a spoon and began to shove porridge into his mouth. Seeing no softening of his attitude, she tried to eat, managing to swallow half what he'd given her. Just as she put down the bowl she heard quiet footsteps, floor-boards creaking.

"Kyala . . ." The voice was weak. She turned to see Bremig enter the room, his feet clad in fur slippers. His face appeared pallid, and he walked with his injured shoulder drooping. But he was upright!

She ran to him, pressing his other hand in her own. "I've got to see Skendron again," she whispered. "Stay here while I'm gone. Lebbon still owes me a favor."

"Cross the forest alone?" he asked with disbelief.

"I have talismans. A few. I'll be safe." Her voice wavered, and Bremig eyed her with concern.

"Wait a day, and I'll ride with you. Even if I have only one good arm, you'll be better off than without me."

"But . . ." Watnojat had warned her. The carver was far too often in her thoughts. She must turn away from him, invite the Lifegiver to return. Surely she and Bremig must part, and what better time than now?

She pushed that onerous thought aside as another voice pleaded for delay. Lowering her gaze, she studied her grimy boots. "Yes," she said softly. "Yes, I can wait a day." The difficult moment had not yet come.

They slipped out of Jannford the next morning, Bremig still sore but able to ride. In place of his shredded jerkin he wore a woven hunter's shirt, Lebbon's gift. And for protection the travelers carried a pole lantern, its light dangling above the pony's head as they entered the woods. In Kyala's pocket lay her talismans against forest beasts. Should trouble come, she had only these charms . . . and the few weapons packed on the carver's horse.

But the ride proved uneventful. Emerging from the trees at the modest inn she knew, Kyala thought of her game of quoits and smiled. As she passed the stable, she noted that the innkeeper's boy was still practicing.

At the junction with the coastal road stood a wayside

shrine, four fieldstone columns supporting an oak log roof. Kyala halted at the humble offering place. Within, she found the stone bowl coated with soot but otherwise empty. Returning to the saddlebags, she brought out the flask of lamp oil and a piece of wick. Bremig was staring at her.

"An offering of thanks for our fair journey," she explained. That was half the truth. She poured oil into the bowl, then went back to light a taper at the hanging lantern. Once more beneath the low roof, she spoke to Ormek softly. "Guide me," she asked. "Help me recover what I've lost." She watched the wick burn until the mare's nicker roused her.

Returning to the road, she soon glimpsed the Reach towering into the afternoon sky. The ascending path seemed surprisingly brief, and Kyala grew more anxious at every turning. Skendron had been civil to her once. On this second visit she did not know what to expect.

Rounding the final bend, she came on a puzzling scene. Workmen were milling about the site where the road gate had stood. One man was digging, while several others shouted orders. On the ground lay the old grating, warped and broken, its sacred disks removed. A smaller, less ornate replacement lay to the side.

The riders dismounted, leaving the animals by a stone watering trough. As there was no longer an obstacle, Kyala brushed past the laborers and approached the hollow-cheeked gatekeeper.

"You? Come back?" he exclaimed. "We thought you'd been eaten with the rest of them." No smile of welcome showed beneath his gruffness.

"I need to see Skendron again," she said without preamble. "This will be quick."

The brown-robe shook his head slowly. "He's retreated to his room. Nobody's seeing him."

"He'll want to hear how I got away from the creature. I know more about it now than any priest or fisherman."

"You don't know what's happened here." The brown-robe nodded toward the workers, who had abandoned their labors and were resting in the shade. "I'd keep this to myself, but what's the point? Everyone in the villages knows."

Kyala glanced at the damage to the old gate. "Draalego?" she asked with alarm. "Did his crew of toughs come up here?"

"They didn't leave their names." The gatekeeper's voice began to rasp. "They carried their Etma filth—their fiendish poles—right into Ormek's temple."

She shook her head in anguish, then turned to see that the carver was out of earshot. Better he did not know how his works had been abused.

"The fishermen threatened us all," said the gatekeeper, now almost in tears. "When they smashed the Beacon, Skendron made a concession."

"The Beacon!" Forgetting Bremig, Kyala tore past the man and refused to hear him calling her back. She arrived at the forecourt winded, and almost forgot to remove her footwear. Within, she saw that the mosses had been trampled and torn up. A group of servitors knelt in one corner, salvaging what they could, discarding what they could not. Ormek's stone circle also bore signs of damage, and a stonecutter was making delicate repairs to the jeweled rays. At the back of the court she saw the yellow-robed Flamen-of-the-disk, who had taken her to Skendron on her previous visit, brooding over the operations with frequent twitches of his chin.

When he saw her coming, his mouth opened in astonishment. He pointed a shaky finger. "*You*. You're the cause of this." Backing up, he clutched the edge of the doorway for support, his robes fluttering across the opening.

Kyala strode forward. "Is that what Skendron says? Let him tell me that to my face."

"The demon-lovers want you. That's all I care about. If they'll leave us in peace, they can have you."

"And keep spreading the lies of their cult?" Kyala had no time to argue with this man. Ignoring his protest, she crossed the threshold and entered the First Flamen's corridor.

Behind her, she heard the priest shouting for assistance. At the far end of the hall, the door to the outside terrace stood open and she noticed fragments of rock crystal littering the polished floor. *The Beacon smashed!* Despite her urgency, she paused to look out at the destruction. The framework of lead that supported the great lamp's windows had been battered from every side. And within, the bowl was dark. The Lifegiver's Flame burned no longer.

Behind her, the clamor of shouting rose. She rapped with a frenzy at Skendron's closed door, and when he did not answer she leaned her weight against it. The panel swung open slowly. The First Flamen lay in his high bed, his bare head on a pillow, his robe covered by a golden cloth. The sharp smell of unguents was strong.

"So. You come back, Balin's daughter." His voice was controlled, his speech measured. He appeared to be staring at the ceiling, but somehow had taken a glance at her.

"I have news of this sea beast."

Skendron's wheezing sigh seemed to fill the whole chamber. "I will hear your news. And also the whereabouts of my Vigen . . ."

The priest was interrupted as two attendants rushed through the open doorway. "Forgive us, Tem Flamen," said the first. "She walked past the open gate." The other man held out an arm in Kyala's direction, but waited for permission to take her.

"I'll ring when I want you," said Skendron, waving them out with a weary flick of his hand. Exchanging raised eyebrows, the pair left the room, shutting the door softly behind them. "Your news?" asked the First Flamen without turning.

"The creature's mortal. A thing of flesh. I've seen the color of its blood."

"And the color of its eyes too, no doubt." Skendron cleared his throat. "Don't you see, you've just made the beast more angry. You and the glassmaker have to keep away from it now."

"Keep away so Draalego's brutes can frighten Ormek's followers?"

She heard the priest breathing softly, but he offered no rebuttal.

"Is it true?" she demanded. "Is it true you said this creature was sent by Etma?"

A long silence. She watched the coverlet wrinkling as he shifted his legs beneath. "*Might* have been sent," he answered at last. "The men were wild. They would have destroyed the whole shrine if I hadn't offered that much."

"And now what will a First Flamen's word be worth? Soon someone will sight the shortened arms. Can a demon's spawn be sliced up by an ordinary poleax?"

Again the covers stirred, and this time Skendron turned his face to her. "A priest can be wrong about such things. I can retract my comments."

"But not the harm already done. Half the landsmen on the coast will be taking down Ormek disks and looking for fiendish poles to replace them."

"Why did you come here?" he said, his voice quavering. "Will you berate a dying man?"

She lowered her head. "I came for another purpose," she said in less strident tones. "To ask a favor."

"What does it matter? If I grant it or not, all is the same."

"I need . . ." She hesitated, only dimly aware of the significance of what she must ask. "I need the Gathering Stone. For a short while."

"Gath—" Skendron began to cough. She saw a pitcher and cup and hurriedly brought him a drink of amber liquid.

"Let me have the Stone," she said. "And teach me how to use it. Is that so difficult?"

Skendron stared at her wordlessly, a tiny froth at his lips. "How. . ." he managed. "How did you ever hear that name?"

"Gathering Stone? I spoke to the spirit of my mentor. Watnojat, the old Vigen of Darst."

The priest shook his head. *"Spirit?"* he rasped, reaching again for the cup. "Your Vigens put too much trust in their necromancy. As for Watnojat, he could never have known of this thing."

"Perhaps the Bright One . . ."

Skendron's eyes widened, and he began to cough again. It was some time before he could speak, and Kyala wondered if she should call for assistance. But she feared any interruption would end the conversation and with it her chance to follow her mentor's plan. "At least let me know what this object is," she said. "Then I can decide the merits of Watnojat's words."

"You'll not see it," he whispered.

"But you've no use for it now," she shouted without thinking. "With the Beacon smashed . . ." She clapped a hand to her lips. What was she saying? But Skendron's face had turned scarlet, and she feared he might truly be in danger. Rushing from the room, she called for his attendants. In a moment they were running past her, leaving her alone in the windy corridor.

What had she said? She could not explain how she knew the connection between the Gatherer and Ormek's Beacon, yet the impact on Skendron had been startling. Somehow Watnojat had told her more than she recalled from his words.

While the priests murmured in the First Flamen's room, she stepped carefully out onto the terrace to view the ruins again. With her bare soles she felt tiny fragments of crystal underfoot. Gazing at the wide, cold wick, she recalled what everyone knew—that the flamens tapped Ormek's heat to ignite this flame. All details were supposed to be secret, shared only by the highest priests. And what she had revealed, evidently, was her knowledge that the Gathering Stone was the instrument.

She toed a shard of quartz while contemplating what to do next. Poor Bremig had been abandoned at the gatehouse, and the sun was halfway down the sky. She could not leave him below indefinitely, nor reasonably bring him up. And she would not depart this place until her plea was answered.

When she stepped back into the hallway, she ventured to listen at Skendron's open door. She heard him speak, but could not catch many words. The Flamen-of-the-disk, standing inside the chamber, turned to stare at her, his expression this time more of bafflement than anger. He beckoned her with a bony finger, and she approached him with dread.

"Tell me," he whispered hoarsely. "Tell me what you know of the Stone." Behind him, someone was spooning soup into Skendron's mouth.

"I know no more than I've said."

"And what is that?"

"That the Stone is clear crystal, shaped to gather . . ." She halted, unable again to explain the source of this knowledge. Yet the priest's look of astonishment told her she spoke correctly. "Shaped to gather His heat to a fiery point."

The priest closed his eyes and began to pace the room. "Shall we make you a flamen, then? Bind you to keep the secret with the rest of us?" He paused and narrowed his eyes. "Or shall we simply toss you from the terrace and be done with it?"

"How would I know these things," she answered softly, "without the Bright One's aid?"

"How? That is my predicament." He continued to pace, finally sending her outside to wait again. Standing by the parapet, she had nothing to do but study the shattered panes. Years of labor had gone into shaping the thin panels of quartz, and now many were broken. If the frame could be straightened, however, she thought glass might be used to replace the missing windows. If her Vigen skills were good for nothing else, at least she might perform that service.

She sighed and looked out to sea. The waves were calm, neither boat nor beast disturbing the glittering surface. Behind her came footsteps, and she heard the closing of the hallway door.

Turning with apprehension, she realized that she was alone with the Flamen-of-the-disk. Though well on in years, he appeared broad-shouldered beneath his robes. With his advantage of size and weight, he might easily push her over the parapet to the sharp rocks below. She tensed, seeking a handhold behind her on the mortared wall.

"We have a consensus," he said, his deep-set eyes betraying nothing. He reached within the robes, plunging his hand inside to his chest. Kyala tensed, ready to confront any weapon he might produce. But instead he brought out an amulet that hung about his neck. "The Gatherer," he said solemnly, offering a disk of polished crystal mounted in a carved wooden ring. The lens just covered her palm, and her fingers trembled at its touch. He hastily put the gold chain about her neck so that the amulet would be safe from dropping.

"It is not yours yet," said the flamen. Kyala barely heard his warning. She turned the ring, noting the beauty of its craftsmanship, the flawless shaping of the crystal. "You must prove you have your knowledge direct from the Lifegiver." From another place within his robe he produced a sooty clay dish that held a bit of dried moss. "Set this afire. With His heat." The priest pointed toward the sinking sun. "Then I'll have my proof."

Kyala drew in her breath. She had guessed—known somehow—that the stone was used for lighting the great lamp; she had no idea how to accomplish that feat.

Peering into the crystal's heart, she understood she was far from the secret. The lens must gather the light to a point, but how was that done? Allowing the sunlight to fall across its face, she squinted into the interior and saw no focus. Had she misunderstood her own words? she wondered. Raising the dish, she cautiously touched the brown wisps of moss to the crystal. She half expected a spark, but there was none.

"So you don't know everything," the priest said in a tone of relief. He stepped forward, reaching for the chain, but Kyala retreated along the parapet. Uneasily, she glanced at the sea below. So long as she held the amulet, he could not dispose of her.

"Either you know it or you don't. There is no half-way." She held out one arm to fend off the approaching priest. A splash of brightness appeared on the front of his robe, moving as she moved the lens with her other hand. Could this be the gathered light from the crystal? The flamen took another step closer, and the radiance became a glowing circle that grew smaller and more intense.

"Wait!" shouted Kyala, edging back again. Only a moment more, and the mystery might be solved. She raised the dish at arm's length so that the brightness fell onto the moss, then drew the clay closer until the ring contracted to a searing point. The brilliance hurt her eyes, but she discerned a wisp of smoke twisting up from the fibers. A tiny flame began to spread.

The priest halted. The smell of burning was unmistakable, and he remained staring at the way she held her hands. "All right," he said throatily. "You've shown you can call down His heat." The flamen closed his eyes, and the lids twitched as he seemed to lose himself in thought. "Now I must keep my word to the others," he said with a woeful shake of his head. "Take the Gatherer. Do what you must."

Suddenly his eyes were open, his gaze fixed straight ahead. He stepped to the parapet and studied the empty sea, his veined hands tightly gripping the wall. "Destroy this creature for us. That's what we ask in return. Destroy it, or the good works of our faith will be lost."

CHAPTER 14

HURRYING down the path, Kyala still saw the flamen's disbelieving eyes. His astonishment could be no greater than her own. How had she gained this arcane knowledge?

Only through Ormek's intervention could the secrets have come to her. And yet she did not *feel* the Bright One's presence as she had at other times. Against her skin lay palpable evidence of His favor—an amulet with a chain so long that it hung at her belly. Already the crystal was warm from her heat; but within her, His fires had not rekindled.

At the bottom of the path she found the road empty of laborers. Though a pair of support posts now stood, the new gate still lay on the ground. Bremig and the brown-robe broke off their conversation as she approached.

The two men parted amicably, but the gatekeeper had only a scowl for Kyala as she passed. Bremig stared at her with curiosity. "Your face shows something new," he said.

"I have what I came for," she admitted as she walked to her mount. "Something to strengthen my talismans. You mustn't ask what it is."

"Ah, the flamens and their secrets. The gatekeeper hinted at some odd practices."

She gazed at his look of bemusement. "This one secret

you must honor. As for the rest . . . I think some of those priests are billy goats dressed in yellow robes."

Bremig laughed, and Kyala regretted her words. She wanted him to respect the flamens despite their human failings. Without the priests, after all, to whom would Ormek's followers turn? Lacking leadership, the faith would falter and soon be lost.

For now, there was no more to be said about it. Following the coast, she and Bremig headed north toward Asep River. On the closest bank lay her destination—a small village where she hoped to cross the swampy delta. Night was coming on; she lit the pole lamp and they continued into darkness.

Even here, on the edge of settled land, lay danger from Draalego's spies. Nearing the village along the narrow track, the travelers came on an abandoned barn. Half the roof had collapsed, but within they found shelter from the night's breezes. As soon as the blankets were unpacked and the animals cared for, Kyala doused the light.

"Be careful of your arm," she said as they nestled in the moldering straw. But regardless of pain, he seemed capable of tousling her hair and stroking her cheek with his long forefinger. This time he was eager as he fumbled with her lacings in the dark. *The Gatherer*! she thought. *He must not even touch it*. Pulling aside, she slipped the chain over her head and secured the amulet inside her discarded boot.

But she could not warm to him that night. Now she was neither his nor the Lifegiver's, adrift with only a spirit's words to guide her. She rolled away from the carver, heard his breath hiss between his teeth. "Something has already fallen between us," he said despondently.

How could she continue her deception? She reached toward him in darkness and her fingers touched the ridges of his back. "I must damp my feelings," she whispered. "That's why I told you to stay with Lebbon."

"Vigens' rules . . ." The words came out bitterly, and she did not blame him.

"More serious than that." How could she repeat the spirit's accusations? She put her arms around him, wishing she could somehow ease the hurt. His skin was warm against her cheek.

"A priest's warning?" Still he sought an explanation.

"They've nothing to do with this." She hugged him tightly, but discovered no words of comfort. At last, she ran her fingers down to his ribs. With some effort, she found she could make him laugh.

Daylight was already filtering through the cracked roof when Bremig woke. He lay faceup, still suffering from the painful stiffness in his arm. But the discomfort was nothing compared with last night's revelations. He glanced at sleeping Kyala, and his despair only worsened. She had warned him days before, yet he had persisted.

What would be left between them now? There was the accursed beast to overcome; that task would keep them together for a time. With a deep sigh, he rolled to his feet and brushed off the clinging wisps of straw. Today he would do what he must—help her cross the delta in secrecy. Draalego's tales, he suspected, had reached even this remote village.

Leaving her breathing softly, he mounted his horse and rode along a lane that passed an isolated log cottage. The chimney was smoking, so he dismounted and rapped at the rough-hewn door. To his surprise, the portal was flung open almost at once, allowing an unfamiliar cooking smell to escape. A short woman of middle years held an unusual weapon while she eyed him cautiously. Bremig studied the long spike mounted on the end of a wooden pole, then returned his gaze to the woman.

"You want frogs?" she asked in a harsh voice. "Come back after noon." Her graying hair had been hacked short, the trimming far cruder than his own work on Kyala. Her chin was wide, her cheeks plump, her eyebrows thick. She wore knee-high boots, with threadbare trousers tucked carelessly into the tops.

"I'm looking for a shortcut north," he said uneasily. "Can't risk losing my horse in muck. Do you know someone who might lead me?"

"Across the delta? Not many go that way."

The distinctive smell grew stronger, and Bremig noticed bundles of stems and leaves hanging from the beams above her head. "I can pay in coppers. And something for you, if you find me a guide."

One shaggy eyebrow twitched, and she lowered the weapon halfway. "I know the paths," she said confidently. "But I've got frogs to hunt when I go. You want to follow me, maybe we can arrange something. Even so, I'll lose time doin' it. Frogs won't be fresh by the time I get home."

The carver had no appetite for haggling that morning, yet dared not let her think his plight desperate. "Maybe I'll try someone else," he said, rubbing his beard and gazing back at his horse. "Your spike makes me nervous."

"You won't get help elsewhere," she warned. "Some know the ways, but none of 'em will take a stranger." When he looked at her again, she had put the weapon aside and was beckoning him across her threshold.

Inside, the strong odors made him eager to be finished. Whether this woman—Nezekra, she called herself—was a healer or a practitioner of dark arts he preferred not to know. With his eyes becoming accustomed to the dim interior, he saw many jars and boxes scattered about the room. A row of crude shelves held smaller vials, as well as an assortment of withered relics. Hastily, he settled her fee and agreed to a meeting place. When he stumbled back into the morning air, he found its freshness intoxicating.

Bremig returned to find Kyala kneeling behind the barn, seemingly absorbed in thought. He saw a flash of a strange glossy amulet, the brightness leaving a dark spot before his eyes. Was this the secret she'd brought from the Reach? She quickly tucked away the piece, dropping a handful of sooty straw in the process. He also noticed a burnt smell, but knew he must say nothing.

Knotting his fists, he railed silently at the mysteries that separated him from Kyala. Yet he harbored a hope that her glass might prevail, and despite all, he could not think of leaving her. "We've a guide," he said, trying to maintain a carefree tone. She nodded, saddled the gray, and followed him across a weedy meadow. Bypassing the cottages, they halted in a copse of birches at the water's edge.

"So there's two of you," Nezekra said, emerging from shadows. "I bargained to lead only one."

"What does it matter?" he answered. "Your effort will be the same." But seeing her sour expression, the carver agreed to pay another coin. The woman shrugged, studied Kyala carefully, then began to walk along the muddy bank. Here the Asep had already broken into rivulets, each only a few horse-lengths across. Underwater the footing was known to be treacherous, and the sandbars had sucked down many riders.

Nezekra stepped into the stream, Bremig noting carefully where she entered. The water reached halfway to the guide's knees as she splashed across. The riders followed through a swampy mire and were forced to wait when the guide spotted a large bullfrog. Her motion was sudden; the pole swung, the weapon rising at once to show the squirming creature impaled on the spike.

The frog went into a sack that she closed with a drawstring. With distaste, Bremig watched the twitching of the bag as Nezekra plodded on. In this manner they crossed nine rivulets and the intervening bars of mud and sand. In some parts trees had established themselves, only to be toppled by spring flooding and then grow up again. He noticed a willow whose trunk ran flat against the ground, then bent up and out to dangle its leaves above the current.

As they continued, the carver kept track of landmarks—a clump of ferns, a mossy slab, a stagnant pool. To return this way might be necessary, he thought. But perhaps they would not be coming back . . . The far side looked familiar. The sea beast's lair was close at hand.

While her sack squirmed with half-dead frogs, the woman accepted her payment. Then she squinted up at Kyala and let a faint smile show. "Go north where no one'll find you," she advised. "Who can blame you for running from a seaman?"

Nezekra plodded back into swamps, leaving Bremig to wonder if she would betray them. But if she couldn't keep silent, her belief that they were continuing northward might discourage pursuit. Only wild mountains lay in that direction.

Putting aside such speculative dangers, Bremig turned his thoughts to the watery cave. "Will you light your lantern?" he asked.

Facing the slope, Kyala hesitated. A short distance higher lay the gap that led down to the undercut cliff. "I'll take care of that when the time comes," she answered at last. "But I must go up without you."

Gritting his teeth against the pain, Bremig managed to raise both arms above his head. "See? I'm not crippled. I can take care of myself."

"Let me go alone. If I need your help, I can call."

I should have stayed in Jannford, he thought. But how could he argue with her when she had told him the same?

Kyala turned her mount and headed up the hill. "You left the spear!" he called after her. She paid no heed.

The carver dismounted, kicked over several saplings in his anger. When his temper had cooled, he tied his horse to a stouter trunk, unpacked the spear, and followed her route. The rising cliffs blocked his view of the sea, but for now he was more interested in the sheltered side of the bluffs. He recognized the path of their recent escape, but hesitated to advance farther. If Kyala was engaged in some private ceremony, he must not disturb her.

Around him all was quiet. yet his fear that she was endangered eventually pushed him on. He found the dropped poleax and picked it up. And then he saw the fang of dark stone, the post he had used to secure the harpoon's chain. Both Sea-snake and iron had vanished!

He bent to the stone's base and saw signs of heavy scraping. Had frantic wriggling slipped the chain? he wondered. Or had the more agile Squid freed its companion? But he turned from such useless questions to notice that Kyala's pony stood alone in a clearing; where was its rider?

Peering over the gap, he spotted her at the bottom of the slope. With the new amulet in one hand and talismans in the other, she advanced on the cave's base. He sucked in his breath, not knowing what folly she was about to commit.

And who is the greater fool? he asked himself. Is it she, who puts her faith in a difficult god, or I, who can find no happiness without her?

The waves were slapping at the cave's entrance, but he saw no hint of tentacles in the water. Kyala leaned her head into the opening and did not draw back at once. *Gone*! he realized. Before she could notice him, he slipped down behind the bluff. He listened until he heard her returning footsteps, then headed back to his horse.

They camped at the overlook, eating Lebbon's provisions and standing alternate watches. The carver promised to turn away when the time came for Kyala to use her talismans, and his oath seemed to satisfy her. Night came, and they wrapped themselves in blankets and bedded down together, yet did not touch each other.

At dawn the watches continued. A day went by and then another, but the beast did not return. For food, and to pass the time, Bremig speared speckled fish that darted about the cave's entrance. These fish were eaten uncooked, out of fear that a fire might draw search parties. Bremig also found scuttling about the shore many small crabs, a delicacy that he had formerly enjoyed. But now neither he nor Kyala could touch them. There was only one Crab in their thoughts.

As time passed, Kyala became increasingly glum, and at last he could keep still no longer. "Do you dare seek Watnojat's advice again?" Bremig asked one afternoon as he watched her attempting to scrape scales from a rockfish.

She answered in gloomy tones. "I've tried twice now. While you were busy with your spear."

"And?"

"I can't reach him." She exposed scarred thumbs, and he realized that she'd been using the bone-handled fish knife not only for cleaning his catches. "His voice may be exhausted," she said with a sad shake of her head. "Or maybe he's already one with Ormek. I can get no answer."

"Then we must find our own." He took the knife from her hand, flipped over the spiny fish, and demonstrated his technique once more. The rock was covered with glinting scales before she spoke again.

"If we try to lure the beast with smoke," she said, "we may attract Draalego first. If we go looking for it on horseback, then he'll surely catch us. But if we had a boat . . ."

"You told me you get sick in a mere river raft." He glanced up at her pale and tired face.

"I can get used to waves."

Bremig considered her words. Seeking the creature at sea would mean an entirely new set of risks. If this new amulet failed her while sailing, what hope would remain of escape? Yet they could not wait here indefinitely while the beast swam other waters.

Sensing her determination, he tried to put aside his fears. "There's a bay just south of here with a few fishing huts. We can probably find something there that floats."

"Only one boat will do," she answered, her eyes fixed far beyond him.

"One?"

"You told me your cousin brought it home. It was built for my sake, so why not use it?"

"The black walnut?" Of all the old tales, one had not lost its grip on him. If she stepped into that cursed craft, what might happen? Perhaps the maelstrom would erupt after all!

"Don't you see the advantage? No one will dare come after me. Not even Draalego, so long as he believes his own tales. We can sail where we please, search as long as we must."

"The boat is in Darst and we are here. And you can't go safely down the coastal road." Bremig sighed, knowing what would come next. He cleaned off the fish knife and handed it back to her. "I may be able to get through alone. I've done it once before."

Kyala frowned. "You may ride safely south, but you'll be *sailing* back. What if the beast catches up with you then?"

The carver pursed his lips, for he had no answer. Should he ask for talismans? Kyala herself had difficulties wielding them. As for weapons, he knew how useless they would prove.

But the answer came from Balin's daughter, and he knew there was no dissuading her. She put a hand on his arm and spoke softly. "We'll ride to Darst together, whatever the risks."

Leaving the camp, Bremig felt a surprising relief, for the time there had both wearied and frustrated him. Now, despite the uncertainties ahead, he was glad to be moving again. The animals were well rested, and made briskly for the delta crossing. He soon found the spot where Nezekra had turned home.

Gazing across the first stream, he realized that there had been no rain for days. The safe path they had taken earlier was still marked by deep footprints. Beckoning to Kyala, he crossed the narrow flow and then a stretch of sand, finally halting to get his bearings. Recalling the landmarks he'd memorized, he looked about for the eddy beneath an overhanging stump. Mosquitoes whined about his ears, and for a moment the scene confused him.

Had he forgotten something? On the mud beyond the next rivulet he saw tracks coming out of the water at *two* different points. Which was the way he'd taken earlier? "Stay back," he warned Kyala. Guessing, he turned his horse toward the closest bank, but the footprints there were so deep that he quickly turned away. The guide's route had been on firmer soil.

The mare halted in the water with her hind leg extended. Recognizing at once that she was caught, he jumped off to relieve the weight and found himself wet to his knees. His mount leaned forward, her muscles straining, but still could not free herself. He felt the soft bottom giving way under his own feet and feared he'd be sucked under.

Kyala shouted something, but he was lost in concentration. Pitching himself forward, he landed with his hands in the mud of the far bank. The suction at his boots broke and he pulled himself up from the stream with his fingers. Behind him, he heard the horse snorting. Turning, he whispered what he hoped were calming words.

He saw Kyala securing her pony to a snag on the other bank. "Don't come after me," he called, but she was already splashing into the water. Shaking his head at her stubbornness, he pulled a long log down the bank, bringing its far end to the horse's caught foot. Only vaguely aware of the old wound now, he stretched out his arms for balance and tried to walk along the pole. But the bark was too slippery, and he tumbled, landing on his back in the chilly water.

"Etma take us all!" he shouted, wishing for a moment that the demon would come and swallow his misery. Then he felt a firm tugging as Kyala helped him sit up. "The bottom's soft," he warned. Drenched through by now, he did not hesitate to flop belly-down into the water. With one hand on the submerged trunk, he reached under the mare toward the trapped foot.

"Shh. Shhh," he said to the roan as he dug his fingers into mire. He felt a tremor. The leg came free with a spray of muck, and he fell facedown into the flow.

When he looked up, spitting river water in all directions, his horse was already standing on the drier of the two trails. Kyala, back where she had left her pony, had turned away to conceal her expression, but he could see that she was heaving with laughter. Bremig followed in the mare's wake, grabbing a hold on the saddle and resting against her flank while he caught his breath. Dripping from hair and clothing, he could only curse silently.

When he looked up again, Kyala was leading her gray across the flood. He could still see twitching at the corners of her mouth. "You're only wet to your knees," he said calmly when she stood beside him. Then, with a sudden lunge, he flung her into the stream.

They stared at each other for a moment, then exploded with laughter. Still grinning, she staggered to the bank and put her arms about him. He sensed more playfulness than passion. "Enough," he said when he realized that she was trying to unbalance him so that both would tumble into mud. "We have to treat this seriously. Maybe I've lost the way."

She gave him one last teasing shove, then danced off to retrieve her pony. Bremig managed to collect his thoughts. He recited his landmarks again, and suddenly the route was clear to him. Ahead lay a familiar pair of rotted logs; he could see the trail on the far side of the next rivulet. "We go that way," he told her, now not even caring that he was soaked.

At last they emerged at the copse, and Bremig stripped off his mud-caked shirt. This hunter's garb of Lebbon's provided little disguise, he thought, but he preferred it to the fisherman's sweater he carried. Turning, he rinsed the woven shirt in the stream, then flung it over his back. To get to Darst unnoticed, they both would need more than a change in clothing.

The sky had clouded over and evening was at hand. Avoiding the main road, they approached Nezekra's cottage from the rear. Above her chimney rose pale smoke that seemed tinged with crimson, a sight that made Bremig narrow his eyes. He hesitated, questioning again his willingness to trust the woman. But he knew no one else in this decaying settlement. With a final resolve, he tied up the horse. Kyala followed as he slipped around to the door.

"You back?" Pursing her lips, Nezekra stared at the travelers. "First, you'd better dry yourselves," she said, pointing to the hearth. A pole scraped as she secured the door behind them. "Then tell me why you want those seamen to catch you."

They sat on low stools by the fire, but offered no explanations. Bremig looked again at the shelves he'd seen on his earlier visit. Uneasily, he framed his request. "Can you change the color of hair?"

"So no one will notice you, my black-crowned friend?" Nezekra thrust her fingers at his scalp and pulled at a tuft until he yelped with pain. Then she briefly tousled Kyala's chestnut strands.

"I'll pay . . . a good price," he said. At that moment, he noticed, to his discomfiture, a collection of lizard skins pegged to one wall.

"Coppers?" She stepped back to study him. "Maybe you have something more interesting."

"I have carvings," he ventured, thinking of what he carried in his saddlebags. But he'd seen no disks of Ormek hanging here.

Suddenly he felt her hands at his waist, and then she was holding Arod's refitted knife. She moved closer to the fire, and the troubled look on her face made Bremig wish he hadn't spoken.

"Tell me what you want," she said deliberately.

"Not in trade for the knife."

"Do you think I'd keep it?" She hastily returned the weapon to its sheath, and he noticed her hands trembling slightly.

"Then tell me your price," he demanded. "To lighten our hair. And my beard as well."

"You paid too much for the crossing," she answered. "I've no mind to cheat you twice." With that she poured water into a wide pot and began to rummage among her jars. Soon steam was rising above the hearth, and a new sharp smell filled the room.

When the brew cooled enough so he could bear it against his skin, he hung his head over the pot. Dipping a cloth, she repeatedly bathed his chin and hair. He heard Kyala hissing with what he took to be surprise. But he was forced to keep his eyes closed, and he gritted his teeth at the indignity of the process. "Am I so different?" he asked her when the bathing was done.

Kyala held a lantern to his face. "You might fool your brother." He rushed to Nezekra's water bucket and tried to catch a dim reflection in lamplight. What he saw made him smile—a coppery red growth covered cheeks and chin. Who would know him now?

Then it was Kyala's turn, and he watched her hair lighten with each application of the cloth. The change wouldn't stay, Nezekra explained. The new growth would again be dark. But this night, he thought, they might easily pass for strangers on the road to Darst.

CHAPTER 15

WITH the pole lantern to light their way, Bremig led cautiously along the coastal road. Now and again a wagon passed, and he watched for any sign of curiosity on the drivers' faces. The carver met with occasional nods and nothing more. But later he heard a rider approaching at a gallop, and felt a clutch of fear. In just such a setting he had met Draalego on the road to Hesh.

He dared not pull aside or make any unusual gesture. At best he could forge ahead, so that his light would not fall on Kyala. The lantern swung wildly from the end of its pole as the mare sped forward. If the flame should go out, he thought, he'd be glad of the darkness. But then the rider rushed past him, so quickly he caught only a hint of his features. As the harsh hoofbeats faded, the carver reined in his horse.

"Who was that?" Kyala called softly.

"How can I know? I just hope he doesn't turn back."

Not long afterward, a drayman hailed Bremig for directions. Halting, the carver heard the pony trot up behind him. Had Kyala no sense? She even spoke to the stranger, telling what she knew of nearby towns. Bremig chewed on the inside of his cheek, wishing the man would be quickly satisfied. When the wagon drove off at last, Lanorik's son turned to see Kyala grinning. "You need another dousing in the river," he told her.

Pushing the animals, they rested infrequently, and reached Darst before the first hint of dawn. They stole into Arod's alley, mare and pony heaving.

"Don't believe what you see," warned the carver when he heard the smith draw back his bar. The gate opened enough to let out a gleam of lamplight, and then Bremig heard an indrawn breath.

"A stranger with the carver's voice," Arod hissed as he widened the gap. "Your face won't betray you, but keep your lips shut. Draalego wants you dead." Then he looked past Bremig and raised his eyebrows. "The daughter here too?"

"I ask you one favor," Bremig whispered. "Take care of the animals. You can say you found them wandering. The pony belongs to a man named Modwetten."

The smith emerged, shuffled closer, and sleepily reached for the mare's bridle. Kyala followed with the gray, and finally they all stood in the shallow yard while Arod secured the gate. "And you, carver," Arod said with a groggy wink. "There's more change than the beard."

Bremig knew what he was hinting at. "Is that all you can think about?" Bending close to the smith's ear, he whispered, "I told you she's like no other. Leave it at that."

The ironsmith shrugged and smiled. "Then tell me whose wine barrel you emptied before you came here. I know fifty men who'd be pleased to rip your belly open. As for her . . ." He could only shake his head in dismay.

"If we get to the harbor soon enough, they'll never catch a look at us."

"Harbor?" Arod stared at him. "You plan to swim again? I heard about you and your cousin . . ."

"The boat. Where is the black walnut boat?"

Clearly flustered, Arod let the mare get away from him. While the roan slipped into his stable, he lifted the lantern to scrutinize the carver's face again. "They left their dark craft in the water," he answered cautiously. "Moored at the quay, where no one dares touch it. But what's that to you?"

"We're going to take her. My cousin proved there's no curse on that vessel."

Arod spat at the base of his high fence. "The others think your cousin a demon himself after the way he rode out the storm."

Bremig gave a weak grin. "Demon he may be . . ."

"But you make no sense, carver. The fishermen want nothing more than to set Kyala adrift. Do you plan to do the job for them?"

"I have talismans, Arod," she said, stepping forward.

The smith frowned. "*Glass?* Watnojat always had faith in his charms, but in this case . . ."

"With Ormek's help, I'll be safe," she said. "But can you tell me where to *find* the sea beast?"

He turned, his attention shifting to Balin's daughter. "Must I point you to your doom? I was Watnojat's friend."

"Then show you trust him. As I do."

Arod hesitated. "I wish I had your convictions," he answered with a sad shake of his head. "If you take that cursed craft, I think you'll have no trouble meeting up with your beast."

"But where was the last sighting?" she insisted.

He answered with a pained expression and a hushed voice. "There was trouble down by Hesh a few days ago. For Balin's sake . . ."

"Then we'll sail south," she replied firmly.

The smith made a sign of Ormek with thumb and forefinger, opened his mouth to say more, but then turned away in evident resignation.

Bremig looked up to see the stars already gone. "We'll have to hurry," he said as he went to seek his mare in the shadowy stable. Arod followed, holding the lamp while

Bremig retrieved a waterbag and the remains of the provisions.

"Let me look," the smith insisted, and before Bremig could protest he went to bring new rations from the house. "I expect to see you again, carver," Arod said solemnly. "And Kyala too. Sitting in front of my fire making sly winks at one other." He clapped Bremig on the shoulders, embraced Balin's daughter, then sent them both out into the lifting gloom.

Laden with equipment and supplies, they crept through narrow alleys, feeling their way as much as seeing. Cautiously they advanced along the beach, crouching to watch for movement against the sky. Was there no guard? Draalego must have thought none was needed, for who would cross a demon? The carver smiled, imagining how his cousin would fume and bellow along the whole length of the harbor.

Suddenly dogs began yapping. Racing ahead, Bremig found the dark vessel at the dock, its mast dipping gently with the waves. He tossed the roll of fishnet and his other parcels over the port gunwale, but did not follow them. Kyala added the weapons and lantern to the cargo, then stood back, awaiting his instructions.

He stared at Balin's daughter with unexpected dread, then turned from her to study the boat's unsettling lines. Now his old fears made a final protest. The profile of his carving stood out against the brightening sky, peering forward as if those oval eyes could see. Was it watching for Etma? he wondered.

If the sea demon wanted Kyala, he thought, then her chance had come. "The boat is yours," he told her. Close by, he heard voices, and boots crunching gravel. "Get in!" he said hoarsely, for the boat was now their only escape. He sucked in his breath as he watched Kyala climb into the stern.

Her hands leaned on the gunwale. He heard her boots against the hull. Yet no waterspout blew, no storm thundered from the west. There was only an angry crowd of fishermen running toward him from the nearby cottages.

Trembling, Bremig followed her into the boat. He was not certain whether he feared land or water more at this moment. Having proven himself a poor seaman as a youth, he had rarely attempted sailing. He knew the rudiments, but could he manage this craft?

He found the halyard to be slick with some foul grease, but was able to pull up the sail and cleat the line to the mast. A breeze filled the cloth despite its deliberate pattern of rents. He reached over to slip the painter. With the land breeze still blowing, the bow swung away from the dock.

"Who steals my boat?" shouted Draalego from halfway down the dock. Bremig hastily cast off the other mooring line. Grappling with the sheet and the starboard tiller, he found himself sliding from the quay.

"You have your wish, cousin!" Bremig called across the waves. "I've delivered Balin's daughter. Now your demon can be satisfied."

"Bring back the vixen!" the fisherman demanded.

"Swim for her," suggested the carver as the boat gained speed. "If you're fast, you may beat Etma to the kill."

"The demon'll swallow you too, carver!" Draalego bellowed. But there was no splash of pursuit. Cool against his neck, the breeze held steady, pushing the craft speedily across the harbor. And now that the sun was emerging, Bremig saw that the sky was perfectly clear. Where was the maelstrom his cousin had predicted? He almost grinned in triumph.

As he headed toward open sea, however, the carver realized he would have to jibe to avoid the islands. Trimming the sheet as he adjusted the helm, he was unprepared for a sudden change in wind. An offshore gust caught the sail, and the greasy sheet slipped from his fingers. "Get down," he shouted to Kyala as the boom swung across the starboard gunwale. Tumbling, he lost his grip on the tiller as well, then felt the craft heeling. *Don't swamp her*, he thought frantically, heaving his body to starboard. He grabbed the helm and tried to regain control.

The boat rolled crazily as he sat up, and he wondered if the wrights had deliberately built an unstable craft. Dropping to his knees, feeling the rough ridges of planks, he wrenched the tiller to avoid the oncoming rocks. Kyala lay huddled beneath the thwarts, and he could not spare her a glance. Was this how he'd lose her, to a puff of wind?

But the boat righted itself as the sail began to luff. Now he was in irons, the wind blowing steadily over the bow and toward shore. Bremig had a vision of his cousin convulsed with laughter at the carver's ineptness. Cursing softly, so that Kyala would not know his concern, he lowered sail and pulled out the crude oars that his cousin had left him.

At last clear of the islands, he turned the prow southward and prepared to sail once more. He wiped his hands clean, but as soon as he touched a line he was greasy again. What slime, he wondered, had the builders used? Someone had elaborated on the traditional curses, and the result had nearly undone him.

"You can come up," he told Kyala when he'd steadied the course. "But keep your head low." Slowly she pulled herself out, and for the first time in daylight he studied her new appearance. She was nearly blond now, the hair making her suntanned face seem darker still. What a change Nezekra had wrought!

From her first moments in the boat, Kyala knew she had no future on the sea. If she survived this one journey, she would be content never to leave land again. She closed her eyes and fought the rising sickness. What had come of her boast that she'd grow used to the ocean's swell?

When the worst of the pitching seemed over, she crawled out and looked back toward shore. Darst's harbor was gone;

she had slipped past Draalego and his crew. Were it not for her stomach, she would have smiled.

"I'm learning to handle this tub," Bremig said when Kyala turned to face him. Sunlight shone on his hair, and for a moment, only his voice convinced her that this was the carver. With his bristling new beard and coppery hair, he looked nothing like the man who had come to her shop. Even the way he held himself was different, as if he had taken on new confidence. Though he appeared uncomfortable, working on his knees, the boat was moving well.

"I want to learn too," she said suddenly, pointing to the tiller. "It can't be much harder than driving a wagon."

"I nearly tipped us over! And you're no swimmer."

"Still, I want to do it."

"And the seasickness?"

She puckered her face. "I'll manage."

He laughed and held his hands steady. "You can't just jump into this," he said. "There's too much to know. If you're serious, we'll have to start with the names of things." She stared at him with curiosity. "Can you guess why they call the side you're sitting on *port*?"

Kyala felt herself frowning as he began the lesson. Not long ago, she had endured Watnojat's endless lists of woods and fires and mixtures. Now she must fill her head with new terms—the fishermen's lore. And what of the beast? She had to watch for its approach while she was listening to Bremig.

When he finished describing parts of the boat, he spoke of choosing a course. "This is called reaching," he said, "because the wind's blowing from the side. Now you tell me if it's a port or starboard reach?" She slapped her hand to her brow, but could not answer.

Meanwhile, the boat's constant rocking made her grip the thwarts so hard that her knuckles were white. She'd eaten nothing since the previous afternoon. How could her stomach feel so rebellious?

Trying to conceal her sickness from the carver, she pleaded for a chance to hold sheet and tiller. At last, he agreed. She had been aware of a foul odor, but when she took the slimy rope in her hand, she realized the source. "Take it back," she shouted as she rushed to dangle her head over water. Her insides, she discovered, had not quite been empty.

After a rest, she felt able to ask for another try. This time she held a close reach, and her confidence began to grow. "Teach me more," she insisted, and soon she could bring the craft about nearly as well as he could. "Were you a changeling," he asked, "snatched from a seawoman's breast?"

"Not likely." She jokingly puffed out her cheeks, but did not hang over the gunwales again. Later, she watched Bremig eat from Arod's provisions but refused the bits he offered. "Find us a place to land," she challenged. "I can't swallow unless I have ground under my feet." He shrugged and kept clear of shore.

And what if the beast should come now? she asked herself. Ever since Watnojat's warning, she had planned to face the creature alone. Yet how could she separate from Bremig if they remained confined to the boat? The longer they traveled, the more likely it seemed that the beast would show itself. She felt the Gatherer against her skin. When the moment came, she must use it.

They passed Hesh and continued south. Kyala found difficulty in maintaining her vigilance. But Bremig, she saw, was constantly scanning the waves. "I think your beast has gone back where it came from," he said as dusk approached.

"We have to keep going."

"Not in the dark." She saw him peering ahead. "And my cousin may be following on horseback. We don't dare touch land."

Indeed, she had seen figures on the shore as they passed. She was certain that the boat's progress had been observed from many lookouts. "Could we stop at an island?" She pointed to starboard at a jumble of rocks hosting only a pair of slender terns.

"We can try. Have you seen an anchor? Or maybe a heavy line?"

Creeping forward, Kyala discovered a thick rope coiled in the bow. Its end was frayed, as if something had been torn away. "That's the hawser," Bremig told her. "See what they've done to follow the legend? A boat that's missing its anchor can't rest." He glanced again at her island. "Now we can prove the tale wrong."

Approaching from the leeward side, he pulled down the sail, then used an oar to bring them closer. With the anchor cable wrapped around a rocky spar, they climbed out, finding a flat place that was big enough for the blanket. Kyala could not wait to stand on this meager sample of solid ground. "Are you sure it's not rocking?" she asked him. Again she refused his offers of cheese and sausage and biscuit.

As dusk fell, she hastened to light the lamp, laying before it the three talismans from her wrist. There was nothing to burn here should the lantern fail. She shook the flask of lamp oil and tried to guess when her supply would give out.

Bremig took the first watch. Having lost an entire night's rest, she found the stone bed as comfortable as any other. But she did not doze long. She told him to sleep all he wished, for now she felt fully awake. Overhead swung the patterns of Ormek's dreams, and she thought the figures were judging her, eager to see her fail.

She recalled the night when she'd gone to Watnojat's shop for her first taste of a Vigen's toil. On the way they looked up into the sparkling sky, and the old glassmaker spoke of new legends. Then he took her to his kiln and let her pump at the bellows until she could not hold up her arms. Yet she kept going, always finding reserves, until the bead was fused. That was the night she helped to make her own talisman, the one she wore even now. . .

In the morning, before Bremig woke, she began loading the boat. But how could she leave him on this bare bit of rock so far from land? No, the place would not do. Moodily, she sat waiting for sunrise. She extinguished the lantern as soon as Ormek showed Himself.

All that day they sailed, at times so close to shore that she watched men waving from beaches or cliffs. They circled the Five Toe Islands and passed under the stone arch of Medhov. At last he pleaded with her to return, arguing that the beast had never been sighted this far south. "We've missed it," he said. "If it's here, we've got to go back."

Kyala had studied the coastline as they went, and knew where she wished to spend the night. Having agreed to turn back at last, she silently greeted the arrival of dusk. The only nearby island lay close to shore, but now Bremig had no other choice of berth. "We'll have to take this one," he said. "Let's hope everyone's still afraid."

Climbing from the boat, Kyala saw lights bobbing along the mainland's beach. "They're watching," she said in a whisper, as if the spectators were close enough to hear her.

They had a narrow stretch of sand to sit on, and Kyala was surprised to find her appetite return. Maybe, if she stayed out long enough, she might accustom herself to the sea. But for how many days must she ply these empty waters?

"What if it's gone?" Bremig asked her, echoing her own thoughts as she lay ready for sleep. "What if the beast has vanished?"

"We can have a new life," she answered dreamily. "We'll sail where your cousin will never come, all the way down to the Mej's fortress."

"Where he'll welcome us, no doubt."

"We'll be guests at his banquet." She tried to imagine the

huge halls she'd heard about, and the glittering tables stretching from end to end. What would wine taste like, she wondered, from a goblet of silver? "First he'll offer us a toast," she said, "and then he'll commission me to make glass for him. And when the cheering's done, he'll appoint you his royal carver."

CHAPTER 16

KYALA again chose the predawn watch, and this time had room to stretch her legs. While Bremig slept fitfully, she paced back and forth along the sandy strip, peering over the low-lying rocks at the mainland. She saw signs of movement in the shoreside settlement—early risers carrying lights as they started their chores. How she wished she could be among them!

Her eyes stung at the thought of what she must do. Fastening the beast-eye talismans to her wrist, she took one last look at the dozing carver. He was a fair swimmer and would not be stranded when she left him here. And she'd be drawing Draalego to another part of the coast. Bremig would be safe, she told herself.

Carrying the lantern and the oil flask, she walked quietly to the boat. Within, already lay the weapons and equipment, a small water bag, and a little food. She had no reason to delay.

The vessel was beached, and only the stern lay in water. She loosened the hawser, then considered how to drag the heavy craft into the surf. Leaning at the gunwale, she put all her strength against the wood. From beneath came a noisy scraping, a hiss of rubbed sand.

Suddenly Bremig was sitting up, watching her. "So

early?" he asked in a sleepy voice. Without replying, she heaved again, advancing another step into the waves.

"Why such a hurry?" Before he could say more, she was straining again, but this time the keel seemed stuck. He was standing up, coming toward her.

"You've done too much for me already," she said. "I have to finish this alone."

"Sail the boat *and* fight the creature by yourself?"

"All I ask is that you help me launch."

"Not if you're going without me," he answered. "I've stayed with you so far, and I mean to finish it. I thought we settled that business of priestly secrets."

"You mean this?" Suddenly she found herself pulling up the long gold chain. She lifted the crystal and dangled it for him to see. "Do you think I care more for the flamens than for you? Here's their mysterious amulet. Look at it all you wish, but still I must leave you."

He shook his head mournfully, ignoring the lens. "What you ask is impossible."

After putting away the crystal, she tugged again at the boat. She could not move it.

"You know how we nearly tipped a few times," Bremig added. "If you capsize, who'll pull you to shore?" Suddenly he advanced a few long steps and gripped the opposite gunwale.

"Don't make me fight you," she pleaded. Yet she'd known this moment might come. The possibility had tormented her, keeping her awake so often that now her thoughts spun with weariness. "I'm sorry," she told him as she dug into her pouch for another charm—one she had hoped never to use. She glanced up to see his features set, the stubbornness clear on his face. Cupping in her hand the gray-green talisman—the last bead she'd cast in Modwetten's shop—she brought it closer to the light.

Did he sense what she planned? "Help me with the boat,"

she said, trying to make the words seem more request than command. He stared at her angrily, and she repeated the order in a firmer tone.

"What have you got there?" he asked in a rising voice. "I feel something. Are you . . ."

"Stay back!" she shouted when he tried to lunge at her.

His body jerked, and he cried out in surprise. "A talisman? A bead to charm *me*?"

"Only because I must."

"You!" he hissed. "You said you'd never misuse your art."

"Ormek will punish me as I deserve. Now help me push the boat!"

He shook his head in fury. "If you're casting me out, then I'll do *nothing* for you. If you think you can finish this on your own, then do the whole of it yourself."

She studied the bead. No, she realized. She could not compel him to do her work. "Then give me room. Move to the end of the beach while I try again."

He gave a cold laugh and stood his ground.

Once more she commanded, and he groaned as his feet pulled away from him.

"You . . ." he gasped as he fought his muscles. "Draalego . . . was right about you."

"Believe what you wish. I do this for your sake, though I can't make you see that." She watched him ignore her words and continue to fight the tug of his legs. His jaw was clenched, his eyes squeezed shut, his fists balled. Tears streamed down his cheeks, and hers also at the sight, but for all his efforts he kept lurching backward.

And then she was grunting and straining, finding a strength in her arms and legs that she had never known. Heaving again and again, she dragged the boat across the last stretch of sand. Bremig had turned away, as if unable to bear the sight of her.

* * *

The sail was a blur, and Kyala could only guess at where shore—and safety—lay. What did that matter now? she asked herself, not bothering to dry her eyes. If the beast wanted her, it would come—a welcome relief from her sorrow. And if Ormek was angered, then soon she would know his wrath.

Had she truly broken His law? It was permitted to force a dying man to drink and eat. Might she not claim that she'd saved Bremig's life? For unless she faced the creature alone, she was certain it would destroy them both.

But this argument left her uneasy, and she wondered what Longval's Vigen would say. He had thought her incapable of such an act, yet now it was done. Modwetten's first trespass had led to another and then another, until now he had dozens of talismans concealed within his wall, dozens of men and women subject to his command.

She pounded her fist against the thwart, refusing to follow her logic to its conclusion. For her there was no future, but only what remained of this journey.

Suddenly she looked up at onrushing breakers. What had she done? In her bitter musings she'd held a landward course, but here she'd find no shelter. Men standing on the rocky shore waved at her, making vulgar gestures. With the noise of their jeering for encouragement, she broke from her reverie, wrenched the tiller, and veered off.

Now she was fully attentive, her gooseflesh still prickling from the closeness of her escape. She forced herself to think only of the wind and how swiftly it could carry her northward. And constantly she scanned the waves for the creature's rusty hump.

One settlement after another slid by, and soon she recognized a spit of land that marked the start of Hesh's bay. Here lay the Thumb-and-Finger, an island that had protected the coast from raiders of old. The beast was said to frequent such places.

Gliding past the "thumb" and discerning nothing unusual, she looked in toward town, studied the empty harbor. That morning, all along her way, she had seen scattered spectators on the shore. Here she could find none. Had Hesh's citizens some matter that preoccupied them all?

And then, as she was about to leave the narrow bay in her wake, she understood why the harbor was deserted. A huge tentacle arching out of the water was battering at a fisherman's shed. The other long appendage probed beneath the wharf, and she heard the splintering of timbers.

Her fingers were slippery, though she and Bremig had scoured the greasy lines. Her hand on the tiller felt wooden. She could not will herself to change course. Even from this distance she discerned the long eyestalks twitching, the Crab keeping watch while the Squid plundered. From the smashed building it pulled sailcloth and nets, flinging all aside.

A moment later, the tentacles retreated below the waves. The float-sacs bobbed as the Crab turned; the water began to froth. The creature had lost interest in deserted Hesh, she knew. The glinting eyes had found her.

To fight from the boat was impossible, and her nearest refuge lay at the Thumb-and-Finger beach. Could she reach the place in time? Staring foolishly at the tiller, she could not choose to move it one way or the other.

Somehow a decision came, for the bow turned and the boom swung past her head. Grappling with the sheet, she lurched into a starboard reach so clumsily that even Bremig would have laughed. *Bremig?* She must think of Ormek now, not the carver, but how was that possible? She tried to focus on the boat, watching how it sped forward despite her awkward handling. Dropping the sail, she let her momentum carry her to shore.

At once she was tossing equipment onto the pebbly strand—the spear, the roll of netting, the poleax. To each side of the beach rose a stark ridge—the "thumb" to her right, the "finger" to her left. Between these towers lay a broad, sandy gap, the ground rising to meet a tangle of thorns. Finding no other escape from the gray shore, she picked up what supplies she could and dragged them through the opening.

Now she saw the bowllike interior of the island with its surrounding lichen-covered walls. The bottom was littered with stunted trees and low bushes, many brown and seemingly dead. The walls were so steep that she could discover no hope of climbing out. Yet atop the "thumb" lay the ruins of a watchtower, and she wondered how the heights might be scaled.

No more time for planning, she realized. The beast was almost here! With the lantern in one hand, a spear in the other, she turned back to watch waves breaking against the side of the boat. The Crab's great claw rose up, and then the creature came apart. The tentacles fell away while the Seasnake, jaws half open, slithered up onto land.

The serpent had survived Bremig's baited hook, she saw, but had not rid itself of the barbs. From the reptile's mouth, the harpoon's straight shaft stuck out like an iron tongue. And beside the creature, as it slithered by the boat, the loop of chain was dragging furrows in wet sand. Surely this burden made the creature more vulnerable than before. But despite the impediment in its mouth, she saw that the fangs could still strike.

Trying first her familiar method of control, Kyala brought the frosty talisman to the lamp. "Hold," she shouted to the Snake, and briefly its wriggling seemed to slow. But a moment later it continued writhing forward. She applied the full heat of the lamp, and even then the serpent merely twitched its oarlike tail without faltering.

She had expected no more. Only with the aid of the Gathering Stone could she hope to prevail.

In a moment she held the amulet ready. The sun hung nearly overhead. Facing the crystal skyward, she centered the glowing circle on the talisman. "Stay back," she cried as she focused Ormek's fire. In the past she had used a lamp or a cookfire or merely the heat of her hand. Now, with this lens, she was bringing the Bright One's heat directly to charge the bead. Her fingers shook, and she had difficulty aiming the light. Then the brilliance came to a point; the talisman was aglow. The beast hissed in anguish, but when she looked up it was still coming at her!

No use! she cried to herself, pushing the crystal back in against her breast. Even the Gatherer, by itself, could not move such a strong-willed creature. What she needed was the Lifegiver within her, channeling power beyond anything a mere amulet could capture. But the Lifegiver had not come.

Had Watnojat betrayed her after all? *Uncle, how could you deceive me?* He'd told her to find the crystal and learn to use it. And now she knew this charm to be as useless as the others. Tears of shame stung her face when she recalled the angered priests and the days of futile sailing.

The reptile was coming for her. What use was bewailing her fate?

If this was her punishment from Ormek, then she swore to face it as best she could. She scanned the surf and saw nothing of the other two creatures. They had sent this one alone, she thought, to settle the score for his hook. And so it must be settled.

Taking the spear, she dodged sideways to put the boat between herself and the creature. The stern of the craft still lay in water, hull rocking as each breaker struck. The Snake's head was already at the bow as Kyala fled toward the stern. And then she glanced in at the hawser, its end carelessly left aft.

This cable had no anchor, yet she might find one. The end of the serpent's chain was just sliding past her on the opposite side. Dropping her weapon, she leaped across the gunwale and into the boat, grabbed the hawser, then leaned out to thread it through the harpoon's loop. Her fingers flying, she knotted the anchor line several times before the rope jerked from her hands.

Then she was out of the boat and hurrying toward higher ground. Taking the spear, she fled into the island's brambly interior. Now she could see nothing of the beach, but a clanking of iron and a hollow thumping told her the Seasnake had run out of line. Again, a thump. The serpent was wedded to the heavy boat now. So long as hook and hawser held, she was safe from its fangs.

But she had two other creatures to deal with—one heavily armored, the second long of reach. She felt trapped in the confines of the island's bowl, and the strand offered no refuge. So she pushed past thorny bushes, following the wall in search of an ancient path upward. How long, she tried to recall, since sea raiders had threatened the Mejdom, since the watchtower had been needed? Not even her grandfather had witnessed such attacks.

Near the canyon's end, Kyala found what appeared to be a series of hewn steps. Needing her hands free, she abandoned the lantern and spear, reached high into a chiseled fingerhold, and pulled herself up. Here a rough ledge jutted out from the wall and above it hung more steps. But seeing how they rose, one so far above the other, she thought that the watchmen of old had been giants. Painfully she lifted her boot as high as her knee, grabbed another hold, and continued.

She was out of breath by the time she gained a clear view. Tangled in rope and chain, the Snake was straining mightily to drag the boat across the beach. And the Crab was half out of the water now, one eyestalk cocked high, the other angled toward the struggling serpent.

The crustacean suddenly wielded its great pincer against the walnut boat, swinging a sideways blow that split several strakes. Again it swung, and she could see a rent opening in the hull's side. The Crab seemed bent on reducing the craft to splinters.

Studying the rusty humped back, Kyala conceived a plan. She must lure the armored one away from the boat before both beasts were free to hunt her. And perhaps, even without the Bright One's aid, she might halt the crustacean.

Her palms were damp with sweat as she made the descent, and several times she thought she might slip. Then she was down again, fighting through the knee-high tangle of brush. The sound of splintering planks echoed up from the shore and set her teeth on edge as she went. At the opening to the beach, she found the roll of netting where she had dropped it. There she stopped, and began to wave the long bundle in the air.

Two eyestalks turned, and then the smashing ceased. The reptile was still caught, she saw, for more than half the boat remained intact. But the Crab was coming after her, its float-sacs bouncing, its mouth parts fluttering.

She dodged back up the trail she'd made and waited for the creature to sight her again. It advanced fitfully, pausing after each few jerky steps. Dancing and waving, she led it to the base of the stairway, then tipped her bundle of netting up onto the ledge above the first step. She tossed the spear up also before pulling herself to the platform. The crustacean, trailing bits of brush, was almost on her.

She grasped the free end of the net and flung the roll down onto the Crab's rising pincer. The mesh crossed its back and the nearest part draped down to foul its footing. But the thin cords were merely an annoyance to a beast of this strength.

Even so, the eyestalks became entangled. It lowered its carapace and scraped with its clumsy pincer to clear the netting. Now she could see into the cavern it carried—the tunnel under its shell where its companions often rode. No weapon she had could pierce the carapace from outside, but what of the *floor* of the compartment? Through the opening, she saw a hint of pinkish flesh.

There was no deliberating the matter, for the beast's distraction could not last. She leaped from her perch and into the putrid maw of the cave. Within, she had only headroom for kneeling, and she touched the sickening pulpy surface with her hand. She felt the pitching and scraping as the creature writhed, flailing with its pincer to be rid of strands and pest alike. Angling the spear, she plunged deep into flesh and felt an answering shudder.

Kyala could not breathe in the confines. Gasping, she twisted the weapon free and found strength to thrust once more. The beast's quaking grew more violent, and she thought she'd be thrown from the cave. Gripping the embedded shaft with one hand, she stretched toward the entrance to gulp for air. Looking out, she saw the pincer trailing shreds of broken net. The claw's sharp end swung toward her and she retreated.

The creature could not wedge its great claw into the cavern, but it had yet to concede the battle. It began to beat the pincer against her roof, tilting at the same time to dislodge her. She clung to the slippery haft, not daring to pull it free again. Her legs swung toward the opening, and she dug in her knees. The spear was working loose!

Her boots kicked frantically, but found no purchase. The shaft slipped halfway out, and she braced herself to be tumbled onto the ground. But suddenly the drumming stopped, and the floor became level again. She sensed the Crab moving, heading, she was certain, back to water.

The crustacean would simply drown her, she realized, unless she could stop its advance. Feeling the lurch of its gait, she tried to imagine how such a creature might be killed. She had often cracked crabs at her mother's table. If this beast was anything like its smaller counterparts, then its insides were a jumble of peculiar organs. Was one more vital than another?

Having no answer, she began to strike wildly, desperate to finish before the Crab regained the shore. Each time she stabbed, she chose a new place for her spear. The pulpy floor became so sticky that she kept losing her grip on the handle. At last, she noticed that all the beast's motions had ceased.

Was it over? Glancing out, she saw the great pincer lying still, the tail not even twitching. Stumbling to the ground, she rushed back to the canyon's safety, dragged herself up onto the ledge. There she lay with her chest heaving, swallowing great draughts of untainted air.

When Bremig was certain she had left him, he flung off his boots and jumped headlong into the brine. Regardless of whether or not he could swim the distance, the carver stroked angrily for shore. If he exhausted himself quickly, he thought, the end would come that much sooner. His muscles began to cramp, and he drifted down into pale-green water. What a cool and pleasant place, he thought, wishing the deep could embrace and hold him for eternity.

But the sea kept spitting him up, and his arms flailed of their own accord. Almost despite himself, he seemed to be nearing shore. Every time he beat at the water, the memory of his pain lessened. Could he forget Kyala so quickly? Perhaps not. But for a while he knew only gasping breath and strain beyond exhaustion.

At last he felt sand scraping his chest. He blinked, saw shadows and milling boots, then closed his eyes again. He felt himself dragged out of the surf, and heard a babble of voices.

"Never saw this man before," said someone.

Fingers tugged at his beard and hair. "Couldn't be the one they're lookin' for."

"But where'd he come from? Just a single boat's out there."

The carver groaned and spat water.

"If he's from *that* boat, you'd better not touch 'im." Bremig heard a woman's voice, harsh and frightened.

"A demon-defier," agreed another. "You might catch his curse."

"Do we leave him, then? He looks to me an ordinary fellow."

The arguing went on for some time, and the carver lost track of it. Later, he opened his eyes to see a roundfaced man leaning over him. "I brought you somethin'," he said with a smile. The little man had short chin whiskers and no beard on his cheeks. Bremig stared at him but did not try to move.

"It's soup," said the stranger. "Come on. Sit up and have some. The others all went away." He draped a raggedy quilt about the carver's shoulders.

"I didn't want . . . to come up," Bremig said slowly. "She . . . spat me out. Etma wouldn't have me."

The other shook his head. "Etma? I've nothin' to say about her. I'm an odd one for a seaman, but I look to the Lifegiver."

The carver sighed painfully. "Not for me. I knew someone who followed Ormek . . ." He could not continue. But he let the man prop him up, and he swallowed a spoonful of broth from the sooty pot.

Sitting with his trousers drying in the day's heat, feeling the languor of spent muscles, he was content to empty his thoughts. The soup soothed him from within, and in time, he was strong enough to stand. He toed the smooth pebbles, warm beneath his feet, and did not miss his boots. I don't know why you helped me," he said, staring at the seaman's bristly chin. "I can't even tell you that I'm grateful. But I have a brother, Wek, who'll thank you. I'm going to find him now."

"I need no thanks," the roundfaced man said. "You've somethin' to do with that girl who follows Ormek—the one in the boat. I've heard all kinds of tales about her, and I still take her side over the others."

Bremig started at those words, but he could not bring himself to argue with his benefactor.

"As for the beast," the man continued, "the Bright One'll take care of it in His own time. Then I'll be back fishin' again, and I'll never think twice about Etma."

"I wish I could promise you an end to the beast," the carver said sadly, getting to his feet. He left the fellow sitting with his back against a rock, his empty soup pot at his side. The road lay ahead, and Bremig was glad the way would be long.

When Kyala's strength returned, she made her way cautiously back to the canyon's mouth. No sound of struggling came from the strand and she wondered whether the Seasnake had exhausted itself or escaped. Peering around the bend, she saw its striped length motionless on the sand. Had the sun's heat dried it out? Perhaps Ormek had helped her in an unexpected way.

She picked up the poleax and crept closer. The body quivered, and she noticed pale foam dribbling from the open mouth. The eyelid was closed. Already flies were buzzing about the tail.

Suddenly the creature twitched and came awake. She had thought it nearly dead, but now the mouth widened to expose the gleaming fangs. There was only a moment's pause. Then, twisting through the tangle of chain and hawser, the reptile lunged straight at her.

In panic, she swung the weapon, bringing the head down as if she were splitting a log. She saw a blur of metal and the oncoming open jaws. The blade bit deep into the flattened skull, and she was spattered by bits of bone and slime. The handle pulled from her grip as the beast rolled in final spasms. Sickened, she looked away.

There was no more she could do here. Though her stomach knotted at the thought of food, she paused by her cache of supplies, hung the small water bottle about her neck, and stuffed the cheese in her pocket. Determinedly she went back to climb the watchkeeper's stair.

This time she kept going, finding at last the ruined circle of wall atop the thumb. The roof of the ancient lookout was gone, the floor littered with bits of stone and wood. She could clear enough room to stretch out if she wished.

More important for now, however, was the view she had from this height. Scanning the sea on all sides of the island, she soon picked out the long, pinkish body of the Squid. It floated beneath the surface, waiting for her just beyond the strand, keeping to the water, where it alone was master. The Squid was her jailer now. She could roam the island in safety, but the mainland lay out of reach.

CHAPTER 17

BREMIG walked barefoot beside the coastal road, avoiding most of the dung piles by treading on the border of weeds. Darst and his mare lay somewhere ahead of him, provided he did not meet his cousin along the way. Perhaps it was this gloomy possibility that slowed his pace. He did not even look at passing carts to see if one might offer a ride.

The afternoon was warm and the air smelled of ripe grain. He paused to watch two youngsters in a field tossing bits of wood to a bedraggled dog. The animal had a trick of leaping high, arching backward, and snatching a stick out of the air so nimbly that the carver laughed. The landsman's life, he thought, was pleasant at this time of year. He swore that he would spend his remaining days away from the sea.

Bremig patted his crusty breeches, now fully dry, and found his coin purse. Approaching a village, he decided to find new boots first, and then a tavern with a washhouse. After he was cleaned up, his belly filled with good food and ale, he would have his first comfortable sleep in many days.

The village turned out to be smaller than he'd expected. He did locate a cobbler, who supplied an adequate pair of boots, but the lodgings were cramped and stank of tobacco. So he joined a large-fisted drayman named Jepp, who was similarly unimpressed with the amenities, and rode with him past a string of settlements until they reached a sizable town.

Here they stopped at the Broken Traces, an inn of modest repute. After a meal of roast pig and buttered yams, the carver called for buckets of hot water. In the musty dampness of the washhouse he wrapped his scrubbed body in a fresh blanket and left his clothing behind to be scoured and rinsed.

Later, at ease by the fire with the blanket still about him, he honed and oiled his knife, idly listening to the chatter of local travelers. There was much talk about a strange boat, but what did that matter to him? He was through with the sea. And if creatures troubled the coast, his advice to all sufferers was to pack up and move inland. The carver slept well that night.

In the morning, the drayman offered to carry him northward. Bremig was in no hurry, but he thought the company might prove agreeable. Jepp had installed a straw-stuffed cushion on the driver's bench, and Bremig felt as comfortable as a magistrate on that seat.

They had barely gotten started, it seemed, when the outskirts of Hesh appeared. Here, the carver noticed a peculiar lack of traffic through the center of town. Though the hour was early, he expected to see more than a handful of people about. Evidently curious as well, the drayman paused to call after a boy who had crossed in front of him.

"Sea beast!" the youth shouted, pointing in the direction of the bay. "Been here since yesterday. Someone's gonna get eaten."

Bremig glanced uneasily at his companion.

"I've heard tales," the husky man said thoughtfully. "Never seen the thing for myself . . ."

"You said you were heading north," Bremig countered, as if the boy's words hadn't shaken him. But the carver's hands were already trembling. If the creature was here, he asked himself, where was Kyala?

"Traffic's light. We can make up the time later." Jepp licked his lips. "Might be able to win a few wagers over this," he added, breaking into a nervous smile. With a few clucks to the horses, he turned his wagon into the street where the boy had gone.

"I . . . I have other business to finish," the carver protested.

"Ah. And you the one with plenty of time. We were talkin' about making up a batch of carvings. I can show you how to turn a tasty profit if you'll come along with me for a bit." The wagon rolled past the boy and was gaining on another running youth. Bremig considered leaping off, at some risk to himself. But what if *she* was out there? He knew from his racing pulse that he couldn't pull away now.

The carver sighed. Though he had forsworn the sea, he was not quite done with it. The driver reached the bay's southern shore, and Bremig scanned the placid water. Gazing out at the twin crags, the famous "fingers," he found the surrounding surf eerily calm.

Jepp drove past the island, turning onto a narrow spit that jutted into the bay. Now they could see a short, gray beach that lay windward of the crags. "Over there!" shouted the drayman. Bremig followed his gaze as the wagon rolled closer. Yes, there was something in the waves. Just off the tiny strand a pinkish mass floated, seemingly lifeless until a tentacle abruptly broke the surface.

A small crowd of onlookers had gathered, and the carver noticed their attention was not on the beast but on the island's shore. He squinted across the water, not daring to believe what he saw. "It's that cursed boat," explained someone who pointed at the beached wreckage. "See. It's broken up. She's been piling brush around it."

She? She still lived? At that moment, a figure carrying a heap of brambles came into view. Of course it was Kyala; it could be no other. *She means to bait the thing*. But with what hope of success? He had seen the new amulet, and it meant nothing to him.

Adding her load to the pile, she turned away with a glance over her shoulder at the waves. She was obviously aware of the waiting Squid. The carver blinked, rubbed his eyes, and she was gone. She soon reappeared, however, and he watched her heap the brush ever higher.

At last she pulled something from her jacket and held it close to the tinder. A flash of light glinted from her hand. Awaiting the outcome, Bremig could not breathe.

But someone was tugging at his leg and would not stop. "So it's you, carver," came a hated voice. "Almost had me fooled." Before Bremig could react, he was dragged from the bench, tossed over a knotted shoulder like a grain sack and dropped heavily to earth. "Clever trick," said Draalego. "But y'r red beard's dark at the roots already." The fisherman toed Bremig's chin with his foul boot.

The carver rolled to his feet and stood back warily, tensing for his cousin's next attack. Why should he feel surprise at Draalego's presence? Undoubtedly, the fisherman had followed Kyala's progress up and down the shoreline.

"You can have your boat back," the carver growled. "And Balin's daughter with it. I've nothing to do with either."

"You can say that now. Who was it at the helm when my boat slipped from the dock?" Pelask's son grinned icily, but a chorus of cries from the throng made him turn his head. Bremig saw past his cousin's shoulder a rising pillar of smoke. *She'll lure it onto land and then* . . . He could not imagine her attacking the thrashing limbs.

At that moment, with Draalego distracted, Bremig had a chance for escape. A few horses and ponies stood idle while their masters were engrossed in watching Kyala's preparations. Perhaps he could steal a mount, outrun his cousin, find refuge in a quiet village, and never be found. But there was a person inside him who was unwilling to run—the one Etma had spewed from her briny mouth.

He felt a hard hand squeeze his shoulder. "We'll see how she fares first," said his cousin, steering him to the front of the throng. "We're in no hurry, are we?"

Kyala's night in the ruined tower had been spent without rest. The odor of the Crab's slime on her skin and clothing had worsened as the stars turned, until she wished she had bathed in the cold sea. But far worse than the stench and the stone bed were her fears about what lay ahead.

The Squid, with its long reach, was waiting for her. She had watched a single swipe of its tentacle lay Bremig's arm open. And she knew the beast would not depart before avenging its companions' deaths.

Facing the comfortless sky, she opened her pouch of beads. She felt Watnojat's charm with her fingertips, sensing the familiar blue-gray hue. An impulse of anger almost made her fling the talisman into the sea. But perhaps she had judged her mentor too hastily. The blame for the failure of the Gatherer lay partly with herself.

For she had not shut Bremig from her thoughts. Even as she recalled his anguished look, his words of rebuke, she could not put him aside. Yet neither could she dismiss the Bright One, who had offered her a gift beyond anyone's expectations. Once she had filled herself with His fierce beauty. Once she had shared a part of His being.

Was this no longer possible? She thought of Balin. Were her feelings for her mother diminished by her love for the carver? And what of her father—dead five years but still fondly remembered? And finally, what of Watnojat himself, the "uncle" who had become more than a father?

The spirit-voice had said nothing about pushing out the others from her heart. Why, then, must she forget the carver? She cupped Watnojat's bead in her hand all the rest of the night, recalling over and again the words of the spirit voice. *Do what is needed, but bring the Bright One back into your soul.* That was the crucial admonition, and one that left room for interpretation. Perhaps she was mistaken after all. "Uncle, I misjudged you," she said softly when at last she stood up to watch the glory of dawn.

Now she knew she must descend. Wearily and with stiff limbs, she climbed back down the steep face. In the canyon she began to gather anything that might burn—driftwood tossed up by storms, dead brush, fallen saplings. Reaching the strand, she found the tide low, the splintered boat perched high above the surf. She dropped her burden beneath the prow-piece, staring one last time at the black-walnut face. Here was an image that belonged neither to Ormek nor to Etma, a face to haunt one's quiet moments for a lifetime. But now she must destroy it.

The dead carcass of the Sea-snake lay tangled in rope and chain. She struggled to lift the beast, and was finally forced to use the poleax to hack it into three grisly pieces. These she placed within the hull.

More brush! She came and went until the boat was barely visible beneath the pile. And all the time she worked, she was aware of the creature lurking in the water.

Satisfied at last, she turned the Gatherer to face the sun. What a simple trick it seemed now, this drawing down of fire. The dry twigs began to smolder and the flames spread from one to the next. Soon the blaze rose on all sides, and she smelled the choking odor of the burnt carcass.

She had seen the Squid devouring charred meat and bones. Would it come to this feast? she wondered. The heat drove her toward the canyon's shelter. She watched a huge appendage rising from the deep, and then another.

This blaze, the reptile's pyre, was her final lure. She had this chance only to conquer the Squid. But ordinary fire could not hurt the creature. It heaved itself up on the strand and dipped its probing limbs directly into the flames. Wood ash and meat it pushed without distinction toward its beaked maw. With such food it was only growing stronger, the colors of its flesh pulsing from pale to pink to crimson. The demon eye brightened, glowing like a fanned coal.

Then the beast saw her and lost interest in the fiery banquet. Already she held the Gatherer, and she took one final glance at its perfect shaping. This was no talisman of power, she now knew, but merely an instrument, a device for concentrating the Lifegiver's heat. Yet the spirit-voice had sent her after it with a purpose. To learn how to use this amulet meant going beyond the secrets of the flamens.

Just as the crystal collected His light, so she must bring within herself all the Bright One's glories. She must become the Gatherer for His greatness. In a few moments, before the creature struck, she must bring together her memories and feelings.

The Squid pushed aside the blazing planks and shot a long limb in her direction. *All the wonders of His works*, she thought, as she cast the sun's light on the demon-eye bead. The clouds at sunset, the fleeting rainbow, wheat quivering before the wind. All of it, His—the blizzards and thaws and mists, the dry crags and flooded valleys. And Bremig, too, was of the Lifegiver's making, another proof of His greatness.

Kyala focused the bright circle, so that a point of brilliance ignited the glossy talisman. And in her thoughts, the fullness of her knowledge came together, collecting with such intensity that she cried out in wonder. The Lifegiver had come at last; His strength poured through her blood and sang at every pore.

The ruddy light reflected from the bead spilled first onto her fingers. The glow spread, leaping toward the smoldering boat . . . In an instant, the beast was engulfed by a maelstrom of fire that seemed to tower as high as the sun Himself. The wind that fanned the flames was the sea's own breath, the bellows of a storm. Kyala flung herself into the sand and covered her ears to shut out the roaring. Here was the cataclysm the boat had been built for, but Etma had no part in it.

Here was the purging that must end the seamen's wrong-headedness for all time. And she wept, as she lay there, for the magnitude of suffering that had been wrought.

Bremig rubbed his eyes, then turned to scan the faces of the others. Had they seen the sudden flash? Perhaps he'd been confused by another reflection from her amulet. But for a moment the bonfire had seemed to engulf even the high crags. Now he saw only the pyre's blaze, its foul smoke spreading in all directions. And the great limbs of the sea beast lay still, the body blackened by heat. The Squid would go marauding no more.

"She's done it!" the onlookers were shouting. "She's beaten Etma. Bested the demon." Some in the group were making circles with their fingers—signs of faith in Ormek. Even seamen stood staring, awed at what Kyala had done.

But the painful grip on Bremig's shoulder tightened, and he felt himself propelled back through the muttering crowd. A few of Draalego's friends glanced at the fisherman, then hastily turned aside. The carver could read their feelings of betrayal. Having watched Kyala triumph, what trust had they left in their erstwhile leader? Yet Bremig's satisfaction was brief, for he knew how his cousin intended to cover his shame.

"Carver, don't leave without me," called the drayman from behind.

When the heavyset driver caught up with him, Bremig nodded toward his cousin. "I've an old matter to settle," he told Jepp in a faltering voice. "You'd best go on without me."

"Old matter? If it's a fight, I'll stand by you."

"I've got to do this . . . on my own." Draalego continued to push him toward an empty clearing away from the bustle of the crowd.

"Then I'll watch," declared Jepp. "And pick up your

bones when he's done with you. Just tell me where you want 'em carried."

"Inland. As far as possible." Bremig grunted as Draalego suddenly flung him forward to sprawl on the sand. Trembling with his old fears, he rolled to face the fisherman. Before Bremig could rise, Draalego closed in, kicking him first in the ribs and then the stomach. The carver lay helpless, unable to catch his breath, but he heard the drayman's frantic call.

"Fish-gutter's got a knife!" Gasping, Bremig managed to glance up and see his cousin warning off the drayman, his stance hunched, the point of his outsized blade aimed at the other's throat. Jepp backed away until Bremig could see him no longer. The carver felt his hand reaching for the sheath at his hip.

He touched the walnut carvings on his weapon's hilt, knowing their appearance without seeing them. In the past, this haft had merely tingled in his palm; now it seemed charged with a furious energy. Draalego bared his teeth, crouched with his polished blade catching the morning light. "Bring it out, carver," he said laughingly. "Make this look like a real fight."

Bremig watched him cautiously, making no move to rise. His cousin's brawling tactics had changed, he realized, for he typically administered a slow beating, dragging out his opponent's suffering and humiliation.

But today Draalego had no admirers to cheer him. The few onlookers, in fact, appeared hostile. Bremig coiled himself, imagining the quick kill that his cousin must be planning. And what did the carver know of fighting tactics? Perhaps, with surprise, he might gain a small advantage.

Without warning, in one motion, Bremig sprang to his feet and thrust his blade. His cousin blocked the blow with his weapon-bearing arm, forcing the carver to spin away from him. Turning not quite fast enough, Bremig felt a track of pain open on his thigh. He retreated well beyond the other's reach, saw his cousin's face burning, his lips coated with foam. Draalego charged like a crazed goat, his underhand jab aimed at the carver's middle, and it was all Bremig could do to smash the arm aside and rush past him. The carver felt dampness oozing down his leg, but did not look at the wound. He turned and prepared to block again.

"First I'll take off your ears," the fisherman taunted as he crouched for his next attack. "The vixen'll want 'em to remember you by. Only part of you she ever had use for." Again he lunged. Another streak of pain opened, warm liquid dripping against Bremig's neck. Retreating once more, the carver put several paces between himself and his cousin.

Now Draalego was panting, and sweat stood out on his brow. This time, no longer grinning, he made a more deliberate advance. The tingling in Bremig's hand grew unbearable, and he felt compelled to stand his ground. The carver saw only his cousin's weapon, the bright blade held high . . .

Suddenly Bremig's knife hand, as if of its own accord, rose for a downward stroke while his other fist punched aside the fisherman's arm. Bremig felt his blade take a strange twist in midair, abruptly changing course, away from, then under, Draalego's block. He saw the fisherman's weapon spin to the ground and could not comprehend what had happened until he noticed his own hand buried in his cousin's guts, the blade finding its way upward to the shuddering heart. The body toppled onto his shoulders, bearing him down until the two lay motionless on the sand . . .

To Bremig it seemed a day and a night that he lay beneath his cousin's corpse. But then the weight was pulled away, and Jepp's worried face hung over him. "You'll need some fixin' up," the drayman said. "Didn't hurt your fingers any, I hope."

"His father and mine were brothers," the carver confessed in a disbelieving voice, his soiled hands quivering.

"Family fight. Worst kind." The brawny arms helped him to his feet.

"I'll . . . have to take him home."

"Not 'til we patch you up some. Come along with me."

Jepp held out an arm and Bremig limped toward the wagon, noting only vaguely the expressions of sympathy in faces he passed. "Take my cousin, too," he insisted when he reached the rig, and the drayman obligingly went back for Draalego's remains.

Bremig refused to lie down. Seated on the driver's bench and facing the bay, he could not help observing that another boat now braved the tide, striking out toward the island. A dory was closing on the far beach. A few more strokes, then the distant figures of two men rushed ashore.

Behind him he heard the drayman grunting. Bremig could not take his eyes from the island. "Heavy anchor-head," Jepp complained. The wagon lurched as something was added to the load.

And then Bremig saw the two men returning from the far beach leading a slender figure between them. They lifted Kyala into the boat, and someone began to row. "So there's more to see," the driver commented as he climbed up beside him. "Maybe learn what this business was all about. How you holdin' together?"

The carver could not speak. He wanted to tell Jepp to drive on, but his lips were clamped shut. He felt light-headed and wondered if he was losing much blood. The crowd grew quiet. Even the birds were silent as the dory glided back toward the spit.

"Why, she's only a girl!" Jepp shouted. "What was she doin' out there, I want to know."

Now the rescue boat was so close that he could hear the oars dipping, the rowlocks creaking. Kyala's face looked colorless and tight-lipped, yet her eyes held a fierce glow. Had she recovered Ormek's gift at last? Perhaps, he thought bitterly, by discarding her carver as if he were a rancid mackerel, she had regained the Bright One's favor.

A dozen men ran to pull the boat up onto the strand. "Go!" he wanted to shout at Jepp, for how could he bear this last view of her? Yet he sat watching, feeling blood and perspiration roll down his back, until the bay rose up on edge and the sky smashed into him.

CHAPTER 18

KYALA rose shakily from her bed of pebbly sand. The great blaze was finished, the sky clear. The charred limbs and body of the Squid lay smoking on the embers of black walnut. She would look at that sight no longer.

With reverence, she tucked the Gatherer away to rest against her skin. She felt Ormek still with her, His strength joined to her spirit, His wonders never far from her thoughts. But He had not pushed out the others. Her feelings for the carver persisted despite the bitterness of their parting. Though she might never see Bremig again, his impression would remain.

What would she do now? For the moment, she could make no plans. Still dazed by all she had seen, she wandered at the edge of the tide, studying the details of seaweed and shell. The ocean was Ormek's also, not Etma's as the fishermen believed. This she had proved for all time. The fish and the tiny crawlers were His. Even the three beasts had been of the Bright One's making, and would have caused no evil had they stayed in their own domain. But she was finished with such worries. The sun's light glittered from the surface He had made . . .

After a time, she heard shouts from the far side of the beach. Before she could even speak, men were leading her to their boat, rowing her across to the mainland. She could not protest. Her thoughts were hazy, and she knew neither where she was going nor where she wanted to go.

When they reached the spit, she stepped cautiously onto the strand. Why were these people staring at her? She glanced from one wide-eyed face to another until she noticed a red-bearded man seated on a high wagon. "Bremig," she said under her breath. How could he have followed her? And why was his neck awash in blood? As she watched, the injured man toppled sideways, his head falling into his companion's lap.

The carver's appearance shocked her from stupor. Tearing free from the hands supporting her, she fought to pass through the crowd. The driver was moving out! She tried to scream after him, but her voice was barely a hoarse whisper. Caught in a knot of new arrivals, she could only stare at the vanishing wagon, its stout barrels bouncing, its loose ropes swinging.

Suddenly everyone was talking, and she covered her ears with her hands. She was lifted, buoyed above the milling throng. She found herself in an elegant cart, the neatly dressed man beside her smiling and prattling. But she made no sense of his words. He was Hesh's magistrate, she realized at last, and he was trying to express his town's gratitude. "Thank Ormek," she said in rebuke. "Thank the Bright One." She could not make him see that she wanted no part in celebrations.

"Let me take you home to my wife," he offered. "After a wash and a rest, you'll feel better."

To get free of the noise and commotion, she reluctantly nodded, and he clucked his fine pony into a trot. As they went, the official shouted his plans to everyone they passed. He was calling out the whole town to honor her, and she wanted only to be home in her bed.

As they left the spit and rolled toward the busier thoroughfares, Kyala thought again of the carver. "Tell me," she asked, though her voice still lacked strength. "Where would a wounded man go for doctoring?"

The magistrate gave her a puzzled look.

"I saw . . . a hurt friend taken away. Just now. I need to talk to him. Only for a moment."

"After you've rested . . ."

"Now," she insisted. "Find him for me, or I'll have nothing to do with your merrymaking."

The magistrate's face darkened, and he huffily turned a corner. Before a squat building stood three white poles, healer's signposts, but no wagon waited at the entrance.

"Could there be another?" she asked.

"Out on the main road." He sighed, turned once more, and drove until the town was largely behind them. A house of fieldstone and timber stood at the edge of a scraggly meadow.

"That's the one!" she cried, spotting the loaded wagon she had watched earlier. She jumped down from the cart, but for a moment she could not approach the house. Bremig lay within, and she knew neither his condition nor what he might say to her. But her life must go on in any case.

She foresaw, now, how her next days must be spent. She would bring Balin and the rest of the family back to Darst. And she would return to the Reach, not only to bring the Gatherer but to offer her glassmaking skills for the restoration of Ormek's Beacon. Fixing those goals before her, she advanced, somewhat unsteadily, toward the healer's dwelling.

Finding the front door open, she stepped into a cool and dimly lit chamber. Cowhides strung on a line concealed most of the interior. A heavyset man with large hands stood facing her, and there was nothing more to see but a rough-hewn bench at his side.

"Your . . . friend," she began timidly. "He fell over on the wagon."

"The carver? Got into a little scrap."

"How bad?"

"That fellow's quite a brawler. Didn't think so when I first saw him."

She wanted to dart past the big man and pull the curtain aside. But his bulk seemed to fill the space before her. "I . . . have something of his." She reached into her pouch and extracted the gray-green talisman. Sensing the hue of the glass, she failed to find the words she needed.

"I've seen you before," the driver said thoughtfully. Suddenly his eyebrows jumped. "You're the one from the boat! I'm still waiting to hear the whole tale."

"Bremig can tell you the rest." She opened her palm and exposed the glossy bead, still not daring to ask to see the wounded man. "Can you give this to him?"

"You'd best give it yourself," the drayman said uneasily, stepping back from her. "I don't have business with such things."

She closed her fist. Having fought all three creatures, was she afraid of a mere carver? Suddenly she rushed past the sturdy driver and pushed through the curtain.

"You! Out!" shouted a thin, heavily bearded man whose hair hung down to his shoulders. Bremig lay on a pallet beneath a dangling pair of lamps while the healer, on his knees, was wrapping a cloth around his thigh. A narrow strip was already wound about his face, covering parts of nose and ears.

Kyala watched Bremig's eyelids fluttering. Ignoring the healer, she drew closer. The carver's eyes opened fully then, but his expression told her nothing. "Draalego's dead," he whispered. "And you were never born."

"Enough," said the healer, collecting his supplies. "That's all I can do for ya. Eat some good meat and you'll be brawlin' again in a day or two." He stalked out past the curtain, and she heard his footsteps vanishing toward another part of the house.

Kyala peered after him and found the drayman still waiting. When he saw her staring, he twitched his mouth and retreated to the doorway. "Tell the carver, I'll be waitin' outside," the big man said. The door opened and closed, and then there was only the sound of breathing.

Turning, she did not speak at once. The still-unfamiliar coloring of Bremig's hair and beard unnerved her as much as the pained look on his face. "I came to leave you this," she said finally, opening her hand and showing the talisman. "A small consolation, I admit. But wear it, and no one can ever steal your will again."

He stared coldly at the bead. "Can it undo what was done?"

"You'll never forgive me for what I did—especially since I lied to myself . . ."

"Believing you'd keep me safe? Did you think you'd follow me all my life? Whenever there was trouble, you could charm me away from it?"

She knelt beside him. "Don't you see my mistake? I couldn't find the Bright One, and believed my feelings for you were to blame. That's the true reason I left you. But when we were apart, it made no difference. I thought of you anyway. All the time. In the end, you and Ormek were with me together."

Bremig shook his head sadly. "To be driven like a beast . . . To have my muscles turn against me . . . How could I know what foolish ideas you harbored?"

"If I'd been able to explain, would the pain have been less?" Her voice trailed off.

"I understood," he said. "After a long, cold time in the water, I knew why you'd cast me aside."

"And now you know why I was wrong." She held out the talisman again. "Take this. I ask you to wear the bead, nothing else."

"And if I wear it, how will I not think of you?"

"I know how to burn fish and scald milk. You can remember that."

"Cooking?" His expression seemed to soften. "There are other things about you I'd remember first." His face began to redden, and she saw the faintest of smiles. Finally, he reached toward her and took the charm in his slender fingers. Holding it by the embedded strand of copper, he studied the glossy piece. "And will this protect me from *you* as well?"

"Only from the power of my glass . . ."

"What else could there be?" He shook his head, but his smile began to grow. "All right," he said as he closed his fist about the talisman. "I'll make you no other promise today. But ask the drayman if he has a tether."